Dornford Yates is the pseudony[...]
Born into a middle-class Victorian [...]
together enough money to send him to Harrow. The son of a
solicitor, he qualified for the Bar but gave up legal work in favour
of his great passion for writing. As a consequence of education
and experience, Yates' books feature the genteel life, a nostalgic
glimpse at Edwardian decadence and a number of swindling
solicitors. In his heyday and as a testament to the fine writing
in his novels, Dornford Yates' work was placed in the bestseller
list. Indeed, 'Berry' is one of the great comic creations of
twentieth-century fiction, and 'Chandos' titles were successfully
adapted for television.

Finding the English climate utterly unbearable, Yates chose
to live in the French Pyrénées for eighteen years before moving
on to Rhodesia where he died in 1960.

ADÈLE AND CO.
AND BERRY CAME TOO
AS BERRY AND I WERE SAYING
B-BERRY AND I LOOK BACK
BERRY AND CO.
THE BERRY SCENE
BLIND CORNER
BLOOD ROYAL
THE BROTHER OF DAPHNE
THE COURTS OF IDLENESS
AN EYE FOR A TOOTH
FIRE BELOW
GALE WARNING
THE HOUSE THAT BERRY BUILT
JONAH AND CO.
NE'ER-DO-WELL
PERISHABLE GOODS
RED IN THE MORNING
SHE FELL AMONG THIEVES
SHE PAINTED HER FACE

DORNFORD YATES

COST PRICE

HOUSE OF
STRATUS

The right of Dornford Yates to be identified as the author of this work has been asserted.

This edition published in 2001 by House of Stratus, an imprint of Stratus Books Ltd, 21 Beeching Park, Kelly Bray, Cornwall, PL17 8QS, UK.

www.houseofstratus.com

Typeset, printed and bound by House of Stratus.

A catalogue record for this book is available from the British Library and the Library of Congress.

ISBN 1-84232-970-7

NOTE

In telling this tale, I have found it impossible not to refer to incidents related in two other of my books. It is neither necessary nor desirable for any reader of this book to read those but, in case someone should wish to confirm the reports of either Punter or Richard Chandos, let me say that SAFE CUSTODY *will bear out the one and* BLIND CORNER *the other.*

DORNFORD YATES

Contents

Prologue   i

1   We Shut the Stable Door   1

2   From Pillar to Post   32

3   Rogues and Vagabonds   69

4   The Play's the Thing   113

5   The Vat of Melody   138

6   The Hard Way   164

7   Two's Company   186

8   Present Laughter   226

9   We Consider a Dimple   260

Prologue

"Where's yer case?" said the valet, cigarette box in hand.

"On the bed," said his master. "Use your eyes."

"Sez you," said the valet. He began to replenish the case. "Too strong fer me, these fags."

"I'm glad of that," said the other. "Give me my coat."

The jacket was entered and adjusted. Edward Osric Friar was a well-dressed man.

"Dinin' at the Club?" said the valet.

"Your supposition," said his master, "is correct."

"Along with bishops an' judges. Enough to make a cat laugh, it is."

"It takes all sorts," said his master, "to make a world."

"I'll say it does," said Sloper – to give him his name. " 'Ere's you, a firs'-class crook, 'ob-nobbin' with judges an' bishops – "

"That is why," said his master, "I am a first-class crook. I am above suspicion – a most important thing. By the way, I shall want you tonight; so be in by ten."

The other sighed.

"An' I meant to go to the flicks. They're showin' – "

"Business first," said Friar. "I meant to go to the play. Ever heard of a crook called Punter?"

"Punter," said the valet, pinching the end of his nose. "A fair-'aired bloke, 'igh-coloured and 'alf a dude?"

"That would be him."

" 'E's knocked about," said Sloper. " 'E used to work with 'Rose' Noble. 'E's done one stretch, I know, but I can't remember why. Auntie Emma's used him. People like 'im, I think: but 'e's nothin' wonderful."

"He's a lazy swine," said Friar, "but he's coming to see me tonight."

"Is he, though," said Sloper. "An' wot does he know?"

"That," said his master, "is what I propose to find out. Give me my overcoat."

Six minutes later, he entered a famous Club, which stands in Pall Mall.

Friar was a fine looking man of forty-five. He was a Doctor of Law, a Fellow of Oxford, and a distinguished Reader of one of the Inns of Court. As such, his duties were slight: so was his remuneration. Yet he lodged in Mayfair, living in very good style. He was a recognized authority upon old silver and a familiar figure at Christie's Great Rooms. He seldom made a purchase, but he was a connoisseur. Physically very strong, he took the greatest care to keep himself fit. He was completely ruthless, as Sloper could tell: but he never 'worked' in England – the risk was too great.

This evening he found himself next to Professor Lebrun: they had a long talk on archaeology: he drank his coffee and brandy with a leading anaesthetist; and soon after ten o'clock he left the Club to walk to his excellent flat.

As he was approaching the block, he observed a figure moving on the opposite side of the street. Experience, rather than instinct, told him that this was his man. The malefactor believes in reconnaissance.

Friar crossed the street.

"Good evening, Punter," he said.

"Er, good evening, sir."

"Before your time, I see. With me that's a very good fault. Come along in."

By no means easy, Punter followed his host. He had meant to 'have a look round', but he had left it too late. He was not at all sure of his host, who had a compelling air.

Friar led the way upstairs and into an elegant room. Then he indicated a chair.

"Sit down there," he said, "and take a cigar."

Punter obeyed.

Friar put off his hat and coat and took his seat on a table, swinging a leg.

"Last night I heard you talking. Who was your friend?"

"We call him Lousy. I don't know his other name."

"Doesn't he work with Auntie?"

"That's right. 'E can play with a car."

"You were talking about a show you had in Austria. A castle, you mentioned – The Castle of Hohenems."

"That was a wash-out," said Punter. "Lucky to save me life, if you ask me."

"I'd like to hear about it."

"There ain't nothin' doin' there, sir. We 'anded the stuff away."

"I'd like to hear about it."

Punter put a hand to his chin.

"A bloke called Harris," he said. "He called me in. A treasure of jools, there was, hid up in a vault. Somethin' very special – there ain't no doubt about that. All carved, they was, an' worth a million or more. 'Istorical – that's the word. Belonged to the Pope, they did: and he'd walled them up."

"That's right," said Friar. "I've seen the catalogue."

" 'Ave you, though?" said Punter. "Well, I seen a photograph – o' the catalogue, I mean. Written down in a prayer book, it was."

"That's right," said Friar. "Interleaved with a breviary. The original is in New York. They were wonderful gems."

"So Harris said," said Punter. "An' I'll say we — near 'ad them. But somethin' went wrong."

"Tell me everything."

Punter took a deep breath.

Then –

"We near — 'ad them," he said. "The jools was there in this castle, an' we was outside: but we knew where they was hid. Ferrers didn't. 'E knew they was there somewhere, but 'e didn' know where – or, if he did, he didn't know 'ow to reach them."

"Who was Ferrers?" said Friar.

"He lived at Hohenems. Owned the place with his cousin – I can't remember 'is name. An' another was workin' with them – Palin, his name was. 'E was the — that laid me out. But 'e didn' live there. 'E 'ad rooms at an inn about thirty miles off."

"Where were they hidden?" said Friar.

"They was walled up," said Punter. "Right down in one o' the dungeons – you never see such a place. But that was nothin'. What was beatin' Ferrers was 'ow to get at the wall."

"Why couldn't he get at the wall?"

" 'Cause o' the water," said Punter. "A — great waterfall, a-bellowin' over the wall. You never see such a thing. I tell you it give me the creeps."

"What, inside the dungeon?" said Friar.

"Inside the dungeon," said Punter. "I give you my word – "

"Why wasn't it flooded?"

"Fell down into a drain, to take it away."

"I'm beginning to see. The water made a curtain over the wall?"

"I'll say it did. Tons an' tons o' water a-roarin' down. An' if you went too near, you was swep' down the drain. Talk about a —"

"So you had to cut off the water, to reach the wall."

"That's right. And so we did. Built a — great sluice – it took us days. On the 'ill above the castle, to stop the fall. Then one night we lets down the sluice an', soon as the water stops, we goes up the drain. I won' forget that in a 'urry – talk about slime. An', as I remarks to 'Arris, 'Supposin' the water comes back.' Nice sort o' death we'd've 'ad, I don' think."

"But you didn't. You got up all right."

"An' wot did we find? You'll 'ardly believe it, sir, but them —
squirts 'ad the wall down. We'd stopped their — water, an' there
they was in the chamber, collectin' the goods… But they made
one mistake, they did. They never thought to watch out."

"What happened?" said Friar.

"We came in be'ind them, an' we was armed. 'Put them up,'
says 'Arris, an' that was that."

Friar was frowning.

"I thought you said that you'd handed the stuff away."

"So we did," said Punter, miserably. " 'Arris sends me to
watch out by the dungeon door, while 'e an' the others was
stowing the jools into bags. An' then somethin' must 'ave gone
wrong. Wot it was, I dunno. There weren't no noise nor nothin':
but after about an hour, that —, Palin, comes up an' lays me
out. An' when I come to, me wrists is tied an' I'm on a stable
floor. I never see 'Arris again an' I never see Bunch. Done in, I
take it. Though 'ow it 'appened, Gawd knows. I mean, we 'ad
them cold."

There was a little silence.

Then –

"What happened to you?"

"Chauffeur took me to Salzburg and put me on board a
train."

"Were you the only one left?"

" 'Cept for Bugle. 'E got out all right, 'cause 'e'd gone to let
down the sluice. Nice fuss 'e made, when we met. Said I'd
double-crossed 'im. 'See 'ere,' I says. 'Three months' – 'ard
labour, the — goods in me 'ands, an' then me block knocked off
an' a third-class carriage to England. Is that wot you call double-
crossin'?' "

"Where is he now?"

"Bugle? He's dead, I think. Working with Pharaoh, he was,
along with Dewdrop an' Rush. They went off on some very big
job, but they never come back. There's the Continen' for you –
if you win, you've got it: but if you lose, you're dead."

"There's something in that."

"I'll say there is... Well, that's what happened, sir. So you see there's nothin' doin'. We opened the safe for Ferrers, an' now the jools is gone."

"No, they're not," said Friar. Punter stared. "I'll lay you any money, those jewels are still where they were."

"Wot, be'ind the water an' all?"

"Why not? They're valuable things: and the chamber in which they were found is better than any safe."

"But Ferrers wouldn' o' kep' them. Wot's the good of – "

"Ferrers has kept them," said Friar. "I don't know why he has, but I know he has. I'll tell you how I know, Punter. Because, if such gems had been sold, the whole of the world would know. There were more than a hundred, if I remember aright."

" 'Undred an' twenty-seven."

"And every one of those a historical gem. All sculptured jewels, that cannot be broken up. The sale of but half a dozen would set the world by the ears."

"You don' say?"

"I do, indeed. And I know what I'm talking about. I move in art circles, myself. That's how I came to see that catalogue. And I tell you here and now that those gems are still there. And another thing I tell you – that such a collection of gems is beyond all price."

There was another silence. Punter's cigar had gone out; but he made no attempt to relight it. The news was too big.

"You goin' to 'ave a stab at it, sir?"

"More than a stab. I'm going to have them, Punter. D'you want to come in?"

"I'm not buildin' any more sluices."

"You won't be asked to. There must be an easier way."

"An' that castle's a — to enter. Walls about ten foot thick, an' the goin' outside enough to break a goat's 'eart."

"I expect there's a door," said Friar.

"There's a — drawbridge," said Punter. "You can't force them."

"No other way in?"

"The terrace ain't bad. A ladder would take you up. But 'Once bitten, twice shy', you know, sir. I'll lay they're watchin' out."

"How long is it since you failed?"

Punter appeared to reflect.

Then –

"Five years," he said.

"Good enough," said Friar, and got to his feet. "But we'd better not wait too long, or Ferrers will take them out. Things are going to happen in Austria. If he can't take anything else, he'll take those gems."

"I wish I knew," said Punter, "wot 'appened to bust the balloon. We 'ad the jools – I saw them, done up in three sort o' bales. An' the squirts was done – they daren't move 'and nor foot, for they 'ad a lady with them and 'Arris was out to kill."

Friar crossed to a little table, on which was a tray. He poured two whiskeys and sodas. Then he returned to Punter, tumblers in hand.

"Thank you, sir. Here's your best."

The two of them drank.

Then –

"D'you want to come in?" said Friar. "If not, I'll give you a tenner to hold your tongue."

"And if I do?"

"I take the lion's share, and you come next. We shan't be able to spend it; there'll be so much. Each gem will be an income: I'll see to that."

"Of course, I know the castle," said Punter. "An' round about."

"Your knowledge," said Friar, "would save me a lot of time."

"I'll say it would. But I don't want another wash-out. I mightn' be lucky this time. If I 'adn' been watchin' out... An' as it was, 'e — near broke my neck. Punch like the kick of a 'orse. My Gawd, I can feel it now."

"You won't have another wash-out, unless you let me down."

"Oh, I wouldn' do that, sir."

"Not twice," said Friar. "But serve me faithfully and you'll find me generous."

Punter fingered his chin.

"I wish I knew wot 'appened," he said. "Somebody chucked a spanner into the works. Must 'ave. It looked like Mansel, you know: but I never saw the —, if he was there."

"I've heard of Mansel," said Friar. "Is he any good?"

"— wizard," said Punter, "an' that's the truth. 'Rose' Noble 'ad 'im cold, but 'e did 'im in. 'E'd lose the race; but, when the numbers went up, you'd find he'd won."

"I'd like to meet him," said Friar.

"Well, I don' want to," said Punter. "I've done it twice, an' I don' want to do it again. I see 'im kill 'Rose' Noble. Shot 'im between the eyes. An' then 'e burst Auntie – I wasn' in on that. His sister's pearls 'ad been taken, an' Auntie was hornin' in. I tell you, Mansel's a —. An' Chandos is pretty tough. 'Alf a giant, like Palin, an' does as Mansel says. Gawd, wot a pair! If I thought they was backin' Ferrers, you wouldn' see me for dust."

"Nobody's backing Ferrers. He isn't backing himself, as far as I know. But that's what we've got to find out. This is the tenth of April. I shall be ready to leave by the first of May. I must get the hang of the country, find out Ferrers' movements and things like that. What I call 'reconnaissance', Punter. And if you're coming with me, I must know two days from now. You'd better think it over." Friar rose and crossed to the door. "Have a word with my servant, Sloper. He will be working with us and he knows my ways." He opened the door and called. "Sloper, look after Punter for half an hour."

"Sez you," breathed Sloper, backing away from the door.

1

We Shut the Stable Door

It was in the early summer of 193– that Jonathan Mansel spent a weekend at Maintenance, which is my country home. My wife and I were never, I think, so happy as when he was staying with us, for we all felt the same about things and had shared the perilous stuff of which friendship is made. 'Life and death, and a close run' – of such is the raw material of which are forged those bonds which nothing on earth can break.

His visit was unexpected; and so I was sure there was something he wished to discuss with me; but not till my wife had retired on the Saturday night did he take his stand on the hearth and fold his hands before him, as I had seen him do when he had some statement to make.

"There's a tale," he said, "which I would like you to hear. I'll cut it as short as I can, for this is a matter, as usual, in which the importance of words is very slight. I mean, it's a case for action...

"One Nicolas Ferrers died a year or two back, leaving his two great-nephews all that he had. This included an estate in Austria, half a day's run from Salzburg – a very beautiful place. It is called Hohenems. I stayed there twelve months ago, with one great-nephew, John Ferrers, and Lady Olivia, his wife. The other great-nephew likes travelling; but they are there all the time. Well, now they are getting uneasy. The Boche has been

1

looking at Austria very hard, and now his look is turning into a glare. They think – and I agree – that before very long they'll be under the German flag... Well, that would be the end of their home: for, even if they could bear to live under German rule, as being English, they would receive an attention which would be as unpleasant as it was particular. And so they will have to go. Sell, if they can, and go. It's a bitter grief to them, for they're crazy about the place. And I don't blame them – it is incomparable. But that is life – today. I'm afraid that in two or three years many other innocent landlords will take the same, hard road.

"But that is not all.

"The Castle of Hohenems is ancient and once belonged to Pope Alexander the Sixth."

"The father of the Borgias," I said.

"That's right. One of the biggest blackguards that ever was foaled. And he concealed in the castle the greatest treasure he had. There this lay, undreamed of, for over four hundred years – and then, at last, it was found by Ferrers and Constable. (That is the other great-nephew – Hubert Constable.) They had, of course, a clue: but it took a lot of finding, because it was well concealed.

"Well, when they had found it, they decided to let it lie. They had no need of money, the finding had cost three lives, and the treasure was of such value that, once its possession was known, it would have been a constant anxiety. So, to my mind very wisely, they walled up the chamber again and held their peace.

"But now the case is altered.

"The castle they must leave to the Boche. And, possibly, most of its contents. But they do not see why he should have the treasure, too. And so they propose to remove it – if they can. This shouldn't be very hard – from what they say, a suitcase would take the lot. It shouldn't be very hard, *provided that nobody knows that the treasure is there*. If somebody knows that secret – somebody ill-disposed, it may not be so easy to take the treasure away. I mean, he might put in his oar…

"Well, somebody does know.

"At the very time that the great-nephews found the treasure, a savage attempt was made to take it out of their mouths. Five rogues were involved, and four of the five are dead. But one is alive – and was seen six miles from Hohenems less than three weeks ago.

"Now, as it happens, we both of us know that rogue: and when I tell you his name, you'll know he's not working alone. Nor is he the head of his gang. But he has spilled the beans to somebody greater than he.

"Well, William, that's the position.

"Every day now the Boche is tightening his grip about Austria's neck: his agents are everywhere: and so, if those gems are to leave that unhappy country, they've got to leave before long. And somebody greater than Punter – "

"*Punter?*"

" – Punter, is waiting to pounce."

Twice we had brushed against Punter in other days. The man was a common thief and had worked for a master villain, who now was dead.

Mansel continued slowly.

"I have been asked my advice – and have offered my help. To tell you the truth, I've other things to do; and, while I like the Ferrers, they're not very much to me. But if they are to be embarrassed by Punter's gang, those gems will most certainly finish in Hitler's treasury. And that I cannot stomach. You see, they're beyond all price. They are one hundred and twenty-seven sculptured jewels…collected by an infamous Pope…and his catalogue is in existence…so that every incomparable item can be identified."

I took a deep breath.

"Such a thing's unheard of," I said.

"And yet it's true," said Mansel. "I've seen the catalogue."

There was a little silence.

Then –

"You can count me in," said I. "I'd like to see Punter again, and I am prepared to resent the rape of Austria. After all, it has been our wash-pot."

Mansel laughed.

"It has, indeed," he said. "But that is the way of the Boche. He's never so happy as fouling another's nest."

I fingered my chin.

"Punter," I said. "Punter, unless he has changed, is a lazy fool. If Ferrers has kept his counsel, why should Punter suspect that the treasure is still where it was?"

"He didn't," said Mansel. "It never entered his head. Punter assumed that the treasure had been removed. He knew of what it consisted and he would assume that it had been turned into cash. Which proves that he mentioned the matter to somebody greater than he – by way of reminiscence, I mean. For they would know at once that no such collection had ever come into the market, or even got into the Press. And that could mean only one thing – that the jewels were still where they were. And don't forget this, William. The same big shot will know that now is approaching the time when those to whom they belong will endeavour to get them out."

Now that I had been shown it, this seemed to be common sense: for Punter's return to the neighbourhood declared his return to the charge. (And there I was wrong, for in all that came to pass, we never set eyes upon Punter from first to last. John Ferrers had certainly seen him – and he had very good cause to remember his face. And I sometimes think the truth is that, though he belonged to the gang and had led them up to the gates, when he saw Mansel, he made some excuse to withdraw: for he had seen Mansel at work and had no desire to try a fall with him.)

"Well, there you are," said Mansel, filling a pipe. "The position is interesting. Our headache will be to get the stuff out of the country. The big shot's headache will be to get it away from us. If he can do that, he's home; for thieves have ways and means of getting stuff out of a country that we have not: it's going on all the time, as, of course, you know. And our joint headache will be to foil the Boche. But I feel that we must have a stab, for German hands are too filthy to finger a treasure like that."

Be sure I agreed with him.

Before ten days had gone by, our arrangements were made.

The Ferrers, at present in England, were to remain where they were: but Mansel and I were to go to Austria. We should not visit Hohenems, but were to stay at an inn some thirty miles off. So, with any luck, our presence would not be remarked; for Punter's friends would have their eyes upon the castle, and not on the neighbourhood. Our object, of course, would be to, so to speak, pick them up: for, if you are to fight someone, it is of great importance to know who it is. Once we had 'placed' the gang, we should send word to the Ferrers to come to Hohenems. Their return would excite the thieves: but we should be ready and waiting to see what action these took – and how they could best be dealt with, so that the field was cleared. For a clear field we had to have, if we were to foil the Boche.

The inn at which we should stay had been for some years the headquarters of a very close friend of the Ferrers, whom Mansel had met. His name was Andrew Palin, and he had been concerned in unearthing the jewels. That we could count upon him, there seemed no doubt: and this was as well, for Constable could not be with us for several weeks. A wire had come from the Congo, to say he had broken a leg…

The final arrangements were made at Maintenance, for there, by my request, the Ferrers had come to stay. To my great pleasure, their visit was to continue, though Mansel and I were gone; for, if I was to leave my very dutiful wife, I liked to think that she had congenial company. And John and Olivia Ferrers were very natural and easy in all they did.

And that, thank God, is the end of my introduction. Never before, I think, have I been so long in coming up to my tale: but I beg that I may be excused, for in this case I had to throw back to action which had been taken before we came upon the scene.

Mansel touched the map with his pencil.

"There's the inn," he said: "about twenty-two miles off. I'd rather get in after dark, so let's take an easy here and have something to eat."

The spot was attractive. A busy stream was tumbling across our road and under a grey, stone bridge; and a little sward, by the side of the hasty water, was kept by a pleasant bulwark of living rock. Above this, beeches were growing, to droop their elegance over its smooth, old face: and I think the truth is that once the stream was broader, and the wall of rock, now idle, had held it back to its bed.

While Mansel's servant, Carson, set out some sandwiches, Bell, who was my servant, began to wash the Rolls; for the way had been long and, at times, the dust had been thick, and no one of us four could endure that a car which was travel-stained should await attention.

There was no pool to bathe in; but, lying on the edge of the turf, we laved our heads and our hands: and I think this did us more good than the food we presently ate, for the day had been very hot, and we had left at dawn and had wasted no time.

It was when we had broken our fast that Mansel lay down on his back and looked at the fading sky.

"I have a feeling," he said, "that we are up against someone who's pretty good. If he is cultured enough to know that these gems have never made their appearance at home or abroad, he is in a different street to most of the crooks we've met. He may not be quite so, er, virile but he's probably more astute – and more appreciative."

"By which you mean...?"

"That he probably knows that every one of those gems is quite invaluable. His desire to possess them will, therefore, be very great. It may approach the fanatic... Punter would sell the lot for thirty thousand pounds: but, if I am right, his chief will be well aware that, if he can bring it off, that sum will be his income, no matter how long he lives."

I fingered my chin.

"Well, it's up to us," I said. "Such stuff should be in a museum."

"That is what Ferrers proposes – if we can get so far."

"Forever England's," said I. "Does Punter know that Palin was in at the death?"

"He does."

"Then they may be nursing Palin."

"I think that's possible."

"Has Ferrers put Palin wise – about having seen Punter, I mean?"

"I'm afraid he hasn't," said Mansel.

"Oh, hell," said I.

"Exactly," said Mansel. "That's why we've come so fast." He sat up and glanced at his wrist. "Andrew Palin's no fool, but of course he should have been warned. I never dreamed that he hadn't, till Ferrers told me at Maintenance two days ago."

I sighed.

"Why will people," I said, "withhold important facts?"

"God knows," said Mansel. And then, "It can't be helped."

Ten minutes later, we were upon the road.

Sitting on the arm of a chair, Palin read through the letter which we had brought. He was a big, fair man, with a merry face. But this was now grave.

When he had done, he looked up.

"I'm to ask you a question," he said. "To prove your authority. I expect that was your idea."

"Yes," said Mansel, "it was. This is a matter in which we can take no risks."

Palin nodded.

Then –

"I played for Olivia upstairs on her wedding night. What tune did I play?"

"*A frog he would a-wooing go.*"

"Good enough," said Palin. "From now on, you may command me. I'm ripe for enterprise. The last time I saw Punter, I had the pleasure of knocking his face through his head. Yet the dog returns to his vomit. I can't help feeling that's rash. Never mind. I fancy all's quiet so far. I was at the castle on Tuesday – three days ago. As you probably know, I have the run of the place."

Mansel nodded.

"I think you've a room there," he said.

"That's right. Complete with changes of raiment. The Ferrers spoil their friends. Of course I never use it, unless they're there: but the servants have orders to receive me at any time."

"And when they're away, you keep an eye on the place?"

Palin shook his head.

"That is not necessary. The steward's a paragon. No; if ever I go, it's to show the place to a friend."

"I see. Was that why you went there on Tuesday?"

"Yes," said Palin. "A wallah was staying here – a most entertaining man, with a caustic wit. A fellow and tutor of Oxford. Great authority on old silver. That's why I took him there the first time – the Ferrers have got some really beautiful stuff."

Mansel sat very still.

"You went more than once?"

"Twice. Friar was charmed with the place – and they don't show it now."

"You took him round?" said Mansel.

"Naturally. He was immensely interested."

8

"No doubt," said Mansel, dryly.

Palin stared. Then he started up to his feet.

"My God," he cried, "you don't mean…"

"It's not your fault," said Mansel. "You should have been warned. But I think it more than likely that Friar is the head of this gang."

"But – "

"Fellows and tutors of Oxford don't leave Oxford in June."

"Nor they do," said Palin. "That never occurred to me. And yet I can hardly believe… Still, he did take an interest in the water. God in heaven, I showed the fellow the sluice."

There was a dreadful silence.

The gems were walled into a chamber: over that wall a cascade was falling down: no one could breach that wall, without letting down the sluice. But once the sluice was down, the chamber could be opened in half an hour.

Mansel got to his feet.

"I think we should be moving," he said. "If they didn't break in last night, we may be in time."

I shall always remember that drive.

Though by rights we should have been tired, the urgency of the business set us alert. And Carson and Bell were a-tiptoe. For such as know its flavour, danger is a wonderful spice.

As Bell took a pistol from the locker –

"It's like old times, sir," he said.

And then we were all in the Rolls, and Palin was sitting with Mansel, to tell him the way to go. I was kneeling behind and between them, to hear what they said.

"The private road," said Palin, "is two miles long. If you don't want to drive that bit, you can berth the car in a wood. By the way, have you got a torch?"

"Be your age," said Mansel. "We're old in sin."

"God be praised," said Palin. "The point is this. If the sluice is down, water will not be flowing down in the woods. I will

9

make my way down there, complete with torch. If the water is flowing, I signal twice. If it is not flowing, which God forbid, I signal five times."

"Aren't you assuming," said Mansel, "that they will go in by the gate?"

"Wrong again," said Palin. "Of course they won't. The drawbridge is up of nights when the Ferrers are gone. They'll go in by the postern steps. Not the postern itself. That's barred. But, if they can reach the terrace…"

"Go on."

"Well, I could do it," said Palin. "A pane of glass and a shutter wouldn't stop me."

"What about the stables? I seem to remember that trees lean over their roofs."

"That would bring them into the courtyard. I'd put the terrace first."

"The terrace has it," said Mansel. "What else d'you know?"

"The water remains," said Palin. "If that's not flowing, they're in."

"Or they've been and gone," said Mansel. "Once they'd got the stuff, they wouldn't pull up the sluice."

"You know," said Palin, "you've got a nasty mind. I've lost quite half a stone since you sprang the mine. I don't say I can't afford it, but must you twist my tail?"

"Sorry," said Mansel, laughing, "but facts have got to be faced."

"Oh, dear. And he made me laugh. The things he said about Gibbon. D'you really think he's your man?"

"Yes, I do," said Mansel. "He's just the sort of wallah I thought would be on this job. But it's not your fault at all. I should have done the same, if I hadn't been warned. How far is the private road?"

"About four miles, now. There's a village a mile ahead."

"Tell me before I get there. I want to put out my lights."

"Then put them out," said Palin. "It's round that bend."

The night was very dark, but, though the way was strange, Mansel drove without lights till we came to the private road: here he had to use them, because of the woods.

"Where is this place," said Mansel, "at which we can berth the car?"

"On the left," said Palin; "about a furlong ahead." A moment later I saw the mouth of a track.

Mansel changed to a lower gear.

As he lifted the Rolls from the road and into the track, he brought her up all standing, and Palin exclaimed.

Six paces in front of us was standing another car.

I was out in a flash and was moving along its off side: but the driver's seat was empty, and, when I used my torch, I saw that there was no one within the car. This was a very nice Lowland and must have been very fast. The switch and the bonnet were locked, but the doors were not.

"All clear?" said Mansel, beside me.

I told him yes.

"Good," says he. "But it's just as well we came." He turned to speak to Palin. "How far are we from the castle?"

"About two miles."

"In that case they're almost certainly using a second car. Bell, keep an eye on that road – towards the castle, I mean. Carson, turn the Rolls, take her back to the highway and cruise to and fro. William, back this car down and leave her across the road: I think her weight will do it, if you take the hand-brake off."

As the Rolls moved out of my way, I did as he said – to bring the Lowland to rest directly across the road. So nothing could ever go by – not even a bicycle.

"Cut the ignition wires, William. I'll attend to the tyres."

Two minutes later, the Lowland was out of commission. She could not be driven: until her tyres were inflated, she could not be moved by hand. And until she was out of the way, nothing could pass.

"Well, that's that," said Mansel. "We've shut the stable door. We may as well go on and have a word with the thieves. Or shall we stay here and receive them? They're sure to come back."

"We'd better go on," I said.

"Palin forward," said Mansel. "He knows the way."

Bell went on, to see if the drawbridge was raised. We waited for the flash of his torch, before descending the road to the valley below. This gave to the postern-steps, by which it seemed certain the thieves would attempt their entry. What was much more important, it led to the running water, the absence of which would show that the sluice was down.

After a moment or two, Bell's torch winked twice, to say that the drawbridge was up.

It was now not quite so dark, for soon the moon would rise: this helped us very much, for the last thing we wanted to do was to show a light, while we were taking the way that the thieves had used. The glow of Bell's torch was directed away from the castle, and so should not have been seen, except by ourselves.

So we made our way down to the meadows below the castle itself, moving fairly slowly, that Bell might have time to rejoin us before we left the road.

Sure enough, at the edge of the meadows was standing a second car, which Palin was ready to swear was the one which Friar had used when he stayed at the inn. No one was with the car, so we took the contact-breaker and let her be.

Then Palin led the way to the water. But this was gushing as usual out of the woods.

"Good," said Mansel. "Tell me about this sluice."

"It's a slab of stone," said Palin "that runs in a groove. Where it is, I don't know. Stout boards would do in its place: but they'd have to fit."

"That may be their trouble," said Mansel, "fitting the boards. I take it you explained this to Friar?"

"More or less," sighed Palin. "This was the castle's supply in ancient days. He said he'd seen the same system once before:

12

but there had been a means of cutting it off. Not to be beaten, I instantly spilled the beans."

And, with his words, the flow of the water diminished, but did not stop.

"That's right," said Mansel, calmly. "They're getting warm. Let's go up and watch them, shall we? As I understand the position, they've got some way to go yet."

I could not see Palin's face, but I saw him take off his hat and wipe his brow.

We climbed the postern-steps, and there, at their head, was standing an excellent ladder, to take us up to the ramparts, hanging above. And a terrace window was open, to let us into the house.

There Palin took charge: and, after what seemed a long time, he led us down into a dungeon, where men were talking quietly and showing a light.

There were, in fact, two dungeons, the inner of which was larger and lower down than the first. It was there that the men were busy, and, standing at the head of the steps which led to the second dungeon out of the first, we could see what they were doing and hear what they said.

There were, in all, four men; and one, with his back to us, was sitting upon a stool. On his knees he had a small searchlight, with which he illumined the scene.

It was a sinister place, with a well in its floor. Its walls were of living rock, but in one, some five feet up, were signs of masonry. I had the impression of a doorway that had been closed: and then I knew that that was the way to the chamber in which the gems were concealed. Above this was gaping the conduit by which the water had passed; the stones and the mortar were reeking with damp and with slime, and the well in the floor was directly in line with the conduit some five feet away from the wall.

The stones were roughly laid, and the layers of mortar between them were finger-thick. With a decent hammer and

13

chisel, I could have cut a way in in a very short time – but not without a ladder on which to stand: and set up a ladder, you could not, because of the well. To this, the floor was sloping, and, since the flags could not be seen for the slime, no ladder could have stood by itself: yet no man could have held it, for he would have slipped; and once he had lost his footing, he must have gone into the depths.

This, then, was the thieves' dilemma. They had uncovered the doorway; they had the hammers and chisels with which to cut their way in: but they could not approach the doorway, because whoever did was bound to slide into the well.

The man with the searchlight was speaking.

" 'And beside all this, between us and you there is a great gulf fixed' – a fact which Punter the Bold preferred to keep to himself." He sucked in his breath. "I wish he was here. Never mind. When he returns to the fold, we'll have things out. Don't forget that, will you? *Suppressio veri* is a practice I cannot commend. I don't mind *suggestio falsi*, because I am never deceived: but its twin is a dart of the wicked, against which no man is proof." Another spoke over his shoulder.

"What we want is a nurdle," he said, "to cover that — well."

"But what a brain!" said Friar, for it was he, of course, that had spoken first. "But I have an uneasy feeling that hurdles are, at the moment, in what is called 'short supply'. A very beautiful phrase. What about a carpet, Orris? A twenty foot square of carpet. I feel that might save your soul."

"That's all right," said a third. "An' a ladder'll stend on that: *an*' cover the well."

"Thank you, Goat," said Friar. "It's always gratifying to have the obvious perceived – and a declaration, however obscure, made to that effect. Orris and Sloper will now go and win a carpet, while you and I await the fruit of their toil. *Get on*, you double —. You heard what I said."

The tone in which he had spoken was like the crack of a whip, and the two men, Orris and Sloper, fairly jumped in their skins.

As they turned to do his bidding –

"We'll 'ave to 'ave the ladder," said Orris.

"I'll see to that. You go and find a carpet, twenty foot square."

We melted into the shadows, to watch, first, Orris and Sloper, and then the others go by.

"What could be better?" said Mansel. "Let's pull up the sluice, while they're gone, and take the boards away."

This took hardly a minute, for Palin showed us the way.

"Can we reach the steps by a window? I'd like to see them out."

"Follow me," said Palin.

Mansel touched my arm.

"See how we go, William. I'd like you and Bell to come back."

So it fell out that, when we had learned how to reach the postern-steps, Bell and I came back to the dungeons, to watch what befell.

Returned to its proper channel, a powerful head of water was plunging into the well: because it fell within walls, the bellow it made was monstrous, and so, if words were spoken, I cannot tell what they were. But, when Friar and his man returned, they seemed, at first, unable to credit the report of their eyes. Then with one consent, they let the ladder fall and turned and ran for the sluice.

Finding their boards removed, they, both of them, drew their pistols, and peered to and fro, all ready to meet the onslaught which did not come. And when the others arrived, dragging a square of carpet and damning its weight, they cursed them into silence, to the others' great indignation, because, of course, they knew nothing of what had occurred. All this we saw very well from behind the first dungeon's door, for the lights were on in the passage which led to the sluice. That I was shaking with laughter, I frankly admit, for few things are more entertaining than to see a man fall into the pit you have digged.

Then Friar gave the word to withdraw, which, using the utmost caution, they presently did. But first they retrieved the ladder – greatly against their will: but they did not know how else to reach the postern-steps. Indeed, I never saw men so much discomfited. Not that I blame them at all, for what had happened smacked of the supernatural, and the passages and the dungeons offered a natural background to such activity.

We saw them on to the ramparts, to join them, later on, on the postern-steps, and we watched them bestow the ladder within the woods. And then, with Mansel and Palin, we watched them deal with the car…

I do not wish to labour the matter, but several minutes went by before it occurred to Friar that the hand that had pulled up their sluice had interfered with his car, and the frantic efforts of his fellows to make the engine fire reduced us to tears of mirth. And then at last they found that the contact-breaker was gone. While they were digesting this outrage, Palin and Bell went on, to intercept Carson and wait at the end of the drive: but Mansel and I stayed behind, in case of accidents.

From what they said, it was clear that it never entered their heads that the Lowland might have been found, and Friar spoke well of himself, as being a man that kept a spare string for his bow. And so, at last, they set off, all very short of temper and two, who had been 'swinging' the shaft, scarce able to stand, to walk the two miles to the car which should carry them home.

As soon as they had started, Mansel and I took the ladder and laid it out of sight by the postern-steps: and then we followed the rogues, to overtake them before they had reached the main drive.

So we moved together, some twenty-five paces apart. And then they came to the Lowland, lying across the road.

For a moment, they all stood still.

Then –

"He's here," said Friar. "This is Mansel. I might have known." He turned in his tracks. "Are you there, Captain Mansel? I'd like to talk with you."

"Then put up your hands," said Mansel. "I'm not alone."

"Today to you," said Friar, and did as he said.

"Your companions will do the same and will stand by your side."

At this there was some hesitation. Then somebody lighted a torch and Mansel fired.

As the torch was shattered –

"I trust that will show you," said Mansel, "that I mean what I say."

Before he had finished speaking, the four were in line.

"Take their arms, William."

I took their pistols away and came back to his side.

"And now," said Mansel, "what do you want to say?"

"Deal with me," said Friar. "If you don't, I go to the Boche."

"I don't deal with thieves," said Mansel.

"D'you think you can deal with the Boche?"

"Nobody can," said Mansel. "That's why you won't try."

"I will – in the last resort."

"I'm afraid I'm not playing," said Mansel. "Do as you please."

"I can get this stuff out of the country. You cannot. I can't help feeling there's room for a bargain there."

"In your eyes, perhaps. Not in mine. Tonight you have shown that you are a common thief. And common thieves are people with whom I never deal – except as I have tonight."

"I see. D'you know a man called Palin?"

"I do," said Mansel. "It's thanks to him that I'm here. When he wired that you were leaving, I left at once."

A pregnant silence greeted this pregnant lie.

Then –

"About these cars," said Friar.

"You can take them both," said Mansel, "provided you waste no time. You see, this is blocking the drive. When you've inflated the tyres, you can push her straight. Then you can bring up the other and tow her away." He turned to me. "The contact-breaker, William."

I took it out of my pocket and pitched it down on the ground.

"You think of everything, don't you?"

"I try to," said Mansel. "How's Punter?"

"He's alive at the moment," said Friar.

"I see. Well, now I've arrangements to make, so I must get back to the castle. I think it would be a mistake for us to meet again."

"The mistake will be made, Captain Mansel."

"As you please. It's now three o'clock. If your cars are still here at five, they'll be taken off the estate and wrecked for good."

With that, he turned on his heel and I followed him down the drive, with the firearms which I had taken still in my hands.

We walked as far as the fork, where one road led on to the castle and the other, up which we had come, to the foot of the postern-steps. And there we concealed the pistols and waited to see that the rogues would do as we said.

Five minutes later, Sloper and Goat arrived – and, having turned the corner, sat down on the bank and lighted their cigarettes.

"Gorblime, said Goat. " 'E can' put this acrost me. Did you ever see such a — in all your life?"

"Give 'im a chance," said Sloper. "Them jools is worf all Bon' Street – an' then some more. Can' expec' roses all the way."

"Roses?" spat Goat. "*Roses*? Bunch o' red-'ot barb wire, if you ask me. Be yer age, Sloper. Led daown the garding path – "

" 'E's bin double-cross," said Sloper. "That Palin's a dirty —. Arms roun' 'is neck – an' wirin' reports to Mansel every night."

"See 'ere," said Goat. "If I fall down, there aren't no excuses for me. Well, 'e's fell down, good an' proper. Danced bung into the muck. An' more. 'Ad 'is nose rubbed in it, Sloper... Well, wot's sauce for the — gander's — well sauce for the goose. I've lorsse me confidence. Mansel's the better man."

"It does look like it," said Friar. The others started to their feet. "And yet I've a feeling that I shall have those gems. You see, they're worth having: and when I want something worth having I usually get it before the end of the match. Palin fooled me, of course. He put up a beautiful show. I could have sworn he was simple. But now I know where I am. And that is back where we started. Well, be it so. Mansel is here, of course, to get those jewels out. I shall let him get them out – *of the chamber*. That will save us a lot of wearisome work. And when they are out of the chamber… Those gems are worth two million – two million pounds. And that's rock bottom. I don't think I can let Mansel in on a thing like that. No, I think we shall have to have them… Sloper, back to the Lowland, and pull your weight. Goat with me. We're going to move that ladder – you never know."

With that, he made for the meadows, and Goat fell in behind: but Sloper turned and went back the way he had come.

Mansel and I followed Sloper for two or three hundred yards: then we left the road and took to the woods, to come out on the main highway in a quarter of an hour.

As we turned to the left –

"Ignorance," said Mansel, "is bliss. If Friar knew what we knew, the knowledge would shorten his life. Honestly, it was a very near thing. And we have emerged triumphant. We have compelled a respect which we in no way deserve."

"You've shaken his fellows," said I.

"Goat, yes," said Mansel. "But Friar will deal with him. That's what he followed them for."

"How," said I, "did he know that you were in on this show?"

"Ferrers must have been watched," said Mansel. "And when my name was mentioned, Punter filled in the gaps."

That that was the explanation, I have no doubt: for Punter had good reason to know what Mansel could do. And Friar's recognition of Mansel's masterly ways shows, I think, what the man had been led to expect.

"What line will he take?" said I.

"I wish I knew," said Mansel. "Of course he'll do as he said and let us unearth the gems. It sounds very fine, but he can't do anything else. But how will he prevent us from taking them out? I mean, he can't watch the castle by day and night. Never mind. Our job is to go ahead as though he didn't exist, and sooner or later he's bound to show his hand."

And there Bell fell in beside us, to lead us up to the Rolls…

As we drove back to the inn, Mansel related to Palin what had occurred.

Then –

"Tell me this," he said. "Tomorrow morning will Hohenems send for the police? I mean, that the castle has been entered will be most evident."

"No," said Palin. "The steward will report to me. I am *in loco parentis*. He will report to me and ask what he should do."

"You're quite sure of that? I mean, the last thing we want to do is to catch the eye of the police."

"I'm sure of that," said Palin.

"Good," said Mansel. "That means we can take our rest."

So we came back to the inn: and twenty minutes later we were asleep.

It was ten o'clock the next morning, when Mansel glanced again at his wristwatch and started to fill a pipe.

"I should have said," he said, "that the steward was late."

"I confess," said Palin, "I thought he'd have been here by now. But he's not the man to panic. After all, nothing has been stolen. The house has been entered and one of the carpets moved – a circumstance, I may say, which will confound the staff. More coffee?" I shook my head. "The steward will certainly acquaint me with what has occurred. But, if he's busy this morning…"

He broke off and shrugged his shoulders.

"I expect you're right," said Mansel. "Hullo, this may be him."

But it was not. It was a delivery van – belonging to a firm of cleaners, that did their business at Robin, the nearest town.

We had broken our fast in the forecourt, and as the driver went by, he lifted his hat. Then he stopped in his stride and came back.

Then he spoke in German.

"The gentlemen will excuse me," he said, "but I have a letter here, addressed to a Mr Palin, said to be staying here. I have brought it from Hohenems."

Palin put out his hand.

"I'm Mr Palin," he said. The letter passed. Palin read it frowning.

Then he gave it to Mansel and got to his feet. "Come," he said to the driver. "You've earned a flagon of beer."

When Mansel had read the letter, he gave it to me.

Sir,

As the police will allow no one to leave the Castle, I cannot report to you in person, as is my duty and desire. But the bearer has promised to bear this note to you.

At five o'clock this morning the stable-telephone rang. It was the stud-groom speaking. The body of a man had been found, not very far from the foot of the postern-steps. He had died from a heavy blow on the back of the head. He was a stranger. I said I would come down at once. I roused the staff and dressed. As I was about to descend the postern-steps, one of the men came running, to say that a terrace window had been broken and that the house had been entered during the night. I saw these things for myself. Then I sent for the staff, and called the roll. But all were safe. I then hastened down to the stables; but the stud-groom, tired of waiting, had sent for the police. I reproved him, for not waiting for my instructions, although I think that I should have had to report the matter, without waiting for your advice. For murder is serious. I viewed the body and gave orders for it to be covered, but not touched. I had never before seen the man. I then returned to the house. So far as I could see, nothing at all had been taken, but a carpet had been dragged from the gallery into a passage in the older part of the house. Why, I cannot conceive: but that is the fact. I had just told Ernst to make ready to drive me to you, when the police arrived. I had, therefore, to postpone my departure. Whilst I was accompanying them on their investigation, more important police arrived from Robin itself. And they had to be dealt with. I then asked them to excuse me, while I reported to you: but they at once declined to allow me to leave the scene. I then proposed to send a letter by Ernst. But they would let no one leave. It was while we were arguing that the cleaners' van arrived: and the driver has kindly consented to carry this note.

Yours very respectfully,

Hans Kirschner.
Steward.

As Palin returned –

"Riposte," said Mansel. "This fellow, Friar, is a very clever man."

Palin put a hand to his head.

"I'm not there, yet," he said.

Mansel fingered his chin.

"Friar threatened to go to the Boche. He won't, and I told him so. But he made up his mind there and then that the Boche must be put on to me. Not on to the gems, of course, but on to Hohenems. His eyes must be fastened on the Castle – *the one thing we do not want*. The question was how to do it, without involving himself. And then he perceived an instrument, ready to hand – 'a *goat* caught in a thicket by his horns'…

"Goat was of no more use. I can't believe such a man was ever valuable; but, after the show last night, he was against going on. More. His outlook was dangerous, for rotten apples tend to corrupt the good. There, then, was Friar's sacrifice. He took him back to the car, and there he offered him up. So he killed two birds with one stone. He got rid of an awkward appendage and gravely embarrassed us."

Palin's face was a study.

"D'you mean to say," he said, "that Friar slew one of his men, to put a spoke in our wheel?"

"Well, we didn't kill him," said Mansel. "Nor did the staff. He was there alone with his master – that we know. He had lately given the latter grave offence, and I think it's pretty clear that his death will embarrass us. A very mysterious murder at Hohenems' gates: a curious house-breaking: and our finger-prints all over that blasted ladder... That's just bad luck, of course. Friar didn't know that."

"And I hobnobbed with that monster. He asked me to play him Chopin, and I complied."

"Oh, he's a big stiff," said Mansel. "You can't get away from that. And now I think you ought to get off. We, of course, must fade out. The wicket is rather too sticky for us to go in. I mean, every stranger will be suspect – and we were abroad last night. And then those fingerprints... Oh, no. We shall reappear all right: three or four days in Salzburg will dry the pitch."

"Shall I stay at the Castle?" said Palin.

"If you please. And write to Ferrers, just for the look of the thing. I'll write to him, too. He'll have to come out, of course. And I think he might bring us with him. Yes, that will be best. And please report to me at considerable length. I want to know the police angle and what you make of the Boche who is sure to be there."

Twenty minutes later, Palin was gone.

The hotel which we used at Salzburg was little known: but that was Mansel's way. Whenever he could, he stayed at a very quiet house: but the service which he received was beyond all praise. Indeed, I know for a fact that we always fared very much better than many people that stayed in the smart hotels. But at times we went forth to dine at a first-class restaurant. And this we did upon our fourth evening at Salzburg.

As we were drinking our soup, Friar came in, with a very good-looking girl.

"What could be better?" said Mansel. "William, you've a way with the ladies. I think you must take her on."

"I'm damned if I will," said I.

"We shall see," said Mansel. "I'll lay he comes up."

"D'you think he'll recognize us? I mean, it was pretty dark."

"He has recognized us," said Mansel. "He might not have known me again, but you took his pistol away."

Sure enough, when dinner was over, Friar asked his guest to excuse him and crossed to where we sat.

"Good evening, Captain Mansel."

"Good evening, Mr Friar. Let me introduce Mr Chandos. You haven't officially met."

"How d'you do," I said.

"May I sit down?"

"You may."

Friar took his seat.

"So you're tired of Hohenems?"

"An occasional visit to Salzburg suits me well."

"You see, I'm a man of my word."

"I have," said Mansel, "no evidence to that effect."

"I said I should go to the Boche."

"And I said you wouldn't go. And nor you have."

"Technically, no. But the Boche has come to you."

"I expect you're right," said Mansel.

"You know I'm right," said Friar. "That's why you're here."

"As you please."

"Do you still refuse to come in?"

"Be your age," said Mansel.

Friar raised his eyebrows.

"An equivocal saying," he said.

"Then let me be plain. I do not deal with thieves or with murderers. Except as I have – and shall. And I never submit to blackmail."

Friar lighted a cigarette.

"Fine words," he said.

"Plain words. You are a thief and you are a murderer. I never strike a bargain with people like that."

"You don't think much of me?"

Mansel shrugged his shoulders.

"Palin beat you," he said.

I saw the man wince.

"That's perfectly true," he said. "I slipped up there."

"If Palin could beat you," said Mansel, "I think I can."

"You'd be much wiser," said Friar, "to do a deal."

"Wiser, yes. But so far I have clean hands."

"You've killed your man, Captain Mansel."

"That's as may be. I repeat that I have clean hands."

"Goat was a blackguard," said Friar.

"It ill became his confederate to put him down. Dog shouldn't eat dog, you know."

Friar threw back his head and laughed.

"It is now seven years," he said, "since I left the narrow path. At the time at which I did so, I made up my mind to one thing – never to resent insult from the caste which had been mine."

"A prudent decision," said Mansel.

"On occasion, it has stood me in stead. And how d'you think I do it?"

"I've no idea."

"By minding a line of Virgil's. *Forsan et haec olim meminisse juvabit.*" He rose to his feet. "Which, being interpreted, means 'It is the last laugh that counts'."

25

"That's a very free translation," said Mansel.

Friar looked at him very hard.

"Are you also among the scholars?"

"By no means. But I can translate *forsan*."

I see. Well, *au revoir*."

With that, he was gone.

As he rejoined the lady –

"And the true translation?" said I.

" 'The day may come when even this memory will make me smile.' "

"I see. And *forsan*?"

"Means 'may'."

"He'll never forgive you," I said, "for 'dog eating dog'."

"I said what I did, to make him step out of his ground. He covered up very well, but I think he must hate my guts. And when you hate a man's guts, you desire to hit him for six."

"He's leaving," said I.

"Good," said Mansel. "We'll give him half an hour's start. And then we'll use our back door. I mean, if it has come off, we shall see him again."

Fifty-five minutes later, I peered through our sitting-room casement, to see a figure erect in an easy chair. I think that it held a pistol in either hand. But of this, I cannot be sure, for the light was dim.

When I made my report to Mansel –

"What could be better?" he said. "D'you think he came in this way?"

"There's dirt on the window-sill."

"Good," said Mansel. "We'll take him as he comes down."

Friar did not come down for three hours – three of the longest that I have ever spent. But they must have been long for him.

As he turned, after reaching the ground, Mansel hit him square on the point of the chin.

I went for Bell and Carson, who were waiting at the front of the house.

By the time I was back, Mansel had searched the man, to find two pistols, his passport, his notecase and nothing else.

Mansel addressed the servants.

"Turn out the Rolls very quietly and keep her here in the yard. In five minutes' time we shall come down as he did, and then we'll be off."

With that, we went round to the front and entered the house with our key.

In our rooms we went through the notecase, to see what it held. But there was nothing but money and two or three visiting cards. These bore no address, but the name of a London Club. I should not think of saying which Club it was; but it bears a distinguished name and it stands in Pall Mall.

As he locked the pistols away –

"Pillows and blankets," said Mansel. "The man is seriously ill. We're rushing him to Munich, in the hope of saving his life. He's had special treatment there from a doctor he knows. A car is to meet us halfway, at —."

Five minutes later we were upon the road.

The plan was a very good plan, but it was very bold. To cross the frontier with Friar was easier said than done. But Mansel was a master of bluff, and would jest with Customs Officials while I dared not trust my voice.

Happily, the frontier was close, though when we came to the post the sky was pale.

While Bell and I succoured Friar – the man was still unconscious, for Mansel knew how to hit – the latter swept the officers off their feet. 'It's a matter of life and death. As you see, we've come straight from a party: we haven't had time to change.' They came and peered at the figure, pillowed and rugged. And then they stamped his passport and let us go.

So we entered Germany…

27

After thirty miles we turned off, and when we were deep in the country, we set the man down.

We kept his passport and notecase and propped him against a tree, with his face to the rising sun. Then we re-entered the Rolls, bypassed the little town at which Mansel had said we were meeting another car, and then returned through this to the frontier post.

Ten minutes later we were on Austrian soil.

As I heaved a sigh of relief –

"I hope and believe," said Mansel, "that Friar will be off our map for nearly a week. He dare not go to the police, for if the police get on to us, well, we know he killed Goat. He'll have to go to a Consul, to get another passport – and that will not be issued for several days. Inquiries will have to be made and references taken up. Besides, he's got to get money."

"He's badly placed," said I. "And Palin said his German was very poor."

"It's a question of time. If he has friends in Munich, they can identify him, and push the thing through. But unless he has friends in Munich, he'll have to wait."

"What would you do?" said I.

"Wire to London for funds, get a pass from the Consul for England – he'd give him that – go to the Passport Office and start again. In case he does that, we'll post his passport back to the Passport Office. That will complicate things, especially if we amend it before it goes."

I began to laugh.

"Your score's mounting up," I said.

"That doesn't matter, if we can get a good start. Besides, for all we know, the Boche is sitting at Hohenems... In which case, Friar's score is very much longer than mine. There should be a letter from Palin, when we get in."

And so there was.

Dear Mansel,

Things might be worse.

The police did not find the ladder. I 'discovered' it later – to their delight. There were then no fingerprints.

This will show you better than anything I can say their standards of efficiency. But since, as you know, the greater a man's inefficiency, the more officious he is, the steward, the staff and myself have been driven nearly out of our minds. Great offence, for instance, was taken, because one of the maids could not spell her mother's maiden name.

And now to business.

The Boche was there. He took no sort of action: he never opened his mouth: he only looked on. But I don't think he missed very much. The movement of the carpet interested him no end. I found him still staring upon it, after the others had gone. And he entered the dungeons and every room on the passage beyond where the carpet was found. In a word, he perceived the obvious – that the robbers had need of the carpet to help them to what they sought. He is a tall, fair man, with burning eyes. A brutal mouth and, I fancy, immensely strong. He was used with a great respect, which he clearly despised. The murder did not interest him. Nor did the statements made. He had eyes for the steward and me. Since he never spoke, it was extremely difficult to read his mind. I think he is quite satisfied that the thieves came for something the staff did not know was there. And I think he is wondering whether, in fact, the thieves went empty away. I did what I could to suggest that they did not. 'But nothing is missing,' says the steward. 'Are you sure there was nothing in some coffer of which you did not know? I mean, the murder looks like a quarrel over the loot.' And so on... But I fear we shall see him again.

As I write, a wire from John Ferrers arrives. So you all arrive on Thursday. Well and good.

A night-watchman is now on duty, as we arranged.

*Let me confess that I am clean out of my depth. I was not
made for such things. And my association with Friar has
taken from me that which I had. Indeed, I am painfully aware
that your little finger is thicker than my loins.*

Yours ever,
Andrew Palin.

"As Palin says," said Mansel, "it might be worse. And the
Boche is not very smart. The trouble is he's devilish thorough.

"He knows that Hohenems Castle belongs to an Englishman:
and he knows that all English landlords must, if they have any
sense, be thinking of getting out. Well, there's no reason why
they shouldn't. But they won't be allowed to take just anything.
Supposing the Ferrers had a dinner service of gold. That they
would have to declare, and I'm perfectly sure that the Customs
would never let it go through. It wouldn't be seized: it'd just have
to stay in the country. So the Ferrers would go, but their service
would stay behind. And one day the Boche would take it.

"Thanks to Friar, the suspicions of the Boche are aroused. He
thinks that there is at the Castle a treasure of sorts. It may be
gold plate or gold bars: it may be anything: but it must be of
considerable value, if even the steward has no idea that it's
there. So the Ferrers' goings and comings – must be very
carefully watched.

"As we know, they're arriving at Salzburg this afternoon. If
they were to leave again, a week from today, I'll lay their
baggage would be ransacked and that, if they travelled by car,
the Customs would search the tyres.

"And now for a bath and some breakfast. We'll rest this
afternoon."

That morning we dealt with Friar's passport.

This had, of course, been stamped when he entered Austria.
Above this stamp, Mansel wrote in German, 'Permit exit: refer
re-entry to Police HQ.' Then he wrote on a slip in English,
'Found in Germany by the side of the Salzburg road.' This he

laid in the passport: then he covered the latter and addressed it as he had said.

The notecase, we sent to Friar's Club, marking the envelope, 'Not to be forwarded.'

It had been arranged that John and Olivia Ferrers should be at Salzburg that evening and stay at The — Hotel. There Mansel and I would dine – and meet them 'by accident'. They would there and then invite us to Hohenems, and we should proceed there together, upon the following day. So all would seem natural enough. They had come out by air; and a Hohenems car would fetch them and lead us in.

At half past eight that evening, we entered The — Hotel.

We had left our coats and were passing through the *foyer* when there was John Ferrers beside me, touching my arm.

I like to think we did the encounter justice…

Then he led us across to Olivia, lovely as ever, in blue. "Now, isn't that nice?" she says. "I knew you were out of England, but someone said you were in France." She turned to her companion. "Captain Mansel and Mr Chandos – Miss Diana Revoke. Her sister was one of my friends, when I was at school."

We, all of us, bowed and smiled, although we had met before. Not officially, of course. But each knew who the other was.

Miss Revoke was the good-looking girl who had been dining with Friar on Wednesday night.

2

From Pillar to Post

Diana Revoke was speaking.

"Mr Chandos, who *is* Mr Friar?"

I looked at the big, blue eyes, twelve inches from mine.

"I really couldn't tell you," I said. "We know one another by sight, but we've never conversed."

"He seems to know all about you."

I shrugged my shoulders.

"There's little enough to know."

"He said that you loved adventure."

"I like it in reason," I said. "But I'd much sooner hunt."

"Are you being adventuresome now?"

"No," said I, "I'm travelling. Often enough, in the summer, Mansel and I join up and wander abroad."

"You don't look a restless person. I should have thought you'd marry and settle down."

"I have done both," I said.

The lady's eyes widened.

"Then, where's your wife?"

"You must ask Olivia," I said. "She left her two days ago."

Diana put a hand to her chin.

"At your home?"

"Yes."

"So she is alone in England, and you are overseas."

"Full marks," said I.

"But I'm sure you're happy with her."

"Very happy indeed," said I.

"But you don't take her with you, when you are on the job?"

"I don't take her with me," I said, "when I go abroad with Mansel for two or three weeks. He and I are very old friends, and Jenny – "

"Friar said you were on the job."

I raised my eyebrows.

"I expect he knows best," said I. "Is he adventuresome, too?"

"I couldn't tell you," said Diana. "I never set eyes on the man till two days ago. But he used to know my father, or so he says. And I think he must have known him, and known him well. Their Club was the same. That's why I went out with him. He's very entertaining, you know. And wonderfully young for his age."

"That's an impression," said I, "that I had already formed."

"How did you form it, Mr Chandos?"

"From a casual observation. He moves so well."

And there, to my relief, John Ferrers put in his oar.

"I may call you 'Diana', mayn't I? Olivia knows you so well."

"I'll answer to that," says the lady.

I turned at once to Olivia, seated upon my right.

"Tell me of Jenny, Olivia. She wrote and told me that you'd been staying with her."

"Won't you return the compliment – just for a day or two?"

I looked across her to Mansel.

"Olivia invites us to Hohenems."

Mansel leaned forward and smiled.

"What d'you know, William?"

"As soon as we leave the table, Olivia and you and I must have five minutes together, undisturbed."

"Consider it done, William. Olivia and I will arrange it, before we get up."

Then Olivia told me of Jenny and spoke of Maintenance.

Conversation became general.

When coffee at last was served, Olivia announced that we must go on to a nightclub, for half an hour.

Thereupon two taxis were summoned: and while John escorted Diana, I followed Olivia and Mansel into the second car.

"Who is this girl, Olivia?"

"Her father was your Military Attaché at Vienna some time before the war. He was a widower. She and her sister were both at school at Salzburg. She came just before I left. I stayed with them once in England, but, though he was then retired, they spent more time in Austria than anywhere else. They never stayed at Haydn – such was my home, I couldn't invite a guest: and then I lost sight of them."

I looked at Mansel.

"Friar's been talking to her." Olivia caught her breath. "About us, I mean. He's told her we're on the job, though he hasn't said what. She's – very curious."

"Is she running with him?" said Mansel.

"I can't be sure."

Mansel fingered his chin.

Then –

"Invite her," he said to Olivia. "Invite her, too."

Olivia's eyes widened.

"Not at the moment, Jonah?"

"At once, if you please. I'm pretty sure she'll come – and I'd like her under our eye."

"I'm in your hands, my dear."

"Then do as I say, Olivia. I'm sorry to put this on you, but the omelette we're out to make is no ordinary dish. I'll be more explicit later."

When the invitation was issued, I do not know: but issued it was – and accepted. When we left the following morning,

Diana Revoke was sitting beside Olivia, in the back of the Hohenems car.

"I told you," said Mansel, "you'd have to take her on."

"Don't be absurd," said I. "If she is running with Friar, she's much too clever for me. Besides, you hooked her and so you must play your fish."

"She may require no playing. She may be innocent."

"She'll still be curious."

"I wish we knew more about her. Never mind. Regard that prospect, William – the great house up on the hill, the hamlet peeping below it, the woods enfolding them both. If I had to name that place, I'd call it 'Jack-i'-the-Green'."

Our way was lovely indeed, rising and falling and curling through country as rich and as friendly as ever I saw. Some of it I had seen, when we had travelled to Salzburg five days before: but the latter part of the run was new to me, and, as we approached the castle, forest and hill and valley seemed to agree together to tell us a fairytale. This famous introduction, Hohenems justified; for it made an enchanting picture and seemed, to my simple mind, the womb of chivalry. Sunk in the woods, it hung on a mountainside, commanding a smiling valley, laced by a joyous stream: the gracious curve of its ramparts swelled out of a quilt of foliage, as I have seen a tiara swell out of a woman's hair: and, on the left, twin towers were defying an elegant fall of water, blue and white – and laughing in the face of a sunshine that magnified all it touched.

Five hours after leaving Salzburg, the cars stole over the drawbridge and into the quiet courtyard, where Palin, with the steward behind him, was standing at the foot of the steps.

As he kissed Olivia's hand –

"The keys," said Palin, "should be on a velvet cushion, for you to touch. Still, a cold collation is ready – I passed the menu, myself. And all is – well." Here he was introduced to Diana Revoke. "My report shall be rendered later. John, you're going my way and putting on weight. And there are Mansel and Chandos. You know, I feel diminished when they are about. They always recall the man who slew a lion in a pit on a snowy day."

It was after lunch, when Olivia had taken Diana out of the way, that we strolled with our host on the ramparts and listened to Palin's report.

"The Boche is active. He came here yesterday, in his vulgar, vile-bodied car. This time, the man was alone, and I ventured to ask his business. After some patent indecision whether to answer or no, he said he was 'of the police' and had been desired to unravel this very peculiar crime. At this I declared my pleasure and asked him which of the servants he wished to see. He replied that it was his intention to study the scene. I, therefore, proposed to take him down to the meadows: but that didn't suit his book: he wanted to visit the passage in which the carpet was found. Well, that was all right by me, and we went there at once. But I fear he was disappointed. You see, I'd decided to have some rooms turned out… And the passage was three parts full of benches and chests and arras and servants and buckets and brooms. Progress was just possible, provided you watched your step; but the industry was against him, and after he'd hit his knee on the edge of a Spanish coffer of a quite incredible weight, he spoke at some length of swinehounds and of the destruction of clues. At that, I drew myself up and asked him to make himself clear. He replied that I should have known better than to 'desecrate' the scene of the crime. To that I rejoined that this wasn't the scene of the crime: that if he visited that, he would find the spot roped off: that, when, in England, a gentleman's house had been entered, it was usual to cleanse the rooms which the thieves might have used. To that, he made no answer, except to look very black: and, making his knee his excuse, he presently took his leave. But I think we shall see him again."

"Be sure of that," said Mansel. "Friar's done his stuff, all right. He's set the Boche on. And the Boche is painfully thorough. He's sure that there's something here and he feels that, after this scare, you will be disposed to unearth it and put it in some safe place. So, if he keeps on coming 'to visit the scene of the crime', he may discern some traces of what you have done. That is why your spring-cleaning upset him – that was a very good move. But he has an instinct, this man: and we must make sure of his movements before we start. I mean, if he reappeared when we were in the midst of the job…" Palin covered his face. "Exactly. And that is the very thing that this wallah might do." He turned to John Ferrers. "From first to last, John, how many hours will it take us to get the gems out?"

"Four," said John. "I think we might do it in less. But the poison may hold us up."

Rodrigo Borgia's age was a poisoner's age; and his gems had been laid up in linen which had been previously steeped in some deadly bane. This had the way of strychnine with such as unwrapped the gems: and though, in four hundred years, it must have lost some of its power, enough had survived to condemn three of Punter's colleagues to a most dreadful death. To this the Ferrers and Palin could, all three, speak; for they had watched the felons unwrap the gems. The linen, then so much dust, had covered their hands and had settled upon their faces, while they worked: as like as not, they had drawn it into their lungs. Be that as it may, before they had gathered their spoil, all three had been attacked and, after some hideous convulsions, had died in agony.

"Not for long," said Mansel. "I'm ready for that. Four hours from beginning to end. I take it you've room in your safe?"

"More than enough: but I think we should clean them first."

"So we will. D'you think we could do the business on Sunday night?"

"Why not?" said John.

"That will give us two days in which to locate the Boche and see that he doesn't 'come down, like a wolf on the fold'."

"And Friar?" said Palin.

"Unless I am greatly mistaken, Friar will be unavoidably prevented from attending, or even attempting to attend, the operation."

"And from watching the waterfall? Where the water emerges, I mean. If he was, a sudden failure of water would tell him that we were off."

"Well done," said Mansel, laughing. "So it would. But Friar has a previous engagement, and I cannot think he'll be free before Tuesday next."

With that, he related in detail what we had done. As he made an end –

"Which brings me," he said, "to Miss Diana Revoke. I felt it was better to have her under our eye: and so I desired Olivia to make her her guest. Now I think the thing to do is to let her in on this show. That will argue our faith in her: and she can do us no harm, unless she can contact Friar: and that, without our consent, will be most difficult. Of course, she may be honest: that, Time will show. And now discourse to me, Palin. I want to pick up the Boche."

"He'll be at Robin," said Palin: "he came with the Robin police. And once you see him, you'll know him – no doubt about that. His car is a bilious green and bears a swastika flag."

"And how far is Robin?" said Mansel.

"Forty-five miles."

On the following morning we saw the German, ourselves. The man was leaving the police-station, and we were within a café on the opposite side of the street: since this was narrow enough and the windows of the café were open, we saw him extremely well, though he did not see us.

He looked the beast he was: and when I say 'beast', I mean 'a dangerous beast'. He was tall and thickset, and his jaw was almost square, because, I imagine, his teeth were forever clenched. So malignant and bitter was his aspect, he gave the impression of being unable to smile, and his eyes seemed to be aflame, as Palin had said.

Over the rim of his tankard, Mansel was speaking low. " 'The glass of *German* fashion, and the mould of *German* form.' "

"A wolf in wolf's clothing," I said. "See how they're bowing him out: but I'll lay they hate his guts."

"They fear him," said Mansel. "That is why he was sent here. To peaceloving folk, he is a fearful man. By God, these Germans know how to do their stuff."

"I give them nothing," said I. "Because your hand is of iron, you don't have to wear a barbed glove."

"You're perfectly right, Aristides. And now come along, – he's going to take his car."

Thanks to Palin's description, we had already located the German's car. This was berthed under some trees, a little way off: and Carson, at the wheel of the Rolls, was waiting as close as he dared.

The man was easy to follow and led us at once to a decent, private house on the skirts of the town. The residence might have been his, for he left his car in the drive directly before the front door and then ascended the steps, to let himself in with a key.

"And very nice, too," said Mansel. "I think we'll come back when he's gone."

And so we did – at a quarter past three o'clock.

This time we came on foot and we went to the back of the house. In the kitchen, a nice looking woman was ironing a dung-coloured shirt with a bright red stripe.

"Good afternoon, Madam," says Mansel, raising his hat. "Surely it is not your duty to iron the shirt of the Boche."

"No, sir," said the woman. "It isn't. But what can I do? When my husband was ordered to lodge him, the servants left. And so I must wait upon his highness, lest worse befall. I must prepare his breakfast and take it up to his room. Our salon is at his disposal; our bedroom is his. He never opens his mouth, except to complain or to threaten. I have, sir, to clean his shoes – and I am an Austrian woman, the wife of an Austrian lawyer and the daughter of an Austrian judge."

"Madam," said Mansel, "you have my sympathy. My friend and I are English – "

"Alas, sir, we fought against you."

"Against your will. We know that it was the Boche that forced your hand. England and Austria were always friends."

"You are very generous, sir."

"I am speaking the truth, Madam. And now please listen to me. We do not like your lodger; and, if we have our way, he will not be your lodger very long." The poor woman clasped her hands. "I tell you this, because I trust you, Madam. Were you to breathe a word – "

"Sir, you can count upon me. Not even to my poor husband, will I mention that you have been here."

"If you please," said Mansel. "And now will you tell me his ways. The Boche, as a rule, is regular."

"This one is not, sir. He is abroad to all hours – except at weekends. He never rises on Sunday before midday. Then he will dress himself up and go off in his car: and he always comes in about midnight. The gardener, whom we have to bribe to wash his car, insists that the mud which it bears is mountain mud. If he is right, then he almost certainly visits The Black Oak Inn – a well-known pleasure resort, some thirty miles off. That is his way on Sundays. On other days, we never know when to expect him, though his meals must always be ready, whether or no he returns."

"I'm much obliged," said Mansel. "You have the telephone?"

"Yes, sir." She gave the number. "And, except on Sundays, I am always alone about noon."

"I shan't ring you up, if I can help it. One can't be too careful today."

"Alas, that is very true."

"Have you a cousin, or someone, whose name I may use?"

"I have an uncle, sir, of whom I am very fond. His christian name is Ludwig. Will you use that?"

"I will, indeed. I shall be Uncle Ludwig, and the Boche will be Cousin Paul. Will that be all right by you?"

"I will remember, sir. But you will not ring up if you can help it?"

"Only," said Mansel, "in the last resort." He put our friend's hand to his lips. "Be of good cheer, Madam. I make no promises. But I hope that, before very long, you will be rid of your guest."

"God bless you both," said the woman, wiping her eyes. As we made our way off –

"The German curse," said Mansel. "Two decent lives made hell by one of that filthy race. Discomfort, indignity, fear – those things are now their portion, thanks to the Boche. D'you ever see red, William?"

"I really don't know," I said. "When I get angry, I seem to get very cold. But I can tell you this. Gems or no, I don't leave Austria until that lease is up."

"Nor I," said Mansel. "What's Hecuba to us? But a sense of justice is something you can't fob off. Never mind. From what she says I think we can make it Sunday."

"I agree," said I. "And then what?"

Mansel wrinkled his brow.

"Out of the castle," he said. "The gems, I mean. Into the ground, perhaps. Then, at least, they'll be safe. But how to get them out of the country, I cannot think."

Our arrangements for Sunday were made with the greatest care.

To remove the gems from the chamber was easy enough: but two most important conditions governed the work. First, no one of the staff must suspect that any such operation was taking place: secondly, no slightest trace of our labour must be left for the eye of the Boche. It was these two provisos that made the exercise hard, for we could make no preparation, yet had to work to time; and, when we had done, must carefully sweep and garnish where we had passed.

Mansel, who thought of all things, had asked John Ferrers to 'wash the night-watchman out' on the day that we had arrived: but we dared not start before midnight or finish later than five.

And there was much to be done.

Planks and trestles must be fetched from the carpenter's shop, for the work would take twice as long unless we had a true stage. And tools and sand and cement must also be brought to the dungeon where we were to work. The mason's tools were kept in the carpenter's shop; and this, as luck would have it, was in the courtyard: but the sand and cement were kept at the foot of the postern-steps.

The original sluice, which was really a slab of stone, still lay in the ancient kitchen, ready to hand. There was a lamp in the chamber, the wire of which Ferrers had cut before he had relaid the stones, five years before: but a reel of wire must be brought, to run from a plug in the hall: and then the connection must be made. When the gems were recovered, they must be instantly washed, to rid them of any poison which might be there. This, in surgical spirit, of which we had a supply. Not till then could we put them in Ferrers' safe. And then, as I have said, all must be swept and garnished against the eye of the Boche.

On the Saturday evening we sat in Olivia's boudoir, debating, one by one, the points of our plan: Bell was without the door, and Carson was keeping an eye on Diana's room.

"And what of Diana?" said Ferrers.

"I advise," said Mansel, "that she should be left alone. All I should like to know is whether or no she leaves her room that night. And that we can learn by setting a mark on her door. If she should leave her room or even find us at work, it will really do no more than clear the air. We shall see that she does us no harm, for we shall allow her no chance of reporting to Friar. If she writes a letter, it doesn't go to the post: if she feels she must leave the castle, she'll be detained."

(Here, perhaps, I should say that 'a mark' may be 'set on a door' by laying across the doorway a very fine thread: this is drawn tight six inches above the floor: whoever comes out will break it, without knowing what he has done, and the proof of his exit will lie in the broken thread.)

"I can't believe," said Olivia, "that she is in Friar's pay. What do you say, Richard?"

I shrugged my shoulders.

"I find it hard to believe that she would betray her host; but Friar may have pitched her some tale, which she has believed."

"Speculation," said Mansel, "is idle. Does everyone agree that she should be left alone – and permitted to rest in peace or to show her hand?"

We all agreed.

"Very good," said Mansel. "I think that's all. I wish the Boche had appeared, for I'm sure he will appear, and I think it just as likely he'll come by night. The idea of surprise, you know."

Olivia had a hand to her mouth.

"What if he comes tomorrow – tomorrow night?"

"He won't be received," said her husband. "No rot about that."

"What'll happen then?"

Mansel laughed.

"He'll come back with reinforcements – four hours too late. Not that it really matters, for, sooner or later, the showdown will have to come. You are now in residence. If you allow him to come here whenever he likes, he will be sure that you have something to hide; for no English man or woman would tolerate treatment like that."

"I entirely agree," said I. "Palin was badly placed. But John, as the owner, must certainly call a halt."

Olivia sighed.

"What a business it is," she said. "D'you think we shall ever succeed in getting them out?"

"I think so," said Mansel. "Friar would manage it somehow: and if he can, so can we."

On the following evening we dined at nine o'clock, for we dared not advance the hour: but Olivia chose a short dinner and we had left the table before it was ten. At eleven Ferrers and Palin went down with Bell and Carson, to get cement and sand to the head of the postern-steps; this, in several tarpaulins, for these would hold fast their contents and could be used in the dungeon as mortarboards. At midnight, Palin repaired to where the water was flowing into the woods. This flow would presently stop – and so would announce, to one who knew the secret, what we were about. So Palin was to keep watch – in case another was waiting to see what this telltale said. At midnight, also, Carson and Bell crept into the carpenter's shop, and brought out the stuff we required to make our attempt. While they were thus employed, Ferrers produced the slab, which, after a deal of trouble, Mansel and I persuaded to play the part of a sluice.

So the dungeon fall was cut off.

By the time we were down there, Carson and Bell were already erecting the stage, and, two minutes later, I was attacking the wall. This was easy to open. Before twenty minutes were gone, I had cut an opening through which a man could pass.

"A little larger," said Mansel. "Another two courses out."

I did as he said.

"Put these on," said Mansel. "I'm not going to take any risks."

I put on the mask and the gloves.

"And now for the light," said Mansel, "or will a torch do?"

With that, he threw into the chamber the beam of his powerful torch…

After a long look –

44

"It's more than enough," said I, averting my eyes.

"I quite agree," said Mansel. "It makes me feel like a ghoul."

In the chamber were lying three corpses, so hideously lifelike, they might have been preserved. Each of them bore the signs of a hideously violent death. There was no actual stench, but a highly unpleasant odour which I can smell to this day. There were the three satchels in which the dead had been bestowing their spoil: and there were the three old bales, two of them empty and one of them, roughly, half full.

"That's right," breathed Ferrers, behind me. "Some gems are still in that bale. The poison got them before they had taken them out."

While Mansel lighted my movements, I entered the chamber of death.

I took up two of the satchels and gave them to Ferrers who passed them to Carson and Bell. Then I turned to the bale which was still half full.

"For God's sake be careful," said Ferrers. "You're going to do as they did."

But I had nothing to fear, because I was masked and gloved. For all that, I went very gently. The look of my predecessors would have made anyone think.

I put a hand into the bale, to encounter what might have been bran: indeed, it made me think of a lucky dip. Almost at once my fingers touched something hard... Drawing this out, I found it a little object, tied up in a padded bag. I thrust it into the satchel, which still remained...

Eighteen more gems, I brought out, each wrapped in its little purse: and I thrust them into the satchel as fast as I could.

Whilst I was doing this, Carson and Bell had carried the other satchels into the ancient kitchen, there to take out their contents and lay them in rows of ten. They were on no account to uncover the gems.

As I held the bale upside down –

"That's the lot," I said.

As I handed the satchel to Ferrers, I heard Mansel speak.

"Into the kitchen, John, and do your stuff. Don't come back when you've done it, unless you're short. If all the gems are there, send both of the servants back."

I had meant to prove the bales and the debris, too; but Mansel would not let me.

"Wait for the count," he said. "Those bales are dangerous. And come on out while you're waiting – I don't like that atmosphere."

I was glad to get out of the place and on to the stage. Treasure chamber, perhaps: but charnel house, too. Indeed, to be frank, no duty I ever did was so repugnant to me; for the dead were dreadful to look on, and, do what I would, my eyes seemed drawn to the features which agony had abused. They were rogues, of course, and had fairly come by their own: but I had a horrid feeling that I was despoiling them, and I cannot doubt that their ghosts were shrieking about me, because I had taken the fortune which they had so nearly won.

For, perhaps, three minutes we waited. Then Carson and Bell appeared.

"Mr Ferrers' compliments, sir, and all correct."

"A hundred and twenty-seven."

"Yes, sir. We counted them twice."

Then Mansel went off to the kitchen, to wash the gems with John; and Carson and Bell mixed the mortar, that I could relay the stones which I had cut out.

Whilst I was thus engaged, John Ferrers brought back the satchels, into which he and Mansel had stuffed the now empty padded bags. I thrust all three through the aperture which remained; and soon after that, I laid the last stone in the wall. Then I sealed the chamber as fast as I dared.

By half past three o'clock, we had removed the stage and pulled up the sluice: and, as I was washing my trowel, Mansel re-entered the dungeon, to say that the gems had been cleaned and were all in the safe.

While the servants returned the gear to the carpenter's shop, Ferrers and I took the sand and cement that remained to the head of the postern-steps. There we found Palin waiting, to say that all was well. Leaving him and Ferrers to take the stuff down, I made my way back to the dungeon, to help to remove any traces of what we had done. There were footprints and grains of sand and little spills of cement: the slab was very wet and had to be dried: and the lens which had fallen out of a torch I had used – but did not seem to have been broken – had to be found.

We had mostly trodden the passage which so much attracted the Boche, but other passages led to the postern-steps; these and a winding stair had all to be scrutinized, as well as the steps themselves up which the cement had come. Three times that night I changed the shoes I was wearing, for fear of leaving footprints on pavement which we had dried; and I think we were all in our socks before the business was done.

It was nearly a quarter to five, and I was counting the cloths which we had used to swab up the mess we had made. (We had brought twenty-four in a suit-case – and used twenty-two.) The servants, with Ferrers and Palin, were looking for the lens of my torch; and Mansel was holding a hand-lamp, to light the scene. Though the door to the dungeons was shut, the rush of the water falling without the gates was loud enough to swallow a footstep, for we were not many feet from the outer wall. Indeed, the first I knew was that Mansel was smiling and bidding Diana good morning and asking her why she was up.

Diana made no answer, but looked at me.

"And you said you weren't on the job?"

The scene was like that of some play.

The girl was framed in an archway that gave to a flight of steps: an excellent dressing-gown swathed her from ankle to throat in powder blue; rose-coloured pyjamas and slippers were hiding her feet. Her thick, fair hair was tumbled, as though she had left her pillow without a thought, and a sleeve had fallen back from her wrist, because she had lifted an arm and was laying her slim, brown hand on the haunch on her right. Beyond her, Palin and Carson, before her, Ferrers and Bell, all of them wearing the havoc of heavy toil, were looking upon her in silence, not seeming to breathe.

"And you said you weren't on the job?"

"I don't think I did," said I. "Anyway, I've finished now. Twenty-one, twenty-two. That's right. Shut that case, Bell, and take it back to my room."

"Very good, sir."

"What have you finished?" said Diana.

"The job," said I. "And now I'm going to bed."

The lady looked at Mansel.

"Captain Mansel, what are you doing?"

"Nothing at the moment," said Mansel; "but I'm just going to put out this light. John and Palin, we'll have to let the thing go. Have you a torch, Diana? Otherwise, William will see you back to your room."

Diana was speaking slowly.

"It must be something that you don't want me to know."

"To be frank, we've been to some trouble to keep it quiet."

"But why?"

"So many questions," sighed Mansel. "Now may I ask you one?"

"Of course," says the girl, staring.

"How do you come to be here...in the ancient part of the castle...between four and five in the morning, when most people are abed?"

"I – I heard a sound," said Diana. "And came to see what it was."

The silence which followed this statement was painful, indeed, for the rush of the water without declared so very clearly that only a monstrous noise could have risen above its din.

Then Mansel put out his light, and I drew my torch. As I threw its beam at her feet –

"Come, my lady," I said; "I'll see you back to your room."

Since that of my torch was now the only light, the girl had to follow the beam or else be left in the dark; and two minutes later we reached the door of her room.

"What do you think of me, Richard?"

"I don't know what to think. I know that you lied when you said that you'd heard a sound."

"Then why d'you think I came down?"

"I suppose," I said, "because Friar told you to."

"I don't take orders from Friar."

"Why did you come down?"

"Because Friar told me that you were up to something – and something big. I've come down every night between one and three: but last night I forgot to set my alarm."

"What did it matter to you?"

"Women are curious, Richard – especially about men. You see, Friar said that you and Captain Mansel were not what you seemed to be. He said you were really two very efficient crooks."

"Did you believe that?"

"No. And I told him so. 'Of course you don't believe it,' he said. 'Who ever would? That's why they've had such a run. But it happens to be a fact. And what is more, you can prove it, if you like to keep them in view.' Well, I said that that was silly. How on earth could I keep observation on people like you? 'Visit the Ferrers,' he said, 'and don't sleep too sound while you're there.' He knew I knew Olivia: I'd told him I'd rung her up, to find that she was away. 'They're on their way back,' he said, 'and Mansel and Chandos will visit them, sure as a gun. I mean, that's why they're at Salzburg.' Well, I honestly thought it was tripe: I simply couldn't believe that he wasn't pulling my leg. And then it began to happen, just as he'd said. The Ferrers arrived the next day, on their way to Hohenems: and you turned up again and were invited to stay. When I was invited, too –

well, nobody who was normal would have spent the whole night in their room."

"I agree," I said. "Placed as you were, told what you had been told, I should have done the same. And now that you've proved him right, you're going to let him know?"

Diana's eyes widened.

"If and when I found he was right, I promised to send him a. wire. We agreed the wording, which was *I apologize*."

I nodded.

"That's only fair," I said. "You wouldn't believe what he said, and you told him so."

"I still don't believe you're a crook. Besides, John Ferrers was with you; so you weren't robbing his house."

"No, we're not crooks," I said. "In fact, we've done what we have at John's request. But I'd rather Friar didn't know that we'd done it just yet. So will you hold up that wire? That's all he wanted, you know. That's why he told you the tale. He knew we were going to work, and he very much wanted to know when that work was done. And then he fell in with you... It was a long shot, of course; but long shots sometimes come off."

Diana's eyes were burning.

"You mean to say he's used me."

"That was the general idea: but if you hold up that wire, it won't come off. He is a crook, you know. And he'd very much like to have done what we have done tonight: but without John Ferrers' knowledge."

"My God," said Diana, quietly. And then, again, "My God."

"Don't take it to heart," I said. "No harm has been done."

"And there you're wrong," snapped Diana. "A rotten blackguard has made a fool of me. Worse. I played into his hands; and, but for you, he'd have won his beastly game."

I fingered my chin.

"Would you like to get back?" I said.

"Just you try me," said Diana, speaking between her teeth.

"Perhaps we will," I said. "Meanwhile, if you'd hold up that wire – "

"Are you being funny?" said Diana.

"Not on your life," said I. "I'd very much like him to have it. But not just yet."

Three hours and a half had gone by, and Mansel was up and dressed and was smoking a pipe in my bedroom, while I was brushing my hair.

We had had two hours' sleep and could have done with eight: but appearances had to be saved.

"I think you're right," said Mansel: "they'll have to go into the car. That secret locker has never yet been found. We can't take them out that way, for the risk is too great. But until we take them out, I think they must lie in the Rolls."

"Can we get them all in?" I said.

"Oh, yes. They don't take up much room. But you must see them, William, for they are beyond all price. The size and glory of the stones, and the fabulous workmanship… Each one is worth a fortune – intrinsically. When you add to them their history, imagination boggles at what the world will say."

I laughed, and picked up a tie.

"I'll see them in England," I said. "I assume we transfer them tonight."

"This morning," said Mansel. "A suitcase goes into the car, and we go for a run. About eleven, I think. We lunch abroad and get back in time for tea."

"You know best," said I; "but why not in time for lunch?"

"*Suggestio falsi*, William. The transfer will take half an hour; but where we lay up our treasure is going to be our affair. Not even the Ferrers will know. John is content, and Olivia is greatly relieved. As nobody knows of the locker, Palin and they will assume that we've either buried the gems or shoved them into some Bank."

"Very good," said I. "And what about the suitcase? Supposing a servant sees it go into the car…"

"It's Palin's suitcase, and Carson will put it in. Palin has need of some clothes which he left at the inn. And as we shall go by that way, we have offered to bring them along. And now about Diana Revoke."

I think," I said, "I *think* she's told me the truth. If she hasn't, she's a beautiful liar. But I'm not entirely sure of that baby stare."

"If she is honest," said Mansel, "provided she's willing to play, I think we may very well use her to string Friar along."

"I hinted at that, and she seemed to jump at the chance." I picked up a coat. "But she mustn't go too far: I mean double-crossing Friar is not a game for a girl."

"She mustn't do it in person. I had a letter in mind. And now let's go down to breakfast – and hope that the Boche doesn't come till we're out of the way."

Though I think our night's work must have been in everyone's mind, it was not referred to at table by look or word. For all that, Diana was thoughtful; and when Mansel announced that, if we might be excused, he and I would drive over to Villach, I saw a look of relief come into Olivia's face.

This was natural enough. So long as no man suspected that treasure was lying within her husband's gates, its existence could be ignored; but once the secret was out, she could not put out of her mind the shocking scene she had witnessed five years before. All for the sake of those gems, she and John and Palin had been condemned to death – and had seen the sentence fulfilled on those that issued it. And now other rogues had arisen, determined to have their way. One man was dead already, and the Boche was waiting to pounce.

"Villach," said Palin. "That means that you'll pass my abode. If I were to give you a suitcase, would you be so very good as to get me some clothes? I've a very elegant suit in gorilla grey, with a flame-coloured overcheck… Then I'm running short of shirts and other accessories. If I had a word with Carson, I think he could make his selection, before you had finished your beer."

"With pleasure," said Mansel: "but give us a note to your landlord, to warrant the rape."

"It shall be done," said Palin. "What time shall you start?"

"We thought about eleven," said Mansel. He returned to Olivia. "May we take some sandwiches with us? I think we'll be back for tea."

"Of course," said Olivia, smiling. "Luncheon for four?"

"If you please, my dear."

So everything was arranged.

Sharp at eleven o'clock, the Rolls stole out of the coachhouse and up to the castle's door, and two minutes later we glided over the drawbridge and on to the road of approach. This was, as I have said, some two miles long, and so we had four or five minutes in which to run into the Boche: but that ill luck we were spared and, in fact, we turned into the highway without having seen a soul.

Mansel put down his foot...

Two hours later, perhaps, some thirty miles from Villach, we left the road for a track which ran into a wood.

We did not know the place, but it seemed retired, and we had chosen a time when husbandmen would be eating their midday meal. Still, precautions had to be taken; and Carson and Bell played sentry, while Mansel and I bestowed the precious stones.

Where the locker was, I shall not reveal: but it was well contrived and cleverly hidden away. Had the coachwork of the car been measured, it would, no doubt, have been found: but even the eyes of those who are trained to observe had never suspected its being for several years.

Each of the jewels was wrapped in a fragment of cotton wool. (As I have said, when I had handled them last, each had lain in its jewel-case – a little, old, padded bag: but these had been discarded, for fear of the virulent poison with which they had been in touch.) There was, therefore, no packing to be done, for the wool was padding enough against any vibration or shock. For all that, we lined the locker with layers of more cotton wool, for its burden had to lie snug and must on no account shift, whatever movement the car might happen to make.

I handed the gems to Mansel, who laid them up, and I told them as I did so and found the tale correct.

One hundred and twenty-seven sculptured jewels…

When Mansel received the last one, he loosed its elastic band and, carefully parting the wool, picked out the precious stone and set it in the palm of my hand.

"Look at that, William," he said.

The jewel was a monstrous ruby.

I never knew that rubies could be carved; but there, before my eyes, was the head of a laughing Bacchante, all done in pigeon's blood. Had it been wrought in marble, it would have filled the eye, so exquisite was the detail, so vivid the air of abandon, so rare were the parted lips and the tilt of the chin: but this was made of a ruby, fit for an emperor's crown.

I gazed upon it in silence.

"There's no deception," said Mansel. "That is a Burmese ruby – the finest I ever saw."

"My God," I said, weakly. And then, "Are they all like that?"

"All," said Mansel. "The Pope was a connoisseur."

We put in still more padding – wool and scarves and stockings, until the locker was tight: then Mansel replaced the partition and screwed it home. The screwheads were countersunk, and when they had been re-covered, I do not think that a coach-builder would have looked twice at the panel which hid the recess. This being so, we were, perhaps, foolish not to have driven for the Channel as fast as we could – indeed, the idea was tempting beyond belief: but it must be remembered that, if the risk was slight, the stake was beyond calculation, it was so high. And if the car had been held and the gems had been found, neither Mansel nor I would have been the same men again.

Then we called our sentinels in and we all of us ate our lunch, after which we drove to Villach and had a word with an innkeeper whom we knew. Then we made for Palin's inn, to pick up his clothes, and just before five o'clock, we were back at Hohenems.

As we slid into the courtyard –

"End of Act One," said Mansel. "I wonder how many there'll be."

Here, perhaps, I should say that Carson always slept in the harness room. This opened into the coach-house in which the Rolls was lodged. Such procedure was normal, when Mansel was 'on the job'. For the Rolls was our magic carpet. More often than I can remember, if Carson or Bell was absent, Mansel or I have slept in the car ourselves.

The Ferrers had nothing to report, and, taking tea on the terrace, surveying as gentle a prospect as ever I saw, I found it hard to believe that Violence, Battle and Murder were, so to speak, in the wings. The valley was floored with meadows, through which a lively stream was making its wanton way: its sides were all of woodland, close and deep and reflecting each whim of the foothills on which it grew. Cows and sheep were making the most of this pleasance, and a colt, shut into a paddock, was standing beside its dam. And the lazy, afternoon sunshine was arraying the scene with splendour, gilding the green of the foliage, printing the shadow of substance upon the sward and turning the water into a ribbon of silver, so that its flash betrayed the course of the torrent after the law of Distance had ruled it out of our sight.

Then the butler appeared upon the terrace, to say that the German had come.

"See him with Palin," said Mansel; "William and I are not coming on in this scene."

But, while Ferrers and Palin made for the gallery, Mansel and I passed upstairs and so to the head of the steps down which Diana had come some thirteen hours before.

As we descended quietly, footfalls rang in the passage and then came Ferrers' voice.

"This is the place, I am told, at which the carpet was found."

No answer was made, and presently Ferrers went on.

"You asked to see this spot, which Mr Palin tells me you've seen before. Now that you've seen it again, is there anything else you want?"

" I am investigating. I desire to be left alone."

"In a house such as this, no stranger is left alone."

"I am of the police."

"That is why you were admitted. What else do you wish to see?"

"You would be obstructive!" spat the Boche.

There was a little silence.

Then –

"I asked you," said Ferrers, coldly, "what else you wished to see."

That he should ignore the German's offensive charge was more than the latter could bear. At least, so it seemed to me, for the fellow burst out in a voice which was shaken with rage.

"Show me the hidden treasure for which these bandits came. They left alone your silver. They never entered a bedroom, in search of jewels. Your private safe was untouched. Why was that, Englishman? Because you know, as I do, they came for none of those things. They came for something greater – something which lies down here. Why did they want that carpet?"

" If that is your theory," said Ferrers, "you'd better ask them. I never heard of a treasure lying within these walls – and I don't believe there is one. I can explain the carpet no more than anyone else. I've no idea why they moved it."

"Because they required a carpet, to bring them to what they sought."

"So you say," said Ferrers. "You may be right. The position is simply this – that so far as I am concerned, there is nothing gone. The police were summoned, because a man was found dead – not because the house had been entered, for there had been no theft."

"Why are you so sure there was no theft? Is your treasure still safe?"

I heard Ferrers expire.

"I have told you," he said, "that there is no treasure here. If the thieves believed that there was, they made a mistake."

"And I tell you that thieves make no such mistakes." This was, of course, perfectly true: and I could not help feeling that the German had scored a point.

"As you please," said Ferrers. "Perhaps they found the treasure and took it away."

"Of that there was no indication."

"So far as I understand, what indications there were are so many signposts pointing to nowhere at all."

"That is because you are obstructive."

For the second time Ferrers expired.

"You have," he said, "been admitted – more than once: you have been allowed – "

"Allowed?"

" – allowed to visit the place you desired to see. I don't call that obstruction."

"Yet you refuse to disclose what it was the thieves sought."

"I have told you," said Ferrers, "I don't know what they sought. I don't know why they came, and I don't know why they went. I don't know why one was murdered. I don't know anything."

"Yet you withstand assistance. I find that strange."

"You have offered me no assistance. All you can do is to say that there's treasure here."

"Which happens to be the answer to all that you are pretending you do not know." I heard the man suck in his breath. "The day will come, Englishman, when – "

"I think," said Ferrers, "that you had better withdraw. This is a private house in Austria – not a prison cell in Germany."

"You would insult an officer of the Reich!"

"Not at all. I prefer your absence to your presence. I don't put it higher than that."

There was another silence.

Then –

"I go," said the German. "I go, but I do not forget. One day I shall come back – and you will show me the place where the treasure lies."

As the footfalls receded –

"You must give Friar best," said Mansel. "We may have bruised his head, but, by God, he's bruised our heel."

That night, after dinner, we told Diana the truth. This seemed the best thing to do; for, if she were honest, such trust in her would grapple her to our cause; but, if she were running with Friar – well, we had told her nothing she did not know. Indeed, by my advice, we used her exactly as though she were one of us, concealing nothing at all, except, of course, how we had disposed of the gems.

"So there we are," said Mansel. "The stable is empty: the stable door is shut: of its having been opened, there is, I think, no sign: all we have to do now is to get the horse out of the country."

"All," said Ferrers, and laughed.

"It mayn't be so bad," said Mansel. "But I think we should leave the castle on Thursday next."

"The day after tomorrow?" said Olivia.

"I think so, my lady. Not that we want to go, but Time is not in our favour – he never seems to be. In spite of all the checks upon passports, the Boche may not know that we're here. You see, at the moment, this isn't Germany: and Austrian police staff-work is not too good. I'm afraid he's bound to find out that we have visited you: but I'd very much sooner he watched an empty stable than that he shadowed us wherever we go. So if we could get a short start... Yes, I think we should go on Thursday. Our rooms will be waiting at Villach on Thursday night."

"And Friar?" said Olivia.

"We shall know when he's back all right. But, unless I'm much mistaken, it won't be just yet." He turned to Diana. "Where were you to address him?"

"C/o the Bank of Austria, Salzburg."

"Would you like to wire him on Wednesday?"

"If you think it's wise, Captain Mansel."

"I think it's natural. And later, perhaps, you shall write."

"You'll tell me what to say."

"Of course. But I want you to remember, Diana, that if you come in with us, you must do as we say. You can't play Friar on your own – he's the very hell of a fish."

"I swear," said Diana, quickly.

"Will you stay on here for the present?"

"If Olivia and John will have me."

"That goes without saying," said Olivia.

"And what about me?" said Palin. "You must admit that I pull my weight as a clown. I showed the robber chief how to get at the jewels. That's more than Columbine's done: so give me another chance to make a fool of myself."

"Your host was to blame," said Mansel. "He never warned you that Punter was hereabouts."

"I entirely agree," said John. " It wasn't your fault."

"I must confess," said Palin, "that if you had told me that, I should have repaired to this mansion, armed the servants and had the drawbridge raised."

"You can serve us best," said Mansel, "by going back to your inn and standing by. I'm perfectly sure we shall need you: but when and how we shall need you, I cannot say."

"It shall be done," said Palin. "But I shall be very lonely. If Friar should come back for a night..."

"Keep him," said Mansel, laughing. "And let me know. Our address is The Sickle at Villach, but keep it quiet."

"And we," said John Ferrers, "for whom you are doing all this, to save whose property you two are risking your lives, are to sit still here and let you lie out in the rain."

"John," said Mansel, "I don't have to argue with you. The moment you leave the castle, they'll know that the gems are gone. Though you stay here, they may suspect that they're gone. But the moment you leave, they'll *know*. And I don't want them to know. I want to keep them guessing right up to the last."

"And now," said Olivia, rising, "Andrew shall play us upstairs. Jonah and Richard are abnormal, but Andrew and John are half-dead for want of sleep."

Palin passed to the piano.

"It'll have to be 'Bohème'," he said. "But that I can play when I'm tight."

So, to the strains of Puccini, we went to our beds.

This, at a quarter past ten: and I must confess that, despite what Olivia had said, I liked the look of my sheets. I promised myself a good night… But Fortune ruled otherwise.

It was almost half past twelve when Mansel slipped into my room. Weary or no, I am a very light sleeper; and so I was sitting up, ready, before he spoke.

"Mansel speaking, William. Don't show a light."

"More trouble?"

"It might be. The Boche has come back."

I sighed.

"Only a German," I said, "would do such a brutal thing."

"And he's brought a posse with him. They're searching the castle now."

"My God, he's hot stuff," said I.

"He's a cunning swine," said Mansel, "and I'll say he had me on. He deliberately gave us to think that he wouldn't be back just yet; and he led us to see the wisdom of getting the treasure out as soon as ever we could. And then, within six hours, at dead of night he comes back. Good work, you know – you can't get away from that. I mean, be honest, William. Had we not got the stuff out, after his visit this evening, I'll lay any money we should have done it tonight."

"So we should," said I. "And have been caught out. And that would have been a party. What do we do?"

"We must leave it to Ferrers. I hope he goes off the deep end. But if they search the whole castle, we are going to be found. To withdraw would be worse than futile, for we couldn't conceal the fact that these rooms have been occupied. But please expect a visit. The Boche is right up in the air."

With that, he slipped out of the room, and Bell slipped in.

"It's Bell, sir. Have you any orders?"

"Tell me the worst. Where's Carson?"

"With Captain Mansel, sir."

"Thank God," said I. "They didn't see him come out?"

"Oh, no, sir. He heard them drive into the courtyard and watched his chance."

I might have known.

Bell deserved his name, for he was the soundest man with whom I have had to do. In times of stress he was my rod and my staff. He knew what I needed, before I knew myself: before I had time to call him, he was at hand: he set my life above his, because, perhaps, he knew that I set his above mine: he was the finest servant and true as steel. But Carson had caught from his master the precious trick of foresight. He could see the move that was coming, and take his place; so that, when the move was made, Carson was ready to meet it, however startling it was. Twice over, by such a manoeuvre, he saved my life – and when I made bold to thank him, he very respectfully said he was glad he was there. Working together, the two were incomparable: indeed, without their service, Mansel and I would never have taken the field.

"Well, that's all right," said I. "You'd better be found in bed. The Boche would not understand it if you were outside my door."

"Very good, sir. You'll ring, if you want me?"

"I promise I will."

When Bell had gone, I lay down and closed my eyes; and since I was still very tired, I soon fell asleep.

Half an hour later, perhaps, somebody rapped upon the door.

I switched on the bedside lamp, propped myself on an elbow and cried "Come in."

A plain-clothes man opened the door, shot a glance round the bedroom and then drew back for the Boche.

"Who the devil are you?" I said.

"I am of the police."

"And what do you want at this hour in a private room?"

"Excuse me." He drew himself up. "I bear with me a warrant to search this house."

I put out a hand.

"I wish to see it," I said.

The fellow turned to the Austrian, standing behind.

"Give me the warrant," he said.

The thing was indeed a warrant, worded vaguely enough, authorizing the bearer to enter and search Hohenems.

"Very well," I said. "We do things better in England, but let that go."

"You are not in England," said the Boche.

"No," said I, "nor yet in Germany."

"May I see your passport?"

"I suppose so." I left my bed, took my keys from a table and opened the little dispatch case in which I kept such things. "There you are," I said.

The German glanced at the passport and back at my case.

"I observe that you carry a pistol."

"I carry a pistol whenever I travel abroad."

"I see. Do you also carry a torch?" Remembering the lens which was missing, I felt rather tired. But I could not say no; for the torch lay beside the pistol, for him to see.

"I do."

"Quite so. May I look at that torch?"

I put the thing into his hand.

As he turned it about, smiling, I could have broken his neck. At last he looked up.

"Its lens is missing, Mr Chandos."

"That's quite true. I lost it a night or two back."

"Where did you lose it, Mr Chandos?"

"In the older part of the castle. There's no light there, and you have to watch your step."

"Why were you there, Mr Chandos?"

I raised my eyebrows.

"Old places interest me. This is a 'show place', you know; the older part of the castle used to be shown."

"Quite so." He took a lens from his pocket and fitted it into the torch. "There! It is all right now. Strange that it should not have been broken. Did you use a carpet, too?"

"A carpet?" I said, frowning.

"Like the robbers, Mr Chandos...who came to look for the treasure...that wasn't there."

"Look here," said I. "I don't understand what you're saying, but it is perfectly clear that you mean to be rude. And that I will not have."

As the man recoiled, I took the torch from his hand.

"*Will* not?" he spat.

"Will not. I pass over your intrusion, because I know better than to expect manners from your race. But you have no shadow of right to molest, much less insult, a soul in this house."

"I am of the police. I have my duty to do." I looked the brute up and down.

"To define your behaviour as duty is to defile the word. Your duty is to succour the public – that's why you're paid. Not to locate possessions which one day you hope to steal."

The fellow's eyes burned in his head, and I saw the tide of scarlet rising into his face.

"Before we are done," he said thickly, "you will regret those words."

"Don't you believe it," I said. "You Boches always split on England, because we're the better stuff."

For a moment the man stood trembling. Then he turned on his heel and stamped from the room.

As I listened to his footfalls receding, I had an uneasy feeling that Friar had done very much more than bruise our heel.

Mansel was speaking.

"It is written, 'No peace to the wicked'. So far as I can see, there isn't much to the good."

Be sure I agreed with him.

Less than two hours had gone by, and we were upon the road. In view of what had happened, it would have been folly to stay at Hohenems. And so we had taken our leave. Although we had not said so, we were not bound for Villach, but for a tiny hamlet some thirty miles from that town. It went by the name of St Martin and boasted an excellent inn, at which Mansel and I had rested a number of times. Since the little place was retired, it was fair to expect that we should not be disturbed there for forty-eight hours; and that, so to speak, would give us a breathing space. By moving at once and by night, we hoped to cover our tracks; but this meant that our run must be rounded with a respectable sleep, for out of forty-eight hours we should have spent four in our beds and our labour on Sunday night had been very severe. And so we should be too weary not only to take any action, but to make any valuable plans.

Driving as fast as he dared, Mansel brought us to St. Martin soon after half past six, to find the inn's doors wide open and the host himself supervising the sluicing down of the hall.

When he saw who it was, he came running, with outstretched arms.

"Oh, my good friends – the best that ever I had! Give you good morning, sirs. Drive the car in, I pray you. See, her stable is ready, all clean and fresh."

Because the inn had no coach house, by the landlord's express desire, we always drove the car clean into the great, flagged hall, and there she was lodged for so long as we lay at his house.

Mansel leaned out of the Rolls.

"If I do that, will you shut the doors upon her?"

"Oho! Sits the wind in that quarter? Yes, indeed. The wicket-door shall be used, and no one who passes by will know that a car is within." He called his good wife. "Breakfast at once, Elise. An omelette and coffee, to start with. Our friends have come back."

At this, the good woman came running, to welcome us in, and to meet such honest goodwill was better than any breakfast, for food may comfort the body, but kindliness warms the heart.

"And after breakfast," said Mansel, "a bath and a bed, for we have had next to no rest for forty-eight hours."

"Sir," said our hostess, "permit me to know you of old. By the time you have broken your fast, the water will be boiling and the bedrooms will be prepared."

With that, she bustled away, calling her maids about her and issuing orders as if we were Royalty, indeed.

So it fell out that we very soon sat down to a truly excellent breakfast under the limes. Then we strolled for a little, to give our digestions a chance; and then we bathed and lay down, to sleep for a full ten hours.

By seven o'clock that evening we were all different men, and, while Carson and Bell were busy about the Rolls, Mansel and I took counsel under the limes.

"By tomorrow at latest," he said, "the hunt will be up. We must leave here tomorrow evening and go to ground. If Wagensburg is empty…"

Wagensburg was a castle in which we had spent some time a few years back: in fact, for a while we had owned it, though we had never lived there as owners usually live. And then we had sold it again to a youth with more money than brains, who was sure that his wife would be charmed with such a residence. I fear that he was mistaken, as husbands usually are, for the castle was again in the market before a year was out. But in that time the house had been modernized and, what was more to the point, a road of approach had been made to the back of the house.

Now if Wagensburg was empty, we could come and go by this road and could use the servants' quarters in secret; for, though we were, in fact, in possession, the main drive would never be taken, the courtyard would never be entered and the front of the castle would argue a desolate mansion for all to see.

I took a deep breath.

"And then what?"

"We reconnoitre a route from there into Italy: and when we are sure of that, we fetch Diana Revoke."

"I thought that was coming," I said.

"I can't say I like it," said Mansel, "but, thanks entirely to Friar, we cannot share the passage, as I had hoped. Either you or I must cross, while the other covers his going with all his might. Now the best way to cover A's movement is to direct attention to that of B. And there Diana can help, for she is the very type that appeals to the Boche. If, therefore, she works with B – and pulls her weight, the Boche will persuade himself that he is doing right in sticking to B. And I have an idea that she'll be a new one on him. When he asked who was in the castle, Ferrers suppressed her name."

"I think she's all right," I said.

"So do I," said Mansel. "I'm almost sure. But I'm not too good at women, and many a man's come down on the lady's mile. Still, we shan't trust her a lot. She will believe that A is in Italy. And that B is going to meet him, bearing the swag. In any event, I don't see what else we can do. She wires to Friar tomorrow, and Ferrers will vet the wire. She writes to Friar tomorrow, and Ferrers will steam the letter, to see what she says."

"Friar should be still off the map."

"He should," said Mansel. "I very much hope he is. But I'm not going to bank upon it. I've seen Friar's shape before."

At dawn the following morning we left for Wagensburg. This, on reconnaissance only. We had to know what to expect.

Each of us knew the way as he knew the palm of his hand, and, before an hour had gone by, Mansel had brought the Rolls to a spot within two miles of the road of approach we sought. Though the ways hereabouts were lonely, nearer he would not go, lest the car should be marked by some husbandman, early abroad. So there we left Carson, with orders to keep out of sight, and Mansel and Bell and I continued our journey on foot.

Soon we crossed the river we knew so well, and twenty minutes later we came to the road of approach. This must have cost much to make, for the ground was difficult; but it had been well done. It ran through a valley or combe, to rise by an easy zigzag past blowing meadows and Wagensburg's famous well. Then it passed into the coppice which masked the back of the house.

Moving along it quietly, we saw no sign of life, and when we emerged from the trees, there was the mansion before us, grey and cool and silent, its venerable walls in shadow, its roof already alight with the morning sun.

After a careful reconnaissance, we cut a pane from a window and entered Wagensburg.

There was certainly no one there; but the house was dry as a bone and the servants' quarters were now much more convenient than had been the masters' rooms a few years back. There were basins and running water, a mighty electric stove and a refrigerator fit for an hotel. Better still, there were two bathrooms, each furnished with water heaters, to beat the band. This proved, as did the stove, that the house was supplied by the mains, and that, if we could make some connection, we might enjoy all the comfort that power can bring.

"Carson's job," said Mansel. "If the thing can be done, he'll do it. We'll leave a flyer behind, to square the account."

And there we left the mansion and made our way to the car.

On the way back to St Martin we purchased such gear as we needed, here and there: and we took in a store of tinned food and two cases of beer. *Mens sana in corpore sano* is what some wise man said.

When at last we sat down to our breakfast at half past ten, we had a free day before us, to spend as we pleased. Mansel, of course, went fishing; and I must confess that I passed the time in a meadow behind the inn, resting in the shade of some chestnuts and, when I was not dozing, composing a foolish letter to Jenny, my wife.

At nine o'clock that evening we took our leave of the inn-keeper and his wife, charging them to forget our visit and to expect our return. And less than three hours later we were installed in the mansion we knew so well, the Rolls was fast in a garage built on to the house, and Carson had done his job and had given us power and light.

3

Rogues and Vagabonds

We were now quite close to the frontier – no more than eighteen miles: but none of us knew the country through which it ran, for on all our other visits we had come and gone by the West: but now we must go by the South.

Had not the Boche been set on, we should, no doubt, have gone back by Germany: but now that was out of the question, for there his writ would run with the power of the Rhine itself.

Now the border was mountainous, and was not defined by some river, as so many frontiers are. But to guard a mountainous frontier is easier than it looks, for, if frontier posts are well placed, Nature will keep the country which lies between. I have known, upon such a border, two posts nine miles apart; but though one would have declared that any young, strong man could contrive to pass between these, only a beast, I think, could have made its way by. A crag would force him aside, and when he had passed round this, a torrent he could not ford would be barring his way: he would find a sudden valley which promised well, and after some weary miles would end in a *cul de sac*. And so, if the posts are well sited, though they stand some distance apart, it may be most hard to go by. Add to this that the guards know the line which the frontier takes and have their private viewpoints to which they send out patrols: though these are withdrawn at dusk, no man can cross by night, unless he has first made sure of his way by day.

When we were at Salzburg, Mansel had purchased some excellent large-scale maps: and we passed our first morning at Wagensburg studying these. So we divided our frontier into three parts. And this we did with three pencils – red and blue and green. The red were the portions commanded by frontier-posts: the blue were the portions which were, on the face of it, hopeless, because of the opposition of monstrous heights: the green were the portions by which a way might be found.

Our greatest hope was, of course, to strike some smugglers' way.

That afternoon Mansel wrote a letter for Diana to send to Friar, as well as a letter to Palin, which I will set out.

Dear Palin,

Please leave for London at once. When you are there, please leave at once for Trieste. There is a hotel at Trieste, called The Heart of Gold. A letter will go to you there, telling you what next to do. When you are in London, go to St James's Street and buy the best mats of the Italo-Austrian frontier that you can buy. Study these carefully.

Yours ever,
Jonathan Mansel.

PS. Say nothing to the Ferrers. Just go.

When the light was failing, Carson left for Villach, taking the Rolls. He was to post the letters and to call at The Sickle, in case some letter or message was lying there. He was to be very careful in all he did. He was to leave the Rolls in a thicket without the town and to make his way in on foot, keeping, so far as he could, to the meaner ways.

I confess that from ten o'clock on I could not keep my eyes from my watch, for Villach was not very far and if the Rolls had been taken, our cake was dough: but Mansel refused to worry, "for Carson," he said, "will never walk into a trap." Sure enough, soon after eleven, the Rolls stole into the yard, and two minutes later Carson made his report.

This was significant.

"I posted the letters, sir, but I couldn't touch The Sickle: it's practically cordoned off: there's plain-clothes men all round it – I counted five. They've trestles across the roads in, and they're stopping all cars."

Mansel looked very grave.

"Where did you post the letters?"

"At the post-office in the square, sir. I watched my chance."

"I'm sure you did. What I'm getting at is this. There's a proper hotel in the square – I forget its name. Were there police about that?"

"So far as I saw, sir, not one. I specially looked for them. Then there's another hotel on the opposite side. I'll swear there was no one there."

Mansel looked at me.

"Who knew we were going to The Sickle?"

"The Ferrers, Diana and Palin."

"Exactly. And when did they know?"

"We told them," I said, "after dinner on Monday night."

"And the Boche arrived two hours later. We said we were going on Thursday – and this is Thursday night. Who told the Boche we were going to The Sickle on Thursday?"

"There's only one answer," I said.

"I quite agree," said Mansel. "But what a show! And that is the Boche all over. He deals himself a truly beautiful hand. But he doesn't know how to play it. Diana Revoke is his agent. He puts her on to Friar, and she picks us up. Luck of the devil himself. We make her free of our plans and she passes them on. He saw her that night, of course, while we were abed. And then he strikes *too soon* – and ruins everything. If he'd held his hand…if he hadn't struck tonight… Well, at least we've looked over his shoulder."

(It is, of course, elementary that a house should be watched, before a raid is made.)

"She had me on," I said.

"Not your fault," said Mansel. "Your eyes were on Friar. But what a lovely hand! And the fellow's thrown it away. We must write to Ferrers at once and tell him to let her go."

"Where to?" said I.

Mansel shrugged his shoulders.

"Report to us at Spittal – wait till we come. But after the washout at Villach, they may be shy. Still, she'll have to leave Hohenems. And since I got her in, it's for me to get her out."

"And Friar?"

"God knows," said Mansel, and laughed. "If he finds out, heaven help her. But that is her affair. The point is that, thanks to Carson, we are now wise."

I put a hand to my head.

"I can't believe it," I said. "She's an English girl."

Mansel fingered his chin.

"I suppose she is," he said. "But what was she doing in Salzburg? And why does she run with the Boche? Oh, I've got it, William. I'll lay her mother was German – which means that, as like as not, her father was, too."

I went to my bed that night, a sobered man.

The next morning, before it was light, we entered the Rolls and drove out. Within the hour, Mansel and Bell and I had been dropped at three different points, and Carson drove back to the castle, with orders to keep the house and to fetch us when dusk had come in. Each of us bore a map and was to explore the district which neighboured the frontier, as best he could. He was to avoid observation at any cost and was to be back to meet Carson not later than eight o'clock.

I was set down some thirty miles from Wagensburg and, if the map was true, almost exactly three miles from the frontier itself. But that was as the crow flies.

I made at once for a beechwood, as offering cover from view, and, once within this shelter, I threw a look round.

The dawn was coming up, and the country was taking shape. Colour was stealing into a lovely world, shading the exquisite contours, in black and green, turning from grey to white the magic of falling water and changing from pall to quilt the glory of forests that hung on the mountainsides.

The wood's recesses were dark, but, by keeping close to its edge, I was able to see. Very soon I was climbing sharply, and, on my left, a valley followed me round. Looking South, from behind a tree, I saw the sun touching a summit a mile ahead. From this, it was clear, I should get a most excellent view and so I set out to get there before I did anything else.

It was nearly two hours before I had my way, for the going was very severe and I had to make more than one detour and then come back to my line. Add to this that I never moved into the open, until I was pretty well sure that no one was there to see. But in the end I got there, to find my reward.

I was commanding the length of a valley system which ran clean across the frontier and into Italy. Of this there could be no doubt, for the map declared that the summit upon which I was lying was little more than two miles from the border itself. And I could see further than that. As though to confirm this conclusion, several cigarette ends and two or three empty tins were insisting that others had found it much to their taste. In a word, it was an observation post: and such posts overlook ways by which frontiers may be crossed.

The valley I had seen on my left, when I was skirting the wood, gave to another valley which ran south-east: this, in turn, gave to another, which ran south-west. More, I could not make out; but by then you were over the border...

This was all to the good: but when such a pass is unguarded, as I have said before, that is, as a rule, because Nature guards it herself. I could not see much water, although I could hear the falls, but I had little doubt that it was water that barred this way. Still, it was well worth proving, and after a little I put my binocular up and, after a careful look round, began to go down.

I should, I think, have done better to make my way back to the wood; but, after three dreadful hours, I reached the valley I sought. This was the second valley, that ran south-east.

I was now in the midst of the waters. On the floor of the valley itself, a boisterous torrent was raising its organ voice; and this was fed by waterfalls right and left. Some were stout heads of water, snaking their way down a mountain and every now and then plunging over some steep: some were cascades as fine as a maiden's hair, that seemed to turn into smoke or ever they reached the ground: and some leapt from ledge to ledge – bow upon bow of blue and white and sunshine, which no painter could ever capture, but only a poet could serve.

But water, lovely to look at, bears a sting. Some can be crossed with care: but some of it no man can cross, except by a bridge.

And then I saw the footprint...

In my exultation, I think that I shouted aloud, but such was the music of the waters, no ear could have heard my cry.

A man had gone by this way a few hours back – in all likelihood a smuggler – to show that there was a passage from here into Italy.

The footprint was pointing due South, and I took the line which it gave me without delay. Be sure I moved with care, but here I could not be seen from the observation post.

Soon I found another, which led me up to an eddy at which I could cross a fall; but then, though I peered, I could find no further traces and had to work out my progress as best I could.

It was after noon when I came to a barrier. This was no less than a gorge, about which there were no footprints, within which a mighty fountain was having its violent way. No man could ever have crossed it without a bridge; and, after wasting some time in moving beside its brink, I hastened back to the footprint which had led me over the fall. For it seemed pretty clear that I had lost the line... Sure enough, after two or three casts, I found another print which was pointing towards the main torrent that raged in the valley's bed.

For nearly an hour I sought for a way to cross this savage water... But for the footprint, I should have thrown in my hand; but the man that had made it had been going down to the torrent, for here the latter was making a miniature horse-shoe bend, and the footprint which I had found was within its heels.

And then, at last, I saw how my man had gone by.

From the opposite side, a handsome beech was leaning over the water, and on to one of its arms was fastened a rope. Its end was now coiled and seemed to be tucked away in a fork of the tree: and, of course, I could not use it, because it was out of my reach. No one, I think, who had not been seeking, as I had, and had not been sure, as I had, that the torrent could be crossed, would ever have noticed the rope, for the leaves about it were thick and only by lying down by the edge of the furious water was I able to see the hitch which had been drawn tight on the bough.

Still, though I could go no further, I was content, for I had now no doubt that I had done as we hoped and had hit on a smuggler's way. To make sure, I searched the bushes upon my side of the flood; and there, sure enough, was a staple, of which but an inch was protruding, which had been driven into the cleft of a rock.

From the other side of the water, taking a very short run, a man could swing himself over the boisterous flood: as soon as he landed, he fastened his rope to the staple against his return: on his return, he had only to swing himself back and then restore his rope to its hiding place in the beech.

I have said that I was content, and so I was. If I was a mile from the frontier, I was no more; and I was ready to swear that my movements had not been seen. I confess that I did not relish the thought of this leap in the dark and I hoped that I might be able to make it by day, for the bellow of the water was angry, as though the torrent was resenting the contemplation of such *lèse-majesté*. But that was 'frightfulness'. To a strong man, the venture was nothing, for, if he failed to land, he had only to climb the rope and come down by the tree...

And there I saw the 'snag', which, had I not been so jubilant, I should have seen before. In a word, *I was on the wrong side*.

The way was there, plain enough, for me to take: I could take it with hardly a thought, for in my time I had trodden more perilous paths: but I could only take it, when the rope was attached to the staple which I had found.

This was serious. When the way is hard and strait, goods are not smuggled on every night of the week. Yet, when the time came, I should have to go at once: I could not watch night after night, waiting on the whim of a smuggler who might not appear for ten days.

And then it occurred to me that a smuggler's path should not be a one way street...

At once I returned to the staple, at which I had scarcely looked.

This, as I have said, had been driven into a cleft or crack in the rock. Stouter than the cleft was wide, it was literally jammed in the fissure, which ran at right angles to the stream. Indeed, this ran into the water, some five feet away, growing gradually wider, as it approached the flood.

Hoping against hope, I felt in the cleft...

At once my fingers encountered a very fine cord, which, when I drew it out, I saw to be an ordinary fishing line: and when I followed this up, I found it was sunk in the torrent by means of leads. How this was made fast to the rock, I could not see; but I fancy a second staple had been driven into the cleft and out of sight.

Pull upon this line, I dared not, because I was sure it would bring the rope from its perch: but at least I had proved my theory and, what was more to the point, I had found I could cross the water whenever I pleased.

Since it was now past one, I sat down and ate my lunch: then I made my way leisurely homewards, that is to say, to the point at which Carson would pick me up. Marking the way as I went and finding seven more footprints, I reached the rendezvous soon after five, and since I had three hours to wait, I crossed the road and entered some pleasant woodland which looked as though it might offer a robing-room for him who was chosen to take the smugglers' way.

I soon found a very sweet dell but five minutes' walk from the road, where a man could lie in comfort until it was safe to move. A little lawn was edged by a tumbling rill, and, after the violence of the torrent, the childish speech of the former fell gratefully on the ear. Here I settled myself, and since I had had a short night and a tiring walk, after a very few minutes I fell asleep.

I awoke, as I sometimes do, in the sudden, certain knowledge that I was not alone.

A middle-aged man and a girl were standing close to my feet and were looking down upon me with curious eyes.

As I sat up –

"He would do very well," said the former. "Ulysses' clothes would fit him as few men that I have seen."

"He is very strong," said the latter. "No doubt about that."

Both wore a 'national dress' that I had seen somewhere in France; but the tongue they used was German and they had the look of being Austrian born. The man, who was fat for his age, had a merry eye and made me think in an instant of one of Shakespeare's clowns. The girl was slight, but well-made: health and sunshine had made up her pretty face, and the thick, fair hair which was curling about her shoulders was crowned by a Juliet cap.

I smiled.

"And who is Ulysses?" I said.

"Alas, he is dead," said the man. "We buried him two days ago. He was our strong man and could lift incredible weights. But the wine was stronger than he. They had many a bout together, but in the end the wine won. And now our troupe is the poorer, for many can sing and dance – or think they can; but few can bend a crowbar into a hoop."

"Few, indeed," said I. "But why do you wear that dress? It is not Austrian."

"Because," said the man, "I am now in Austria. A prophet is not without honour, save in his own country. So in Austria I am a Frenchman, and when I am on parade, my German is very poor. The same in Italy, for Italy does not like those that are Austrian born. If ever I go to France, I shall wear my own dress."

"You move about?" I said.

"From here to Italy. We have come South from Innsbruck and soon I shall be drinking the beer of Padua. The life is hard in a way; but I would not change it, sir, for any that I have seen."

"Nor I," said the girl. "It is very good to be free."

"It is everything," said the man. "For this reason, I am not so sure that we shall return from Italy in the spring."

"Aha," said I. "You have no use for the Boche?"

"None," said the man. "Neither for lord nor for peasant, for matron or for maid. The Boche is no fellow creature. The blood is bad."

"You are perfectly right," said I. "If Europe is to be safe, the Boche should be behind bars."

The fellow turned to the girl.

"How many times, Colette, have I used those very words?"

"It is true," said the girl, smiling. "And Jasper knows Germany."

"Before the Great War," said the man, "I was with a German circus for nearly three years. That is the way, sir, to learn what a people is like; for you pass through the whole of the country, and high and low visit a circus and sit beside the ring." He drew in his breath. "What the Boche enjoys most of all is another being's distress – a bear in torment, sir, or a clown that is kicked by a horse. I have seen a dog, short of a paw, that, because he had a great heart, would try to do his tricks with the rest. And when he failed, the dog cried – I saw the tears on his face. And the Germans roared with delight... I could have been ringmaster: but, once I had learned my job, I went away."

"What was your job?" I said.

"I was a tumbler, sir. Or, if you like it better, an acrobat. The sand, the rope and the horse, I learned to master them all." He sighed. "But after forty, no man can do such work as it should be done. So now I have my own troupe, and I sing a ditty or two and play the fool."

"Believe me, sir," said Colette, "he is the life of the show."

"I can well believe you," I said. "If I were free, I would come to your show tonight."

Jasper regarded me straitly.

"You are a man that has done many things in his time. You have sweated and shivered and you have walked with death. I can read these things in your face, and I know I am right. Add, then, to your wisdom, sir, and be our strong man. Just for a month, till we come to Padua. There, I think, I can find one to take Ulysses' place. I swear you shall want for nothing and shall have a tent to yourself. You will, in fact, be our guest. And the life will entertain you..."

I laughed.

"I'm sure it would," I said, "but I have too much to do. My holiday here is ending, and I must leave for England in two or three days."

"Extend your holiday, sir, for I will wager no desk awaits your return. And your duties with us would be nothing."

"The weights," said Colette, "can be altered to suit your strength. Though you are stronger than most, the lifting of weights is an art. But our weights have a plate at the bottom, by which we can let out the sand. And then even I can move them. It is meant to be used when travelling, but we have given that up, for we had to take the sand with us in any event. Still, the plates are there."

I sat very still.

"In such a case," I said, "what would happen if somebody questioned the weights?"

Jasper fingered his chin.

"The fact remains, sir, that nobody ever has. No ordinary man can judge between forty and fifty pounds. But come, my friend, you do not know your strength. And weightlifting is a knack. After two days you will pick up a hundredweight."

I put a hand to my head.

"I ought to get back," I said, feebly, striving to hide my excitement from those keen eyes. "But Italy is a country which I have never seen."

"Then here is your chance," said the girl. "With us you will see the country as tourists never see it."

"That is true," said Jasper. "You will see the heart of the country – and not the smirk on its face."

"We know," said Colette, "that we cannot offer you money: but do us this favour and you shall be our guest."

Jasper bowed.

"Our honoured guest, sir. Stroll for a month with us, and you'll find that we poor players know our place."

I got to my feet.

"My very good friends," I said, "if I were to come, be sure I should ask no better than to be one of you. To live and laugh, to labour and rest as you do. To be frank, your suggestion attracts me. Once I worked with a circus, because it served my turn. And I know that, hard though it be, the life is good. And Italy is a country which I should like to see. But I must think it over, before I decide. Can you meet me here tomorrow?"

"Name your hour, sir," said Jasper.

"What time is your show?"

"At half past seven. Yes, Colette, we must be going."

"Will half past ten be all right?"

"At night?" said Jasper.

"At night."

"We shall be here, sir, to take our good fortune up."

"Don't be too sure," I said. "I may not be able to come."

"Ah, yes," said Colette. "We will strive to make you happy, and I will wash your linen day after day."

"Bless your heart," said I. "I shan't ask that. I'd like to travel with you. But I have made other arrangements, and whether or no I can break them, I cannot tell."

"Let him be," said Jasper. "He knows his mind." He turned to me. "Until tomorrow, sir."

With that, he made me a bow and Colette, a smile. Then they turned and passed down the dell, by the side of the busy brook. Before they entered the greenwood, they turned and waved.

I put up a hand and waved back.

"William," said Mansel, "I think you've driven the nail. I have no doubt that the gems can go into the weights, and I simply cannot imagine a safer vehicle. Indeed, so far as I see, there's only one fence to fly. And that is, of course, that, unless you resemble Ulysses – and that I beg leave to doubt – you cannot go by a post, but must take the smugglers' way. And that means taking Jasper into your confidence."

"To a certain extent," said I. "That the Boche is laying for me will be more than enough."

"Then that's all right. But, if you go, Bell must go with you. They'll see nothing strange in that. And Bell can come and go, can keep in touch with Carson, and, at the appropriate moment, load your weights."

"Yes," I said. "Bell will be quite invaluable. I only wish they were leaving the country at once."

"You must learn the date tomorrow. If you're to come in, you've got to know where you stand."

"I wish," said I, "you were going to play the hand."

"You'll play it much better," said Mansel. "Besides, I quite expect to have my hands full. Friar will be back before long, and the Boche may stumble upon us at any time. And your absence will take some explaining... Oh, no. I'm better here. But I feel that you should sign on as soon as you decently can. I have a hunch that a tempest is on the way. And you must have disappeared before it breaks loose."

"You said last night that the Boche had put Diana on to Friar. How do you make that out?"

Mansel wrinkled his brow.

"The English police could have done it within twelve hours. I think the Boche could have done it in twenty-four. The ground was hard in the drive, but soft in the valley below. So Friar's second car left prints. And one of the tyres was new, but the rest were old. If a policeman is properly served, it shouldn't be very hard to follow that up."

"Say you're right," said I. "He got on to Friar. But he never took any action."

"The Boche doesn't care about failures: and Friar had failed."

"He'd done wilful murder," I said.

"Be your age," said Mansel. "What's murder count with a German, if he can smell gold?"

At ten o'clock the next evening I left to keep my appointment, driving the Rolls myself, with Bell by my side. I berthed the car half a mile from the little dell, in a convenient thicket, fed by a track.

As I led the way –

"Stay in the background," I said, "and listen to what is said. If I want you, I'll say so, and you will appear. But I don't think I shall."

"Very good, sir."

For this very strange instruction, my instinct was to blame. Not a very fine instinct, I fear, as my tale will show. Still, I had a feeling that Trouble was out that night: and I have learned not to ignore the nudge of Fancy. It may, of course, be misleading; but to take such a hint is worthwhile, though four times out of five your fear is proved vain. For the fifth time you honour the whim that may save your life.

I had been in the dell for ten minutes when Jasper appeared with Colette.

"Ah, my good sir," he cried, "I knew that you would be here. Whether or no, you have come, because you passed your word."

"Naturally," said I. "I keep the appointments I make."

"Not everyone does. Never mind. We await your decision, sir."

"Upon certain conditions," I said, "I will join your troupe."

"There you are," cried Colette. "I said he would."

"We accept your conditions, sir, without hearing what they are."

"Italy attracts me," I said. "Were you not bound for Italy, I should not come. When will you enter that country?"

"In ten days' time," said Jasper.

I frowned.

"We can leave before that," said Colette.

"Yes," said Jasper, "we can. We had not intended to, but we can leave next Thursday, if you insist."

"I insist upon nothing. But if I am to come – well, I was leaving for England, for I have been here long enough. If, instead, I can leave for Italy, well and good."

"Next Thursday evening, sir."

"Good enough. Next, I must bring my servant. He is the best of men and will pull his weight."

Jasper bowed.

"We shall be most happy to have him. Another mouth means another pair of hands."

"You will have no complaints," I said.

"But no man can wash," said Colette. "Your linen will be my affair."

"He shall assist you," I said.

"He shall watch and learn," said Colette.

"Finally," said I, "my incognito must be respected. No one outside the troupe must ever have any idea that I am an amateur."

"That," said Jasper, firmly, "is understood. You will be our strong man, for so long as you stay. And no one outside the troupe will have the faintest idea that you are not what you seem."

"In case of emergency, I think I had better be French."

"You do not look like a Frenchman, but as you will."

"Those, then, are my conditions."

"Thank you, sir," said Jasper. "Now I will tell you mine. You will have a tent to yourself, though, if you like, your servant shall sleep with you. You will do no sort of work, except that you will rehearse and will play the strong man. You will rise and retire when you please, your table will be as good as we can afford and from first to last you will be our honoured guest."

"I think," I said, "that we shall get on very well. But I want no special fare, for I do not do things by halves. If I am to join your troupe, then I shall be one of you. Do you give two shows tomorrow?"

"No, only one, sir, as usual, at half past seven o'clock. And on Monday we move to Godel. That is a handsome village, four miles from where we stand."

(In fact, it was not so far – perhaps three miles and a half.)

"Very well," said I. "I think I should join you at Godel. I mean, if I meet you there, my arrival will cause less remark."

"That is most true," said Jasper, "for I can say I had written and asked you to come. We travel betimes, sir: so we shall arrive before noon."

"I will await you there from ten o'clock on."

Jasper bowed.

"That will be excellent. There is an inn commanding the great cascade. It is known as The Vat of Melody – no one knows why."

"Come there direct," I said, "and pick me up. My servant and I will help you to pitch your tents; and then you shall teach me my duties and I will try the weights." Jasper regarded Colette.

"I cannot," he said, "regret Ulysses' demise."

"No, indeed," said Colette. "And if we are nice to him, perhaps he will stay with us."

"You have my permission," said Jasper, "to do your worst."

At that, we laughed and shook hands. Then we bade one another good night, and I watched them go. As before, they turned to wave at the edge of the trees.

As I rose out of the dell, Bell stepped out of the shadows and fell in behind.

"They're honest souls," I said.

"I think so, sir. I take it they're Austrian."

"That's right. Of the rest of the troupe I know nothing, but we must hope for the best. I think we should be able to manage."

"It's not for long, sir."

"No. And once we're out of this country, I shall not care. Come along. Let's get back to the car."

When we found the Rolls safe and sound, I was greatly relieved; for whilst I was talking with Jasper, a sudden fear for the car had taken hold of my heart. No one, of course, could have moved her, because she was locked: but, had the German found her, to use a colloquial expression, it might not have been too good. The truth is that her precious freight was beginning to loom in the background of every movement we made; and when it was not under our hand, I began to imagine vain things. This may seem foolish enough, and Mansel declined to give the matter a thought: but when you are treating millions much as you treat a spare wheel, contingencies lift up their heads – and may look you down.

We drove back quietly enough – for most of the way without lights, for though the moon had not risen, the air was clear and the sky was without a cloud: so the starlight had a fair field, and for me, who was well accustomed to watching and moving by night, the darkness had lost its sting.

Now Wagensburg had been built on the edge of a cliff, the foot of which was washed by a river, as, a year or two back, we had good reason to know. The road we must use this night ran close to the bank of the river upon the opposite side; and we had to pass the castle, before we could come to our bridge. I knew that I could not see it, for the quarters which we were using lay on the farther side – and, even so, we were careful to keep the curtains drawn: but perhaps because I knew where it was, as we passed, I glanced up at the courtyard – to be more precise, at where the courtyard hung. And as I looked, I saw the flash of a torch.

Without thinking what I did, I set a foot on the brake and threw out the clutch, but the flash was not repeated, and, after a little, I took the car slowly on.

"I saw a light on the terrace," I said to Bell.

"I thought you seen something, sir, the way you stopped."

Thinking aloud –

"And what does that mean?" I said. "It means the devil and all, for they've found us out. I must leave the car at the junction and go on on foot. You will stay at the junction, keeping the engine running, ready to move. If anything comes, you'll have a choice of three roads, so you can't go wrong. And when all's clear, you will return to the junction and wait for me."

"Very good, sir."

(The junction was a spot by the river where three roads met: one ran North to Villach, one East – the road we were using – and one ran West.)

A moment later we came to the junction itself.

I passed the spot and stopped dead: then I took the Rolls back and round, until she was off the road and was facing North. And then I was out of the car and was running down the road to the bridge which lay to the West.

I had about two miles to cover, before I could come to the house; but I dared not make too much haste, for my hand must be steady when I got there, in case I ran into a storm. Then, again, if I was to do any good, my approach must not be made known to the strangers within our gates.

There was, so far as I saw, no car at the foot of the combe or near the house; but the servants' quarters were screened by a little covert, and what there was behind this, I could not tell.

I padded through the meadows, past Wagensburg's famous well: then I slipped into the covert – and stood very still.

A man was stooping by a window which served the servants' hall, trying to peer between the curtains, which had been drawn. The window being open, after a moment I saw him put up a hand and move the curtain a little, just as a breeze might have done. Then he let it go and stood up, as though he had seen what he wished, and, after looking about him, went stealing towards the garage, which had no doors.

I knew as well as he what the fellow had seen – Mansel reading or writing and the table with covers for two, for Carson would be in the kitchen, making ready some soup against my return.

When he had entered the garage, I stepped across to the window and pitched my cigarette case into the room. This was made of leather and made but the slightest sound. Then I moved to the mouth of the garage and stood there, straining my ears.

"Do as I tell you," hissed Friar. "I'm not going to wait any more."

"Or right, or right," said Sloper, "but don' blame me. An' wot if the car comes in before we done? If you'd wait to get Chandos first, you'd 'ave the other for tea."

"I'll have him now," said Friar. "Go and get Orris in."

As I stood against the wall, Sloper left the garage and turned to his left. This almost certainly meant that Orris was in the courtyard – the flash I had seen was probably that of his torch. If I was right, at least two minutes must pass before Sloper came back.

I dared not enter the garage, for, while I could not see him, Friar would surely see me against what light there was: so I stood where I was and willed the man to come forth.

I thought that perhaps he would, for to watch the backdoor was natural – I should have done it myself. And so he did…

As he came abreast of me, I hit him under the jaw with all my might: he made no sound at all, but crumpled and fell.

As I got my hands under his arms –

"Well done, indeed, William," breathed Mansel.

"And where do we go from here?"

"Two others coming," I said. "We move him out of their way and wait for them. Carson round to the courtyard, to see what's what. But he must let them go by."

"Very good, sir," said Carson's voice.

We picked my victim up and laid him down by the door he had come out to watch.

"And now what?"

"They'll enter the garage," I said. "I'd like to hear what they say."

"Right. We let them go in and close up." As we reached the edge of the covert – "And now expound to me, William. Whom have you laid to rest?"

"Friar," I said.

"Friar? And how in the world – "

"It's just occurred to me. Punter."

"Oh, my God," said Mansel. "Of course you're right. When I picked this place, I never thought of Punter. Of course Punter knew in an instant that this was where we should go."

(I have mentioned before that we had known the castle in other days: others, too, had known it, and Punter was one of them. Not to have thought of this was careless, indeed; but we had had much to think of during the week, and the Boche had been more in our minds than had Friar and his gang.)

"Never mind," Mansel continued. "What is the special idea?"

"Your liquidation, I fancy: and mine when the car comes in."

"What could be better? And here they come – to report to the fountain-head. As the fountain is out of order, I wonder what they will do."

Two figures passed into the garage, and we drew near.

" 'Ere we are," said Sloper.

There was, of course, no reply.

"Mus' be outside," said Sloper. "You wait 'ere."

I touched Mansel's arm, and he nodded…

As Sloper passed me, I struck; and Mansel caught his body and laid it gently down.

"Who is the third man? Orris?"

"That's right," I said.

Mansel approached the garage and lifted his voice.

"I want you, Orris," he said. "So come straight out and keep your hands in the air. If you don't within ten seconds, I'm going to fire into the garage; and if you're in the way of the bullet, it'll be just too bad."

There was a moment's hesitation.

Then –

"Coming, sir," said Orris, and out he came.

Mansel drew his torch and threw the beam on the door.

"Walk to that door, Orris. You'll have to pick your way or you'll tread on the dead."

"—!" said Orris.

89

"Exactly. You see what comes of trying to mix it with me. Is Punter with you tonight?"

"No — fear," said Orris. "I wish 'e was."

"Why d'you wish that?"

Orris let go.

The horrid threats which distinguished his lengthy reply soon showed that our assumption was perfectly right. Punter had led his companions to Wagensburg – not, of course, in person – and had furnished them with a plan, the omissions of which were outstanding, few details of which were correct. This was not wholly his fault, for, since he had visited the castle, considerable changes had been made: still, while laying great stress upon the courtyard, as being the castle's hub, and insisting that that was a place at which no light should be shown, he had failed to disclose that in the courtyard itself were four or five well-grown trees, to say nothing of a well, with a parapet two feet high. His unsuspecting colleagues had discovered these picturesque features in the most painful of ways, and to Orris had belonged the distinction of finding the well. This he had almost entered, for, the parapet tripping him up, he had fallen heavily forward, to encounter nothing but space. How he had saved himself, he had no idea, but the venture had deeply shocked him, as well it might. Yet, upon his declaring his repugnance to what he had found, instead of receiving the sympathy which was his due, he had been, as he put it, 'cursed silly', for daring to raise his voice... From that most pregnant moment, Orris had lost all interest in what was toward: for him, the enterprise was poisoned – by pain and fright and, curiously, most of all, because he must keep to himself his agony of body and mind. Indeed, he made no attempt to disguise the relief he felt at being made prisoner.

How Mansel kept a straight face, I do not know: I confess I was shaking with laughter before the rogue was halfway through his recital of blood and tears.

"Go over him, William, will you?"

I found a pistol and torch – the torch, no doubt, which had stood us in such good stead.

We took him into the house, turned him into the stillroom and locked the door.

"And now," said Mansel, "before we go any further, please put me wise. I was awaiting the Rolls: instead, your cigarette case alighted beside my chair: it seems that you've saved my life, but I'd love to know how."

My tale was soon told.

"By God," said Mansel, "but what a stroke of luck. If Orris hadn't been sore, he wouldn't have lighted his torch: if you hadn't passed at that moment, you wouldn't have been forewarned – and Friar would have got you first, and then me, before you were cold. For I should have come to the door, as I always do. William, we must be more careful. Fancy forgetting that Punter knew this place."

Be sure I agreed with him.

Then I went off to call Carson, to send him for Bell, while Mansel inspected my victims and took their pistols away.

I never got as far as the courtyard, for Carson met me halfway.

He was out of breath, for he had been running fast.

"The German, sir," he panted. "They must have been trailing Friar, an' now they've found his car at the foot of the drive."

"Are they on their way up?"

"By now, sir."

"Come along," I said.

I turned and ran the way I had come.

Mansel looked up from the business of searching Friar.

"What is it, William?"

"The Boche."

Mansel straightened his back.

"Where?"

"On his way to the courtyard."

For a moment Mansel considered this very unpleasant news. Then he gave his orders as quietly as if we had hours to spare.

"Carson, our two dispatch cases. Everything else we must leave. Take them through the covert and wait on the other side. William, get Orris out and switch off every light. Between you, pick up Friar and carry him into the covert. I can manage Sloper – he looks pretty light."

Two minutes later, Friar and Sloper, still senseless, were lying out of sight in the thicket; and Orris, now thoroughly scared, was standing on the edge of the meadows, listening to Mansel's words.

"If you don't fancy foreign prisons, you'd better do as I say. Pick up those two cases." Orris obliged. "This is my servant, Carson. From now you are in his charge." Mansel turned to Carson. "Tie a cord to his wrist and make him walk in front. If he gives any trouble, shoot him and shove his corpse in the ditch."

"Shan't give no trouble, sir."

"Bell's got the Rolls at the junction. Get there as quick as you can. Keep her moving till daybreak, always touching our bridge-head once in the hour. When it's light, you must lay her up, and one of you come to the bridge. Bind Orris hand and foot and keep him on the floor of the car."

"Very good, sir."

"They're here," said I. "I saw the flash of a torch."

"Good," said Mansel. "Come on," and led the way back.

As we came to the edge of the covert –

"The garage is empty," said a voice.

"Blockhead!" hissed the German. "Can you be quiet?"

With the greatest caution, five figures reconnoitred the building. Then, after a consultation we could not hear, one, who was not the German, ventured to open the door.

His reluctance to enter the house was very clear, and the German was dancing with impatience before the fellow had done as he dared not do himself. Indeed, he would not go in, till the four had preceded him and had declared the coast clear. Then he stamped his way into the quarters, shouting for lights.

"Excellent," said Mansel. "Those fellows must hate his guts."

"If they had any guts themselves, they'd put him down."

After, perhaps, two minutes, the five reappeared.

"They are clearly out," said the German, "but they will soon come in. Their soup is simmering, and their table is laid. So put out the lights again and close the door. Viller will go down the drive, to announce their coming by torch: Benz will watch for his signal and pass it on. March."

On this blunt command, two of the five moved down the road of approach. "Wessel will go to the courtyard and bring back two men. Hasten, fool. Who told you that Mansel would wait for you to return?"

Wessel plodded off the way he had come.

"And what of Herr Friar?" said the policeman who had not moved.

"God in heaven," said the Boche. "And can you not work that out? We surprised Herr Friar, my friend. And since the last thing that he wants is collision with us, Herr Friar has faded away. Be sure, he is cross – very cross. But that is the jackal's fate, when the lion appears. He can have what is left, of course."

There was a little silence, during which, after cocking an ear, the German took out his case and lighted a cigarette.

The other man cleared his throat.

"You will forgive me, Herr Boler, but what, when they return, are you proposing to do?"

"Arrest them, of course," said the Boche.

"Upon what charge?"

"Of failing to register."

"So far as we know, they have stayed at no hotel."

The German stamped his foot.

"They are living here without the owner's consent."

"Perhaps," said the other. "But that is the owner's affair."

"Then think of some other charge. These men must be detained."

"It is all very well," said the other, "but they are Englishmen."

"That is in itself good cause for letting the swine rot in prison for twenty years."

"I am thinking of this," said the other, "that, if, as a result, there is trouble, the blame will fall upon me. You have no official position and cannot be touched: but I am the Chief of Police and I shall have to answer for any action we take."

The other tapped the ground with his foot.

"You white-livered hound," he said. "The Reich has sent me here to stiffen your rubber spine – to drain the tea from your veins and introduce blood. I have laid bare an attempt to smuggle out of your country – "

"All surmise," said the other. "Proof, you have none."

"I have the proof," screamed the Boche. "My agent was in the castle and found them at work."

"I know nothing of that. I confess their behaviour is strange. They can be asked to explain it. But we have no right to arrest them for what we cannot prove they have done."

"They shall be detained," said the German. "On that I insist."

"Of what is the use? Detention will not give you the treasure you say they have seized."

"My friend," said the German, "you have a great deal to learn. Detain them for forty-eight hours, and I will guarantee that, ere that time has expired, the treasure will be in our hands. I know how to make people talk."

The other stood very still.

Then –

"Herr Boler," he said, "the line you are seeking to take is extremely grave. And *I* am responsible."

The German leaned forward.

"Play me false," he hissed, "and you lose your job. Within twenty-four hours of your failure, a note will leave my country, desiring the instant dismissal of the Chief of the Robin Police.

Do you think that desire will be questioned?" The other drew in his breath. "Exactly. No post, no pension, no money. You and your wife and daughter, begging your bread. But render me all assistance to lay these swine by the heels, and you shall be promoted to Salzburg within the week."

"Salzburg is not vacant."

"If I wish it to be vacant, it will be. Depend upon that. And Robin will be vacant, if I choose to say the word."

On a sudden he threw up his head. "Is that a car? Where the devil's that booby, Wessel? Go and get him. I'll call the others in."

With that, he ran to the drive, while the other stood watching for a moment and then strode off to the left.

This shows how poor a soldier the Boche would have made. There was no car to be heard: he did not wait for the signal which Benz was to give: instead he kept flashing his torch, to call in the men he had posted, to warn him of our approach.

Until I saw Mansel behind him, I never knew he had moved. Then he touched the German's shoulder...

The latter let out a whoop, and started about, when Mansel hit him square on the point of the chin.

As I came to his side –

"Three's lucky," he said, shortly. "Into the covert with him, and let Viller and Benz go by. Then we carry him off and make for the bridge."

And so we did.

First Benz and then Viller came by at a steady trot, but we were too far from the house to observe the return of the rest. At once we entered the meadows, bearing the German between us and making what haste we could.

There was a byre in the combe, and we carried his body in and threw it down.

"And now for the Rolls," said Mansel. "God send they haven't just left."

We had to wait twenty minutes before the Rolls came by...

As Bell brought the car to rest –

"Free Orris," said Mansel, shortly, "and turn him out."

A moment later the fellow was down in the road.

"Listen to me, Orris. The police are up at the castle and have your car."

"Gawd 'elp."

"I think I'm the better bet. Walk back down this road till you come to a village called Lerai. That is the one you went through to get to the castle drive. You turn to the right at Lerai and cross the bridge. Get back to the foot of the drive and use your eyes. When the police go away, come up to the house and report. You can, of course, try to double-cross me, but, if you do, Orris, as sure as I'm standing here, I'll blow your brains through the back of your rotten head."

"That's all right, sir. Punter's tole me your shape."

And then we were in the Rolls and were flying over the bridge.

Three minutes later, perhaps, we were back at Wagensburg.

This time we had run with lights, and, as we slid out of the covert, these revealed two figures standing against the wall.

"Hullo, who's there?" cried Mansel, and set a foot on the brake.

There was a hurried consultation.

Then one of the two came forward and took off his hat.

"We are the police, sir," he said. "Our chief will be here in a moment. And he will explain our presence better than I."

"That's all right," said Mansel, and left his seat. "Put her away, Carson, and Bell shall give us some food. Tell your chief we've gone in, will you? If he's as thirsty as I am, I'll lay he can do with a drink."

We had washed and were sitting at table, before the Chief of the Police made bold to enter the room.

The man looked ill at ease and worried to death.

"Sit down, pray," said Mansel. "No, I insist. You must forgive us for dining, but three of us have eaten nothing all day. But we cannot dine, unless you will drink with us. May I pour you a brandy and soda?"

The poor man looked helplessly round, and Mansel mixed the liquor and put it into his hand.

"Monsieur is very kind."

"Nonsense," said Mansel, "nonsense." and raised his glass.

The other did the same and drank long and deep.

"And now," said Mansel, "what can we do for you?"

The man put a hand to his head.

"Forgive me," he said, "but your movements interest us."

"Do you find them irregular? I mean, we know Austria well and have very often made her our hunting ground. There is hardly a stream hereabouts that I have not fished. And I used to own this castle – not very long ago."

The man was staring.

"You owned Wagensburg?"

"Yes. I spent a summer here, but I tired of the place. And then, you know, I had a whim to come back. I fear I have asked no permission, but we are doing no harm, and are using the servants' quarters, as you can see. But we shall not be here much longer. We have to get back to England – and, to be frank, your country is not what it was."

"Alas, that is only too true, sir. I am but one of many who are alarmed."

"No doubt you know more than I do. But I can tell you this, that I have not visited Germany since the war. I never liked the Germans, but I can never forgive them for what they did. Austria was a cat's paw – I bear her no such ill will. But upon this, my latest visit, a German enters my room in a private house. It was when I was staying at Hohenems, Mr Ferrers' home. He enters my room with a warrant – a German in Austria. He vapours about some treasure which I am trying to steal… Well, I do not like such treatment. That is why I left Hohenems. That is why I sought refuge here, for I wished to avoid his attentions for the rest of my stay. You see, I dislike the German. For me, he taints the air. So when I leave Austria this time, I do not think I shall come back."

The man had his eyes on the ground.

"I have always liked the English," he muttered. "All that has happened has been most distasteful to me. But, believe me, sir, I cannot help myself. So long as this beast is at Robin, I have to do as he says."

"Do you refer to that very vulgar upstart who came to Hohenems?"

"That is the German, sir, whose orders I have to obey."

"Has he sent you here?"

"He brought us here, sir, this night. And now he has disappeared."

"Why did he bring you here? What wrong have we done?"

"None that I know of, sir. He maintains that you have a treasure, which you are seeking to smuggle out of the country, as soon as may be."

"But – "

"Monsieur, it is his idea. He has no evidence. Again and again I have asked him to give me something to go on – some grains of foundation for his hypothesis. But all I receive is insult... I have not, perhaps, a very outstanding brain, but I was walking my beat when he was in swaddling-clothes. And I know the law and my duty. If I had a case against you, English or no, be sure I should follow it up. But I have nothing against you – except that a gang of thieves led us here tonight."

"A gang of thieves?" said Mansel.

The other nodded his head.

"A gang of English thieves, whose leader is one Herr Friar."

"Friar?" said Mansel. "Friar? Is Friar a thief?"

"What do you know of him, sir?"

"I saw him in Salzburg," said Mansel, "about a fortnight ago. He came up and claimed my acquaintance. I told him that he was mistaken and thought I had shaken him off. But that night he came to my rooms, and, to cut a long story short, I knocked him down. D'you say he's here now? I suppose he hopes to get back."

The other spread out his hands.

"All I know, sir, is this – that he led us here and his car is at the foot of the drive. And now tell me this, if you please. Could he have known you were going to Hohenems?"

"No," said Mansel, "he couldn't. I didn't know it myself. He may have known that I was a friend of the Ferrers."

"Had you stayed at the castle before?"

"Certainly. A year or two back."

"Then that explains it," said the other. "That is why he forced himself on you. He has entered Hohenems once – but not as a guest. He desires to repeat his visit, and knowing that you had the *entrée*, he sought to improve an acquaintance that did not exist."

Here our soup was served, but though Bell brought in three plates, our friend excused himself and proposed to withdraw.

"One moment," said Mansel. "Your fellows would like some beer?"

"Monsieur is very considerate."

"See to that, Bell, will you?"

"Certainly, sir."

Mansel returned to the Chief of the Robin Police.

"Before you go, Herr…"

"My name is Kerrelin, sir."

"Before you go, Herr Kerrelin, please tell me two things. The first is, where is Friar? If he is meaning mischief, since you and your men are here…"

The man put a hand to his head.

"Sir," he said, "I do not know where he is gone. Herr Boler – that is the German – declares that when we arrived here, he beat a retreat."

"But his car is still there. That means he is somewhere about."

"He must be, sir, for he would not abandon his car."

"You know him for what he is. You say that he entered Hohenems in an irregular way. Why don't you pull him in?"

"You may well ask, sir," said Kerrelin, looking from side to side. "Herr Boler will not let me, because he maintains that you and Mr Chandos are bigger game. He insists that there is some treasure, of which I have very grave doubts. He insists that you are here to carry it off, which, to my mind, is absurd. He insists that is also Friar's object, and that if we leave him alone, then Friar will embarrass you."

Mansel expired.

"What a fool the man is," he said. "We shall have to leave the country, if this goes on."

"Until you do so, sir, you will know no peace. Herr Boler desires to detain you – and put great pressure upon you, to learn what he calls the truth. But when you go, you must expect to be searched. All frontier-posts are waiting. They have been warned that you will be laden with treasure, and, believe me, sir, they will take the tyres from your car."

"Well, I hope they'll like their contents: in any event, they can damned well put them back."

Kerrelin spread out his hands.

"I tell you these things, sir, because it is right you should know. We do not molest the English – we never have. Mr Ferrers and Lady Olivia command my great respect. But now my hand is forced. Their guests must be insulted, and thieves that have entered their home must not be touched."

There was a little silence.

Then –

"But where is Boler?" said Mansel. "I understood you to say that he brought you here."

Kerrelin shrugged his shoulders.

"He was here," he said. "He sent me off on an errand, and when I came back he was gone. That is one of his ways, sir. I have waited hours for that man. If I am leaving my post, I tell my men where I am going and when to expect me back. But

Herr Boler will disappear when my back is turned – and I must wait, like some servant, until it pleases his highness to come again."

"Such behaviour is intolerable," said Mansel.

Kerrelin swallowed.

"I find it discourteous," he said. "It makes a fool of me. If my men were not sympathetic, it would be bad for discipline."

"Perhaps he's outside," said Mansel.

The other shook his head.

"No, sir. My men would warn me of his approach. Still, if you will excuse me, I should be outside."

"What happens when he returns, to find that we have come back?"

"I hope he will see the wisdom of going away. I think, perhaps, he will enter and issue threats. But you will not be arrested. On that I have made up my mind."

Mansel inclined his head.

"I'm much obliged. When I return to London, I shall report this affair. And you may be sure I shall say that, in spite of foreign pressure, the Austrian police decline to be deflected from the duty they swore to do."

"That is very kind of you, sir."

"No, it isn't," said Mansel. "You'd do the same for me."

Then, in spite of his protests, we poured him a glass of wine, and we touched one another's glasses, before we drank. After which, he took his leave, to resume an obnoxious vigil, which, though he did not know it, was going to last a long time.

Mansel sat back in his chair.

"What happens when Friar and Sloper recover consciousness?"

I began to laugh.

"I think it's just as well that we took their arms."

"Yes, they'll be ripe for murder they cannot do. And, though they can't think straight, they'll have to take on the police.

When once they're alone again, Sloper's strictures will be worth listening to."

"And Boler?"

"Ah," said Mansel. "And Boler. We should have put him in the river, instead of the byre. But it's too late now."

"How long is he out for?" I said.

Mansel shrugged his shoulders.

"Four or five hours, I should say. I hit him hard."

"Will they wait so long?"

"I don't see what else they can do."

"And then what?"

"Friar will be suspected of knocking him out. Friar or Sloper, unless they find them first. Our alibi's very good. It doesn't really exist, but the Boche was sure we were out and Kerrelin saw us come in."

I began to laugh.

"This," I said, "is really too good to last."

"That's very true," said Mansel. "Any moment now we shall go down the drain." He sank his voice to a whisper. "Tell me, William, why did we take this on?"

"God knows," said I. "I've been asking myself for days. The brutal answer is – because we're a couple of mugs."

"I don't like that one," said Mansel. "Let's say we're altruists. When d'you join up? Monday?"

"That's right," I said. "But I can't take over at once."

"Tuesday night, perhaps: but not before. You must get the hang of the, er, receptacles."

We had finished our simple meal, when we heard a flurry outside and then Sloper's voice.

"— 'avin' tea, I was, with the Consul's wife. An' the las' thing the Consul says, as 'e brings me 'at, 'Arthur,' 'e says, 'don't you stan' no — from — ' 'Ere, wot's this?" We heard the click of handcuffs. "Nasty, vulgar, 'abits. An' wot would you say I'd done?"

Another voice was reporting – in German of course.

"This man was found in the meadows, moving cautiously East. He was proposing, I think, to gain the entrance drive.

"And his car," said Kerrelin.

"I imagine so, sir. There is, I think, no doubt that he is one of the gang."

Kerrelin spoke in English.

"Where is Herr Friar?" he said.

"Sick," said Sloper, promptly. "Cort a cole or somethin'. Left 'im at 'ome."

"What are you doing here?"

"Come to see Capting Mansel – on private business."

"Did you expect to find him out in the fields?"

"Out when I called, smartie: so I went to 'ave a laydown and falls asleep. Then I got into them meadows an' lorse me way. Wanderin', I was, when 'e foun' me – bless 'is soul."

Mansel and I began to shake with laughter.

"How did you know that Captain Mansel was here?"

"Gov'nor tole me: 'e's a friend of 'is."

"That is a lie," said Kerrelin.

"Sez you. Frien'? 'E's a — crony. Mansel, Palin an' Friar…all at Eting together an' always kep' up. Talk abaht the ole school tie…"

"What was your business with Captain Mansel?"

"Well, you see, Capting Mansel don' know that the gov'nor's ill. If 'e did, 'e'd come an' see 'im, sure as a — gun. Bring 'im some books to read, an' a bag o' grapes. So the gov'nor sen's me orf. I'm 'is servant, I am – 'ave bin for years. 'Sloper,' 'e says, 'you go an' fin' the Capting,' 'e says; 'an' tell 'im ole Ned Friar's sick. As like as not,' 'e says, ' ' e 'll come back in the car wiv you.' "

A silence succeeded this truly admirable effort on Sloper's part. Then a knock fell upon our door, and Mansel cried "Come in".

Kerrelin entered the room.

"You have heard?" he said.

"Yes," said Mansel, "we have. Your Mr Sloper has made us laugh very much. He may be a knave, but he is a comedian. His flights of imagination are very fine. Still, to come down to earth, his master, Herr Friar, is not on my visiting list. And Sloper did not come here to tell me that he was ill. For one thing, I have no doubt that Friar is here himself."

"Nor I," said Kerrelin. "I have told my men to look out for any movement. He will almost certainly try to approach his car."

"I agree. But he must be extremely cross. He came to offer me violence, and you put a spoke in his wheel. And, but for you, it might not have been too good. If we had come in, as we did, to find Friar here… My impression is that he will be very cross: so I think your men should be careful."

Kerrelin bowed.

"I am glad to think, sir, that we may have spoiled his game."

"Thank you, my friend. But don't let him turn upon you."

Kerrelin smiled.

"To do that would be very foolish. Still, I will take precautions. And now I say 'Good night.' "

"One moment," said Mansel. "We're both of us very tired and, if you have no objection, we're going to bed. Is that all right by you?"

"Sirs," cried Kerrelin, "I beg that you will retire. When we shall go depends upon Herr Boler. Leave without him, I cannot. But I assure you that you shall not be disturbed."

We thanked him and bade him good night.

As I shut our bedroom door –

"I've sown the seed," said Mansel, "and we must hope for the best. Of naughty temper Friar knocked Boler out. Damned thin, I admit. But it may be good enough."

"For Boler?" said I.

"Why not? The man's a fool. He may suspect it was either you or I: but the evidence will be against him. Very strong evidence, William. He had been gone half an hour before we appeared. And Kerrelin is our friend. All the same, we mustn't stay here. And now call Carson, will you?"

A moment later Carson entered the room, which lay directly above the servants' hall.

"Carson, you will watch for one hour and then call Bell. When Bell has watched for one hour, he will come and call me. The general idea is not to be seen or heard: the special idea is to keep an eye on the Rolls. So stay by the door from the garage that leads to the hall. Of course if you should hear something you think would interest me…"

Carson smiled.

"Very good, sir."

As Carson withdrew –

"You've three hours, William," said Mansel, "so do your best."

Less than five minutes later I was asleep.

The daylight was broad, when Mansel touched my arm.

"Nothing?" I said, sitting up.

"Nothing," said Mansel. "Neither Friar nor Boler. Kerrelin must be cursing the latter's guts. But he's sent two search-parties out."

"To me, the honour," I said.

"Perhaps. But mind you wake me."

Three quarters of an hour had gone by, when Boler emerged from the covert, supported by two stout policemen and looking more dead than alive.

Almost before I had touched him, Mansel was out of his bed.

"What is this?" cried Kerrelin. "I thought – "

"Damn your thoughts," cried Boler. "I have been more than half murdered and you are to blame."

"That I am not," said the other. "You call in the sentries and then go off on your own. How can I be expected – "

"I never went off," screamed Boler. "I was here, in the drive: then came a lightning pain and I knew no more. I awake in a cattle-pen; and, wandering forth, not knowing at all where I am,

I encounter these two boobies... My God, shall you pay for this? My body was put in your charge: and by your negligence, I have been done to death's door." Here he let out a scream. "To move the eyes is fatal. My God, I will make you suffer for this night's work."

Kerrelin drew himself up.

"Herr Boler," he said, "I protest. You send me off after Wessel, and when I return, you are gone. How shall I know what has happened? I have, to my great inconvenience, awaited you all through the night, and – "

"*Your* inconvenience?" raved Boler. "And what of my death? I have been murdered, I tell you. And only my will to live has enabled me to survive."

"I regret," said the other. "But it was not my fault. You sent me away; and Friar, who was lurking here, has vented his spleen upon you, because you had spiked his guns."

"Friar?" howled Boler. "Show me the treacherous swine. I will tear his eyes from his head."

"It can have been no other, for Mansel did not return for fifty minutes after you had been gone."

"Was Chandos with him?"

"Yes. And the servants, as well."

"Are they under arrest?"

"They are not," said Kerrelin. "I saw no cause to arrest them. I see no cause now."

"But they have the treasure, you booby. They must be clapped into prison and made to talk."

"Herr Boler," said Kerrelin, "I will give no such order. So far as I know, they have committed no crime."

Before this blunt refusal to toe the line, the German abandoned the remnants of self-control. Shouting and stamping, he raved and cursed like a madman, now threatening with hideous dooms the Austrian police, now execrating Friar, and now, like some wilful infant, condemning the pain in his head. This indulgence of his emotion naturally made the pain worse, and he soon confined his reproaches to the agony, which, as he put it, dared to afflict an officer of the Reich. Had I not heard his words, I would not have believed that an adult could so debase the image in which he was made; for he addressed the pain as though it were some monster that understood what he said and actually argued with it, laughing to hideous scorn the justification which he pretended it lodged.

At last the tempest blew itself out, and Kerrelin told two men, one to bring a car to the courtyard and the other to escort Sloper to the foot of the drive.

"That is one of the gang," cried Boler.

"Certainly," said the other. "I would have pulled them in: but you have insisted that they should be left alone. Sloper walked into our arms, and I had no choice but to put him under arrest."

"And the treacherous Friar?"

"We have sought high and low, but he is not to be seen. That is not surprising in country like this."

"Yet it was he who would have done me to death. I shall not forget this, Kerrelin."

Kerrelin shrugged his shoulders.

"I am tired," he said. "If you are ready, I think that we should be gone."

"You must leave two men here," said the German, "to watch these English swine. Ere twenty-four hours have passed, I will produce to you proof which you cannot ignore. And then you will have to arrest them, my Austrian friend."

"That is as may be. In any event, I cannot leave a man here. They are all worn out, as I am. What is the use of a guard that cannot stand up?"

"Very well. And if when we come back, they are gone, you may expect no mercy."

Ignoring the threat, Kerrelin turned to Wessel.

"Are the others here?"

"Yes, sir."

107

"You will go to the courtyard, and they to the foot of the drive. Are you ready, Herr Boler? By now the car should be there."

Glowering, the German moved off in the wake of the plain-clothes men, and, after a glance at our window, Kerrelin brought up the rear.

"There goes a good man," breathed Mansel "I'm sorry to have him on. And what did I say about moving?"

"I assume," I said, "that he's going to produce Diana."

"That's right," said Mansel. "On her sworn deposition, Kerrelin's bound to act. We slipped up there, William."

"You're telling me."

"Friar, too – and Olivia Ferrers. One to the Boche, William. You can't get away from that. Never mind. Let's bathe and breakfast. I don't think we need fade away until after lunch."

Mansel had moved from the window, but I was still looking out, when Friar emerged from the covert and stood looking round.

"*Exeunt omnes*," I said. "Enter Friar."

"Go on," said Mansel, turning.

"It's like a play," I said, laughing. "Of course he's been listening in."

Friar raised his voice.

"Captain Mansel." Mansel moved to my side and, after a careful survey, put out his head. "Ah, there you are. I do hope I didn't disturb you."

"Not at all," said Mansel. "What do you want?"

"I suppose some breakfast would be too much to ask."

"Yes," said Mansel, "it would."

"Quite so. No doubt you were present at the conference lately held about here. Not to be seen, but present – as I was myself."

"I heard what was said."

"Good. Within thirty six hours from now, the hunt will be up. Our well-disposed Chief of Police will be forced to act. It seems a pity, you know, that all those incomparable gems should fall to the Boche."

"I hope they won't," said Mansel.

"What can you do?" said Friar. "But I have ways and means. Even at this late hour, I can get them out of the country without any fuss. I will hand them to any agent you like to appoint. And all I should ask, is twenty per cent of the proceeds, when they are sold."

"There's nothing doing," said Mansel.

"Quite sure?"

"Quite sure."

"Then, as sure as God lives, you'll lose them."

"Whose fault will that be?"

"Yours. You are trying to do a thing that no amateur can do. You are treating this stuff like a packet of cigarettes."

"Listen to me," said Mansel. "When the curtain went up, the fight was between you and me. I was content to fight you. I should have done my best to get the gems to England, and you would have done your best to steal them *en route*. But those terms didn't suit you, because you were afraid I might win. And so you turned to blackmail. You told me in so many words that, if I wouldn't do a deal, you'd go to the Boche... Well, I don't submit to blackmail. And when you realized that, you set the Boche on. You meant to frighten me. You never dreamed he'd get as far as he has. And now *you're* scared, Friar. You meant to pull up a sluice, but you've burst a dam. You've attended one conference only: but I have attended three. Had you attended the others, you wouldn't feel so good. And in case you think I'm bluffing, here's something for you to go on with – Diana Revoke is in Herr Boler's pay."

Friar jumped, as jumps a man who receives an electric shock – and then stood still, as though frozen, with his lips a little apart and his eyes like cold, grey glass.

Presently the lips closed, till I saw the set of his jaw: then the eyes began to move, shifting from side to side; but his head and his body stayed still. At last, very slowly, a hand went up to his lips.

"Hers is the proof," he said thickly, "that Boler is going to produce."

"I imagine so," said Mansel.

"Use me," said Friar, "and beat her. I meant to kill you last night, but I'll work with you now."

"Not on your life."

After a long look, Friar shrugged his shoulders and turned. Then he spoke over his shoulder.

"'Cry havoc!''s all very well: but not when you've got a nonsuch under your arm. I assume you know what you're risking."

"The like of which," said Mansel, "the world has never seen."

Friar nodded.

"That's right. And it's not yours to risk?"

"No. It belongs to Ferrers."

There was a little silence.

Then –

"Oh, well," said Friar, looking up. "What did you do with Orris?"

"Orris was deported," said Mansel.

"I beg your pardon," said the other, cupping his ear.

Mansel made to lean out. Then he dropped sideways against me, forcing me to the left.

A bullet crossed the room, to enter the opposite wall. When I peered over the sill, the man was gone.

"And there's a viper," said Mansel, as Carson entered the room. "It's all right, Carson. Friar took a chance and missed it. I didn't think he was armed. Don't show up this side, for he may be in the covert. All the same, I think it likely he'll make for his car. So try the courtyard, will you? Use one of the corridor windows. I don't have to say 'Be careful', but I'd like to know he was gone."

As Carson shut the door –

"You said he'd be cross," I said.

"I know. Had I said he'd be cunning, that would have been more to the point. The fellow set out to make me lower my guard. And damned near did it, William. If I had leaned out... When he turned, and then went on speaking, that made me think; for his right arm was out of my sight. And then he allayed my suspicion, by being so natural... I've only myself to thank. And I searched him, too."

"I should have bought it," I said.

"No, you wouldn't," said Mansel. "He shouldn't have cupped his ear."

I left it there, although I shall always think that very few men would have read that gesture so well. Looking back, it is easy to see that, if Friar had been hard of hearing, he would not have heard what Mansel had said before, and that he made his movement as well to make Mansel lean forward as to enable him, Friar, to bring his pistol to bear: but Mansel's brain was so swift that, even as the man acted, he could interpret his action and save the game.

Twenty minutes later, Carson returned, to say that Friar had driven away in his car, which the police had left. Sloper was certainly with him: but whether Orris was there, he could not say. Still, after what had occurred, we were taking no risks, and Bell or Carson played sentry from that time on. For one man to watch both drives was quite impossible; but by moving to and fro at the end of the house, he could keep an eye on the courtyard, as well as upon the covert, which lay on the other side. And since the neighbourhood was extremely quiet, he could have heard a car coming while it was still a great way off.

So we came out of a pass which was quite unpleasant enough, but might have been worse.

And here perhaps I may say that what both of us found so trying throughout those hours was the forbidding fact that the treasure both parties were seeking was actually under their hand. Thanks, no doubt, to Diana, Boler believed that we had bestowed it somewhere six days before: when he found it was not in our quarters he very wisely decided to make us talk, rather than search a castle he did not know. (To search Wagensburg with effect, would have taken three or four men at least three days.) Where Friar supposed it to be, I do not know. But had either dreamed that the gems were in the garage – within six feet of them, as they passed its mouth, the 'show-down' which must have followed would have been awkward, indeed. Still, all ended well – thanks entirely to Orris who gave me the danger signal just in time.

4

The Play's the Thing

At five o'clock that evening we left the castle for good. This with regret, for we had been comfortable there and the place had suited us well. But, while it made a handsome retreat, once we were known to be there, it became a trap; for it could be approached from two sides, and unless we had been able to keep a continuous watch, a car could have been upon us before we knew it was there.

But now we had nowhere to go.

Orris had not reappeared, and we had little doubt that he had gone off with Friar. This was as well, for the man would have given more trouble than he was worth. Still, I had thought he would do as Mansel had said; and I was faintly surprised that he should have returned to Friar.

That night we passed in a forest, some thirty miles off: and though we had not the comfort of bed and bath, I confess I was glad to be sleeping beside our charge. Since the weather was fine and warm, we did very well.

Early the following morning, Bell packed into two kitbags the stuff he and I should need; and after an ample breakfast which Carson cooked and served, Mansel and I went strolling under the trees.

"I decline to worry," he said. "You have found out the way, and you are going to take it as quietly and firmly as if it were Jermyn Street.

"As soon as you are able, send Bell with a written report about the weights. I'd like to load them as soon as ever we can, for if I should be taken, a hundred to one the Rolls will be put in balk. If you want another reason, once I'm rid of the stuff, I can distract friend Boler by trailing my coat. In other words, I call attention to B. I can be seen in Salzburg, lunch at Villach, be recognized in Innsbruck and generally take the stage. But I must lie dead low, until we have made the transfer.

"Now for the smuggler's way. That, of course, is your road. How you explain this movement I leave to you. I suggest that you should tell Jasper about the Boche. Say that you knocked him down and he's out for blood. And so you prefer to leave by a private path. But I leave it to you, William – you have a remarkable flair for picking up cues." (This was untrue; for I am not 'quick in the uptake', as Mansel is. If a thing is thrust down my throat, I can usually swallow it: but Mansel can persuade his opponent to serve him with what he chooses, and, as often as not, to stand behind his chair.) "But one thing is clear as paint – that is that you must not attempt to take with you the weights." I bit my lip. "I know. You'll be on tenterhooks, until you see them again. But for you to stick to them would be insanity.

"I'll tell you why.

"In the first place, both Friar and Boler know that we dare not depute another to carry the treasure out. They have, therefore, eyes for us and for nobody else. So the stuff will be far safer, if you are nowhere near when it comes to the frontier-line.

"In the second place, Jasper may well accept your decision to leave the country in an unorthodox way: but he would never swallow your proposal to take the weights – for that would be out of all reason. They are stage properties and go with the tents, costumes and drums and whatever they have. Departure from such tradition would make a half-wit think…

"Thirdly, strong as you are, to take such a way, so burdened, might well be beyond your power: while, if you met a patrol, you would be sunk, for the first thing that they would do would be to inspect the weights."

I nodded reluctantly.

"I'm not going to argue," I said, "for any one of your reasons is good enough. But to leave such stuff to make its own way out is a fearful thing."

"Of course it is," said Mansel. "I don't have to tell you about the stuff I've carried, because on the greatest occasion you were there."

"I know. And it shortened my life."

"So it did mine. But I was never nervous – as I am now. To nobody else would I make this confession, William: but, honestly, I am nervous about this stuff. If I were superstitious, I could believe that Alec the Bad had laid a curse upon such as should handle the treasure he was at such pains to amass."

I shrugged my shoulders.

"That may be so," I said. "Three men died, trying to lift it five years ago. And Goat has been sacrificed."

"That's four," said Mansel, and fingered his chin. "And Friar is in the running. I'll take no more chances with him, and neither must you.

"One thing more. You're to leave on Thursday: on Thursday evening, therefore, I shall get out. I shall make straight for Strasburg. I may be a little late, for they're pretty certain to stop me and search the car. But I shall sit at Strasburg, until I have heard from you. Don't wire there direct: wire, instead, to London – you know the address. They'll forward it instantly. ALL WELL will mean what it says: any other statement will bring me at once to the office of origin. If I get ALL WELL, I shall leave for London and then for Trieste; so have a line waiting for me at The Heart of Gold.

"Finally, give me your passports – yours and Bell's. Smugglers don't have to have passports. But others find them useful now and again."

Then we consulted the map, for we had to settle where Bell should go to meet Carson and other things. Then I wrote a letter to Jenny, saying I hoped to be back in another ten days – as, to tell the truth, I did; for I felt that, once I had entered Italy, we were as good as home. Friar could go to the devil – to whom he belonged. Once we were shot of the Boche, if Friar ran between my legs, I would break him in two. And that, without compunction, for of pure spite he had hanged a very millstone about our necks. And the man was a murderer.

Godel was very charming and made me think at once of the picture books I loved as a little boy. I saw it first from above, for the road from the East drops into it very sharply, in spite of a double bend. Indeed, it lies at the foot of a waterfall and athwart the tumbling torrent which this becomes. The torrent is spanned by a crooked, covered bridge, a rare enough feature to make a tourist gasp: but, lying there in the sunshine, Godel itself would have warmed a painter's heart. White walls, red roofs, black shadows, wearing, as though it were some order, a sash of the liveliest blue and, because of the meadows about them, seemingly set upon a cloth of emerald green – of such was the village that morning at half past nine.

Bell and I gazed for a little, before we descended the hill. Then we began to go down, in search of our inn. But this we found almost at once, by the side of one of the bends.

The Vat of Melody hung by the side of the fall. This, its terrace commanded – the parapet was wet with the falling spray. And though it was but one of the village inns, because it boasted this valuable belvedere, its table was ready for strangers at any time. Few, no doubt, came across it, for Godel is off most maps: but a board, declaring its virtues, stood by the road, and I know that if I had been passing, I should have stopped.

It was there that Jasper joined us at half past ten. I introduced Bell to him and called for wine.

"And where is the troupe?" I said.

"The troupe is coming," he said, "but not to this inn. It will go direct to the meadows, where we shall pitch our camp. They will not come by this way: but as soon as we see the caravan, we will go down. I usually walk on ahead, for the pace is set by the mules, and does not suit me. Once I had to conform, sir: but, now that I am the master, I give myself leave."

"You will have," I said, "to give up calling me 'sir'."

Jasper shook his head.

"I have informed the troupe that you are a famous artiste, not long retired. Because once I did you a service, you have most handsomely offered to fill the breach."

"But this is absurd," I cried. "I have a certain strength; but I know no tricks and I am not excessively strong. The troupe will see through me at once."

"Believe me, they will not," said Jasper. "In the first place, I think I can judge your strength even better than you. In the second, I have explained that you are not now in training and so will be unable to do as you used. So you will be perfectly safe. And everyone understands that you have only come on condition that your identity is not disclosed. So you will be Monsieur X." He turned to look to the West. "See. There is the caravan. It is entering into the meadows, beyond the village itself."

I got to my feet.

"Then let us be going," I said. "If I am to take the plunge, let me take it as soon as I can."

Looking back, I shall always consider that Jasper's tale was far better than any that I could have told. All my shortcomings were forgiven, because I was a notable man: my eccentricities were accepted, and the honour which I was conferring upon the troupe blinded them to the *gaucherie* which I must have constantly shown. Happily, I was able to do what Ulysses had done – a fact which made me think that 'a strong man's' reputation may not be always deserved. There are, of course, certain tricks which cannot be mastered at once, which appear imposing indeed, when they are grandly performed. But these are not truly the feats of strength which they seem. But, then, 'a strong man' is a showman, and the efforts he seems to make at a country fair would not be made if he was a stevedore.

Early that afternoon I tried the weights.

These were six in number, all more or less bell-shaped, with handles above by which a man could take hold. They were not marked, and I really have no idea how much they weighed. Each one was greater than the other, and I must confess I was glad to set the greatest down. The point is that I could lift it without any fuss.

Colette was clapping her hands.

"Bravo, bravo," she cried. "Oh, but I knew you were strong. The poor Ulysses could never have done so well."

"But, then, he drank," said I. "Before he took to drink, he was probably very good."

"But not like you," said Colette. "Can you lift this chair by its leg?"

"I will try," I said. "But that is a matter of practice, and I have not done it for years."

Still, I managed to do it – not very well.

"Splendid," cried Colette. "Now I will go and find Jasper, and we will rehearse."

The moment she disappeared, I examined the weights. Precisely as she had said, at the base of each was a plate which could be unscrewed. I judged that the four largest weights would accept the whole of the gems. But I had, of course, to make sure, by removing the plates: for I could not tell how much space they really concealed. To do this, I required a square pin, to introduce into the sockets sunk in the plates – a tool not so easy to come by: but each of the weights had its box, and when I looked into the largest, the pin was there.

Here Jasper appeared, with Colette.

"What did I say?" he said. "We shall have to look to our laurels, Colette and I. Now, sir, if you will allow me, I play your part: and when I have done, you shall play it – as you will play it tonight."

I had supposed I must give an exhibition: but now I found that this was wrapped up in a play. Hardly a play – a masque, which ran for about twenty minutes to music and song. Of this I was the hero, Colette the heroine. The plot is not worth setting down, so I will only say that Colette was to dance, but found her floor strewn with boulders which none of her swains could move. These, of course, I removed, for they were the weights. Then she dismissed her suitors and danced about me, while I made play with the 'boulders', to show my strength. In the end, she sat down on a mushroom – really a stool – and I lifted the mushroom up and, finally, held it high with one of my hands.

All of this I very soon mastered, to their content. Featherweight as she was, to raise Colette, stool and all, was as much as, at first, I could do: but very soon I found that this was a matter of balance and that, taking the strain as I should, I could have easily lifted a heavier girl.

Here, perhaps, I should say that, when they were on the stage, the weights resembled boulders, if you stood back: for each had its painted jacket, cunningly stuffed and padded to give it the shape of some rock. But, of course, their handles were free, and the little illusion was shattered as soon as I picked them up.

When the rehearsal was over –

"Sir, I foresee," declared Jasper, "a great success. They are sure to demand an encore: but that I forbid. You see, if you do it twice, they will not believe: but when I step forward and say that you are too much exhausted to do it again, all will be sympathetic and deeply impressed."

"And now," said Colette, "he must rest; for no man can do as he has, yet not be glad to sit down."

I smiled.

"I will rest for an hour," I said. "And while I am resting, my servant shall polish the weights." As Bell stepped forward, "Don't try to move them, Bell: that's my affair: but take their boxes and put them into the tent. From now on, so long as I use them, the weights will be in your charge. Is that all right, Monsieur Jasper?"

"Sir," said Jasper, "such treatment is more than they merit. But I knew, without being told, that you would do all things well. Employ the stretcher, I beg you. It is one thing to lift those weights when you are properly poised, but quite another to carry them to and fro."

Perhaps he was right: though I knew that, with one in each hand, I could have fairly carried four out of the six. Still, I felt it was best to comply, and, while Bell bestowed their boxes, Jasper and I conveyed the weights themselves.

Our tent had been pitched apart, and its mouth faced away from the others on to the countryside. So soon as we were alone, I bade Bell stand in the mouth and be ready to say I was sleeping, if anyone came. Then I spread a towel on the ground and set a weight in its midst; and then I turned the weight over and took out its plate.

The weight was not so capacious as I had supposed it to be. Still, when I considered the sand which I had released, I knew that the six, between them, would certainly take the gems. The weights would then be much lighter, but that, of course, could not be helped: and if nobody touched them but Bell, the difference would not be remarked.

I, therefore, restored the sand and put back the plate. Then I wrote a short note to Mansel, to tell him that all was well and that I could receive the gems as soon as he pleased. That done, I lay down and rested, for the show was to come and I had been up betimes: and, while I dozed, Bell sat in the mouth of the tent and polished the weights, which were plated, as though they belonged to me.

Here, perhaps, I may mention the rest of the troupe. Besides Colette and Jasper, there were three men and two girls. Two men sang very well and played the mandolin. The third was the quartermaster: he purchased and cooked the food, laid out the camp, cared for the mules and supervised every move. He did not distinguish himself, except as a cook, and Bell and I groomed the mules and watered and fed the poor beasts: but he cooked extremely well, and the table he managed to keep was quite remarkable. I cannot remember eating more savoury food, and the coffee he made was the best I have ever drunk. Which is, of course, why he survived; for Jasper was impatient of his conduct, except as a cook. The two girls could sing and dance, to my mind, admirably. They were not so good as Colette, but she was exceptional. All of them treated me with the greatest respect, and there was quite a scene when I took charge of the mules. Indeed, except at meals, I hardly met them at all; and then Colette and Jasper sat on my right and left. Of these two charming people, I came to grow very fond. They were of the salt of the earth, and I always felt the better for having to do with them.

A light meal was served that evening at half past six, and, when that was done, Colette produced my costume. This may be described as a doublet and hose of light grey, with soft leather shoes to match.

"They are spotless," she said. "Myself I have washed them twice. The hose, of course, will stretch, but I fear that the jacket is small. Ulysses was not your stature. Will you put them on, please? And then I will come and see."

With Bell's help, I was very soon dressed. To my relief the shoes were an excellent fit: but the jacket was far too tight. The hose expanded to meet the demands I made.

"May I come in?" said Colette.

"Come in and take charge," said I. "I shall split this jacket to ribbons, doing my stuff."

Colette came into the tent and looked me up and down.

"Is the jacket too tight at the waist?"

"No. Except for the shoulders, it fits me well."

"Good. Split it now, if you please. It does not matter at all."

I stooped, to pick up a weight, and the seams gave way.

"Are you easy now?"

"Yes," said I. "I have made the room I require."

"Then all I shall ask you to do is to wear a hood. That will cover your shoulders and hide the rents. We have one of scarlet face-cloth, and it has never been used."

With that, she left the tent, to reappear in two minutes with one of those excellent garments, worn, I believe, in the time of King Edward the Third. It was a hood and short cape, made all in one. You could cover your head with the hood, or throw it back on to your shoulders and let it lie. Why we do not wear them now, I cannot conceive, for they are most simple to make and offer a fine protection against the wind and the rain.

I put the thing on and let the hood lie on my back.

Colette clapped her hands.

"But that is superb," she cried. "It is an immense improvement. You see, out of evil comes good. Oh, sir, you will cause a sensation. Never before – "

"Don't call me 'Sir', Colette."

"I will not, then. But I do not know what to call you. You have no name."

"Call me 'Feste'," I said. "He was a famous clown."

To my great dismay, Colette burst into tears.

"A clown!" she sobbed. "Because I dress you up, you think that you are a clown. I knew that you would resent it, but what could I do? But a clown – no. Though you were to daub your face and – "

I took her hands in mine and put them up to my lips.

"Colette, Colette, you must let me laugh at myself. As a matter of fact, I think that I look very well, and I wish that Jenny could see me – that is the name of my wife. And now you shall give me a name – and I will answer to it so long as I am with you."

Colette looked up.

"Your wife? I had not thought of you married. What is she like?"

"I think she is rather like Eve was, before she slipped up. When I get back, I know she will write to you; for she must always thank whoever has been kind to me."

Thoughtfully, Colette wiped her eyes.

"I will call you Adam," she said.

The performance went very well. Jasper was really immense – and far too finished an artiste to be 'on the road'. In London he and Colette would have had a *succès fou*. And the very lenient audience seemed pleased enough with my mediocre display. When I lifted Colette on high, there were roars of applause, but I think that this was because she had won their hearts and so they were glad to see her presented so well. When she caught my fingers and hailed me before the curtain, to be perfectly honest, I did not know where to look; so I kissed her hand and then put her up on my shoulder and bowed our way off.

Behind the scenes, Jasper was radiant.

"Sir, you have given full measure. Tomorrow night the whole of the place will be here, for those that have come this evening will come again. Shall I tell you your secret? It lies in your quiet smile. Ulysses was always grim. But what you did seemed to please you, and so it pleased everyone else."

"I'm afraid I'm no actor," I said.

"No, indeed," said Jasper. "But you are yourself."

As soon as the show had begun, Bell had left to meet Carson, taking my note: and at half past ten he was back with Mansel's reply.

This was short as ever.

Dear William,
Very good. Let Bell come again tomorrow, to get you 'some
clothes'. These will be ready for him at half past eight. On his
return you can unpack and bestow them, as you suggest.
  And then you must wash me out, until you come to Trieste.
Palin is under your orders. You know where he is or will be.
I think I should get him to meet you as soon as you can.
  As soon as you are over the border, cable as I have said.
No sign of Boler so far; but then I am lying low.

Yours ever,
JM

I read the note twice. Then I burned it to ashes, and Bell and I
went to our beds.

The next evening, as Jasper had predicted, we had a full house.
My friends were jubilant, and supper, 'after the show', was a
festive meal: but, while I was very glad, I was, I fear, something
distrait, because I was soon to bear a burden which no one
could share.

Look at it how you will, my charge was fearful indeed. The
gems were not mine, yet they were beyond all price. Were they
to be moved in London, they would, no doubt, be accorded an
armed guard: but Bell and I were to pack them, as though they
were so many buttons, behind a sheet of sailcloth in a strolling
players' camp. Tomorrow a thousand fortunes would lie in
those polished weights. The sale of one single jewel would make
Jasper, Colette and their company rich for life. And I was to care
for this nonsuch. On Thursday I must, so to speak, allow it 'to
go in the van' and hope very hard to claim it upon the following
day. While it was passing the Customs – warned, of course, to
be on the tips of their toes – I must defy the law by taking the
smuggler's way. To cover this curious whim, I must tell Jasper

some story which he would accept. And I must arouse no suspicion – I could not afford suspicion, in case an errant breath of it happened to fall upon the weights… Little wonder, I think, that my smiles were something forced.

As I left the board, Colette's arm slid into mine.

"What is the matter, Adam? You are not yourself."

"I have worries," I said. "You can allow me to share the excellent life you lead: but I cannot leave behind the cares of the life I led."

"Then I will share them with you. If I am troubled, it always helps me to talk."

I shook my head.

"You are very sympathetic, Colette. But I cannot do that. Perhaps in a day or two my worries will disappear."

"You share them, I think, with your servant."

"That is what Bell is for. He is my man, and the fortune I meet with is his."

"This morning I showed him how he should wash your shirts, and in return he told me about your home."

"It's his home, too," I said. "He is as happy there as I am myself."

"Yet you leave it – and your wife, to wander abroad."

"Sometimes, Colette."

"If I were your wife, I would not let you go."

"I know. She's terribly good. I think I must not do it again."

"Had you not done it this time, you would not have met us. What will she say, when you tell her what you have done?"

"She will wish she had been here, too."

"If she were here, you would share your worries with her."

"I might or might not. I do not like laying my burden on somebody else's back."

Colette set her head in the air.

Then –

"Why did you join us?" she said. "Jasper maintains that the English are whimsical. But I am a woman – and it was more than a whim."

"So it was," said I. "I liked you both, and it happened to suit my book."

"To masquerade?"

"To lie low, Colette, and pass into Italy."

The fingers closed on my arm.

"The police?"

"The Boche," said I. "I have offended a Boche. And he is powerful here and is seeking to bring me down. So I must get out of the country."

"But if he is truly powerful, the posts will be watched."

"I shall not go by a post. I shall leave you on Thursday evening and you will see me again the following day."

Colette stopped dead and clapped her hands to her face.

"But you can never – "

"Oh, yes, I can, Colette. I know my way and I shall be there before you. And now you must please forget this. You may tell Jasper, of course. But the others must never dream that I did not come out by the post in the ordinary way."

With her eyes on my face –

"Yes, you will do it," she said, "because you mean to do it and know no fear. And because you know no fear, you are not afraid of the Boche. It is not that, then, that concerns you, but something else."

I put out my hands for hers.

"It is not my secret," I said. "I have not the right, my dear, to share it with you."

Colette nodded.

"You shut my mouth," she said. "But I would have liked to share it, because I have a feeling that I could help."

"You've helped already," I said. "You've done me a world of good."

"That is what I am for, Adam. Bell is to share your fortune: but I am to distract you, when you are dull."

"But – "

"May I not do it, please? Look at what you are doing for us. And the money we took this evening and shall take tomorrow night. May we make no return? You are doing this thing because – it suits your book. That does not diminish our debt. And it is my pleasure to pay that, as best I can. Besides, I have a book, too." Before I could stop her, she whipped my hand to her lips. "And I do that, because it suits it. Sleep well, my dear."

With that, she was gone.

Two hours later, I packed the last of the gems.

Whilst I was at work, Bell moved without the tent, ready to give me warning of anybody's approach. But, mercifully, nobody came. I managed to pack the gems into five of the weights: in this way, one could be opened without any harm: this one I proposed to leave on the top of the rest, so that, if, by some dreadful chance, it should occur to the Customs to take out a plate, they would perhaps choose the first weight that came to hand. When I had packed the rest, I restored as much of the sand as I could get in, for I could not see that it could damage the gems and I wished the weights to weigh as much as they could. Besides, with a layer of sand directly above the plate, a careless examination might bear no fruit. Then I screwed the five plates home with all my might; and since I had made up my mind to take with me the opening tool, I felt that whoever desired to take them out might well be discouraged before he had his way. Then I carefully garnered the sand which I had displaced and, tying it up in a towel, gave it to Bell to get rid of, by dropping it little by little about the fields.

More, I could not do, though I daresay someone could tell me of something I left undone. Indeed, I felt that the matter was now upon the knees of the gods and that all I could do from now on was to show no concern for the weights and to devote myself to playing out the role I had taken, as well off the stage as on. It follows that when, upon the following morning, a radiant Jasper announced that the host of The Vat of Melody desired us to perform upon his terrace on Thursday afternoon, I did my very best to rejoice with him.

"A shortened performance," said Jasper, "lasting little more than an hour. If we strike the tents in the morning, we shall have plenty of time to cross the frontier that day. And it is a great compliment, sir – which we owe very largely to you: for your fame has gone round, as I was sure that it would. And quality may be there, for motorists often lunch at that agreeable inn."

Subduing my natural emotion,

"Rest assured," said I, "I shall give the show of my life."

"There!" cried Jasper. "Colette said you would not like it; but I said that of your good nature you would be glad at the news."

"It's part of the game," I said, smiling. "Where you go, I go, Jasper, until the end of the trick. What time do we 'open' there?"

"At half past one, sir. So we shall catch any customers stopping for lunch that day. These may be generous. I have known such a one put as much as we take in an evening into the plate."

"It shall not be my fault, if someone does not do it again."

"You are very good, sir," said Jasper. "I knew we could count upon you."

There was really little to fear, for the odds against one of our enemies choosing tomorrow not only to pass that way, but to lunch at The Vat of Melody were very long.

But I think I should not have been human if I had liked the idea. Still, there was nothing to be done. It was, of course, the masque which had won us the invitation to play at the inn; and if the strong man declined it, the whole invitation would probably be withdrawn and the company's disappointment would warm to resentment before the day was out. And that, I could not afford...

I did my best to put the matter out of my mind, but I had an uneasy feeling that the wind that had served us so well was beginning to back; and, sure enough, that evening I found I was right.

Because he had been meeting Carson, Bell had not seen the performance on Monday or Tuesday nights. This evening, therefore, when he had helped me to dress, he left to sit with the audience and see the play out. Now although I did not appear till towards the end of the show, I used to watch the whole from what might be called 'the wings'. And so I did, as usual – to find Bell standing beside me before ten minutes had passed. And his hand was up to his chin. (This meant that he had something to say for my ear alone; for that was the gesture the servants always used, when they wished to communicate something which other ears must not hear.)

Casually enough, I led the way into the shadows...

"Orris is here, sir. Sitting right at the back."

I thought very fast.

"Alone?"

"I think so, sir. There's no sign of Friar or Sloper. Nor any car."

"I must appear," I said. "Don't let him see you, but watch him. He may not recognize me. If he does, he'll certainly show it: and then we must pull him in." I bit my lip. Then I went on slowly, thinking aloud. "If he's still running with Friar...and he reports that I'm here, Friar will join us before we know where we are...and Friar will know in a flash that those gems are within the weights...This is damned awkward, Bell. We can pull him in all right: but, when he doesn't report, Friar will smell trouble and come to look for him. We must pray that Friar gives him some law, for this time tomorrow we shall be off the map."

"You say 'pull him in', sir."

"If he seems to recognize me. Wait till he does, of course: but don't let him get very far. Friar may be at the inn, for all we know. And take him into the tent and wait for me."

"Very good, sir."

And then he was gone.

I was now much more than uneasy – and would have given the world to be able to talk with Mansel for only five minutes of time. But trying as was Bell's news, for some strange, merciful reason, I was immensely relieved that I had to deal with Friar and not with the Boche. Had it been one of the police that Bell had seen, I do not know what I should have done, for by now Diana Revoke would have made her deposition and Kerrelin would be forced to act upon what she deposed. And he would be well aware that we had thrown dust in his eyes.

An hour and a half later, I entered my tent.

As I did so, Bell jerked his head, and Orris got to his feet.

I took my seat on a stool and lighted a cigarette.

Then –

"Your orders were clear," I said. "Why didn't you carry them out?"

Orris swallowed.

Then –

"The Capting says 'Come to the 'ouse', an' so I did. But when I gets there, there isn't nobody there."

I nodded.

"By the time you came, we had gone. But he didn't say 'Come with Friar.'"

This was a bow at a venture, but from the fellow's face I saw I was right. Friar had come back to Wagensburg, only to find us gone.

"I'm through with 'im now, sir. 'E picked me up that night, an' wot could I do?"

"Quite sure you're through with him?"

"Strike me dead, sir."

"What are you doing here?"

"Jus' lookin' noun', sir."

"For Captain Mansel or me." As the fellow began to protest, "Your only chance with me is to tell the truth. There's a river a mile away, and I've carried a blackguard's body further than that. You'd better get this, Orris. I'll put you down, like a dog: but I'll never give you away." Orris moistened his lips. "And think this over, Orris. The police have their hand on Friar for the murder of Goat." I saw the man start. "But they're waiting to pull him in, till he's served their turn. Anyone running with him will naturally be involved."

With vehemence and at some length, Orris declared that he had no hand in the deed.

"I know you hadn't," said I. "But police will be police, you know. And if I were you, I'd get out while the going was good."

" 'Arf a chance," said Orris. "That's all I want. — about, I've bin. Firs' the stuff's in a castle, be'ind a wall. Yes, but 'ow joo get at the wall? Nice sort o' death, I don' think – to go down that — well. 'Oh, we mus' 'ave a carpet.' An' when I gets back, wiv me fingernails arf tore out, cursed silly an' tole to beat it... An' then you comes up an' smears 'im – all over the — road. 'But that's all night,' he says. 'Let 'im crack the safe. An' when 'e's full up, we'll meet 'im an' take the jools.' An' orf he goes to Salzburg... Never see 'im again for the nex' ten days, an' Sloper an' me on tick, an' the lan'lord as rude as rude. But we 'adn't no money to pay 'im. Never a drink nor a smoke for seven days. That's wot I've 'ad to put up with, an' that's Gawd's truth. I tell you, sir, I've 'ad some. Seven — days wivout a fag or a drop of anythin'. An' the victuals the lan'lord give us not fit for a — dog. An' then 'e comes back, an' orf to Wagensburg. Another — washout... 'E an' Sloper buys it, an' I'm picked up. Talk about claowns in a circus... An' then 'e 'as the nerve to talk about comic relief. 'I can see the comic,' I says; 'but where's the relief?' An' then 'e turns nasty. 'Goat's found that,' 'e says. 'D'you want to find it, too?' An' then he talks about fortunes an' bein' made rich for life. Course 'e's got them jools on the brain; 'e'd sell 'is soul to 'ave them, an' — cheap at the price. ' 'Istorical gems', 'e calls them, 'an' wurf 'alf Lombard Street.' But wot I says is wot fence is goin' to touch 'istorical gems? 'Coz they can't be broken, I says. But 'e says 'That's all right; I'm goin' to sell the stuff. An' I'm goin' to sell it big.' Then back to Wagensburg. Not up to the 'ouse. 'Ave to crawl the las' three miles, to catch you out. An' when we gets there, you've gone. Another — wash-out... So 'e says, 'They're for the border. I'll 'ave them yet.' So 'e gets out 'is maps an' starts in. 'Alf mad, 'e is, for fear you'll beat 'im to it. Seems 'is passport ain't right for enterin' Italy. So it's got to be done this side. So Sloper's dropped at Doris, an' me at Godel, while 'e drives up an' down like a rangin' beast. 'Look everywhere,' 'e says. 'They're somewhere about. Be on the main road at 'alf past seven tomorrow, to make yer report.' Well, I don' work that way. So I 'as a bite at a pub an' comes to the show. An', Gorblime, there you are, sir. An' then Mr Bell pulls me in. 'E ain't up to your weight, you know. Punter said 'e wasn't, right from the first."

Of this I was not so sure. Friar had a very fine instinct – and now he had got a long way. If Bell had not seen Orris...

"Where were you to meet him?" I said.

"A mile towards Doris, sir, where 'e set me down. Jus' the other side of a bridge, with 'alf its parapet gone."

"And if you don't meet him – what then?"

Orris wrinkled his brow.

"I take it," he said slowly, " 'e'll come to Godel, 'isself."

There was a little silence.

I dared not trust the man. He might have been honest with me: but once he was out of my hands, he would make a bee-line for Friar. Apart from anything else, he would not return empty handed: he had an offering worth having, to lay at his master's feet; for he had run me to earth.

I glanced at my watch.

Then –

"Take him outside, Bell. I'm going to change."

Godel was eight miles from Kalitch: and Kalitch was a small junction upon the main line. The Salzbung express would stop there – so far as I could remember, at about a quarter past two.

And Orris must take that train – and must not leave it until it came to Salzburg at eight o'clock.

I changed as fast as I could. Then I unlocked my dispatch case and called the two in.

"Let's see your passport, Orris."

Slowly and with obvious reluctance, Orris produced the thing.

I took out a cheque book and sat down and wrote a cheque. *Pay Mr Samuel Orris the sum of fifty pounds.*

This, on a Salzburg Bank.

Then I wrote a note to the Bank, stopping the cheque. I handed the cheque to Orris, who read its burden, wide eyed. Then he looked up.

"I'm sure it's very good of you, sir. An' you can take it from me I 'aven't seen nothin' tonight."

I regarded him grimly.

"The trouble is, Orris, you'll have to cash it damned quick." I passed him the note to the Bank. "Give that the once over, will you?"

As Orris read its contents, I watched his face change.

" 'Ere, wot's this?" he cried.

I took the note out of his hand.

"Bell will post that letter tonight in the box of the Post Office van on the Salzburg express. At a junction called Kalitch, Orris, eight miles from here. The train will reach Salzburg at eight, so the letter will be delivered about ten o'clock. But the Bank will open at nine. So if you were to take that train, you could cash your cheque before the letter arrived."

Orris' face was a study.

The man had thought me a fool and had hoped to eat his cake and to have it, too.

At length –

"Orright, sir," he said. " I'll jus' nip back to the pub an' – "

"You'll leave with Bell," I said, " in two minutes' time."

"But – "

"Hold your tongue." I covered the letter and stamped it and gave it to Bell. "Take him to Kalitch, Bell, buy him a ticket for Salzburg and put him on to the train. And post that letter in the van. If he wants his fifty quid, he can damned well go and get it. If he gives the slightest trouble, bump him off."

"Very good, sir."

"You should be back here by five. Any way, I'm going to meet Friar. So, if you should be late, you'll know where I am."

"I shan't be late, sir."

"All right."

Bell turned to Orris.

"Come on."

Looking ready to burst, the other went out before him into the night.

(If what Orris had said was true, I had cooked his goose, for when I met Friar the next morning, Friar would know that Orris had opened his mouth. That being so, for him to return to Friar would be bad for his health. Indeed, as I saw it, he would be well advised to draw his fifty pounds and make his way back to England as fast as he could. But if, in fact, he had lied, any useful attempt to reach Friar would entail his casting the money into the draught.)

As soon as their footsteps had faded –

"May I come in?" said Colette.

"Of course," I said.

She came in.

"I saw you had someone there."

"That's right, Colette. A blackguard. Bell's seeing him off."

She looked at me very hard.

"But not the Boche, Adam?"

"Oh, no," I said. "Much smaller fry. Still, I didn't want him around."

"I think you are in danger," she said.

"Not at the moment, Colette. And on Friday morning I shall be out of the wood."

"In thirty-six hours. Dear God, how I wish that we had been leaving tonight."

With an effort, I shrugged my shoulders.

"Tomorrow will serve, Colette."

"Oh, it will serve – yes. At least, I suppose it will." With a sudden movement, she pushed back her thick fair hair. "You are very good to play at The Vat of Melody. I begged Jasper not to ask you; but he said that you should decide. And I think you are a very good actor, for he came back and said that you were as pleased as Punch."

"I don't suppose the Boche will be there."

"But someone who knows you may."

"Then I shall have to beat it. I cannot be taken now."

A hand went up to her chin.

"Why did you join us, Adam? If you knew a way out, you ought to have gone at once."

"I had to wait for a message."

"You have it now?"

I nodded.

She caught my arm.

"Then leave at once, Adam, I beg you. The night is young. And I will explain to Jasper. And you shall join us when we are in Italy."

I took her hand and put it up to my lips.

"You are very sweet, Colette. But I cannot do that."

"And you are very – resolute, Adam."

"I try to be."

Colette looked out of the tent and up at the moonlit sky.

"I still do not understand why you joined the troupe. You could have waited for your message without doing that."

"Call it a whim, Colette."

"I will call it what you bid me. I may not share your secrets – as others do."

"This is not mine – I told you. And one day you will thank me for not revealing the truth."

135

Colette shook hen head.

"Never. If you had done murder, I would be glad to know it, for two can bear such a burden better than one."

I smiled.

"I have done no murder, Colette."

"You need not tell me that. And if ever you slew a man, it would be because he was better dead than alive."

"Listen," I said. "You have not yet told Jasper that I shall not leave with you."

"I shall tell him, tomorrow, Adam, when you have slipped away. Then he cannot try to dissuade you, because it will be too late. He has a great regard for you, Adam, and he will be very much troubled until we see you again."

"He is a good man," I said. "I like and admire and respect him with all my heart."

"I have no parents," said Colette: "but for twelve years now he has been my father and mother – and more than that. He has often gone hungry, that I might eat. When I had typhoid fever, he spent the whole of his savings to put me into a ladies' nursing home. And once he sold his watch, to buy me a length of silk. He is but a strolling player, but he has a great gentleman's heart."

"You're perfectly right," I said – and so she was.

Had Jasper been born to a title, he would have adorned the estate of, say, some landowner of the Victorian age. Shrewd, benevolent, masterly, he would have used his tenants as tenants should be used: his servants, I think, would have loved him: and he and his would have prospered, because he was in command.

Colette smiled.

"I like great gentlemen," she said.

"Tomorrow," I said, "I may be late for breakfast. I have an appointment to keep a little way off. But I shall be back in time to help strike the camp."

Colette regarded me gravely.

"I shall be glad," she said, "when you are in Italy."

"So shall I, Colette. And I have a friend there whose coming will warm your heart."

Colette raised her eyebrows.

"I do not think that is likely. Now I must go. Do not be too late for breakfast, or – Jasper will be concerned."

I laughed.

"Give Jasper my love and tell him not to worry." Colette looked down at the ground.

"I did not mean – Jasper," she said.

I took her fingers and kissed them.

"Neither," I said, "did I."

She raised a glowing face.

"Good night, Adam."

"Good night."

5

The Vat of Melody

At a quarter to seven the next morning, I was lying behind a hedge. Peering through this, I could see the end of the bridge which was short of a parapet, and the road running off to Doris for half a mile. Bell was a little behind me, watching the road to Godel, which I could not see.

Between the hedge and the road was a ditch which was half a gully, which gave to the stream which was tumbling beneath the bridge. This ditch was covered with bracken, and I had been much inclined to take cover in that. But, moving across the country, I had come first to the hedge, and since I was not yet sure of the line I should take, but Friar was 'quick on the trigger', I felt that I should be wiser to stay where I was.

That I did so was just as well, for, after, perhaps, five minutes, I had the shock of my life.

On a sudden, a match was struck – I heard the scrape and the flare – and smoke rose up before me out of the ditch.

Somebody, sitting there, had lighted a cigarette.

Then –

"Wake up, you —," said Friar. "This isn't Mayfair."

"You're telling me," groaned Sloper. "Why did I come?"

"For the same reason as I did," said Friar. "You like the fat of the land."

" 'Aven't seen much of it lately. — 'aunch o' gristle, if you ask me."

"Cultivate faith," said Friar. "You've been with me fourteen years, and when have I let you down?"

"Orright, orright," said Sloper. "But you didn' ought to 'ave let that — Boler in."

Friar raised his head, to peer up and down the road.

"I think we've lost him," he said. "That's the Boche all over. The — can't do his job, so he sticks to someone who can. I'm to rake out his chestnuts, but he's going to pick them up. But you're wrong, Sloper, as usual. To hang Boler round Mansel's neck was a very nice move. The mistake I did make was to touch Diana Revoke." I heard the man suck in his breath. "By God, I'd like to meet her – one of these nights. I'd wring her head from her body and – Gently. I hear a car."

I had heard a car coming from Doris before he declared the fact. He lowered his head and Sloper rose into my sight. The three of us watched the car pass at a pretty high speed. It was grey and closed and I could see men within.

"Police," spat Friar. "God — their — souls. If Orris is coming, will he have the sense to drop?"

"I think so," said Sloper. "I — well rammed it in."

I saw Friar glance at his watch.

"He ought to be here any minute – with nothing, of course, to report."

"Lazy," said Sloper. "That's Orris. 'E won't go after 'is man. But point 'im out to 'im, an' 'e'll never let go. An' talk about deception…You ought to of let 'im go back that night at Wagensburg. They'd 've bin trustin' 'im blind in twenty-four hours."

"Not Mansel," said Friar. "Chandos, perhaps: but not Mansel. He's nobody's fool. Three times he's bested me."

"Twice," said Sloper.

"Three times. But I'll get him at last, Sloper. It's time his score was paid. He could have come in, but he wouldn't. And now

he's stuck. He cannot get the stuff out. I told him he couldn't –
you heard me. And now my words have come true. And if we
don't find him first, he'll lose to the Boche." He started up. "By
God, where is this – ?"

"It ain't seven yet," said Sloper.

"Five minutes to," said Friar. "And he's not in sight."

(Orris had said 'half past seven' – not 'seven o'clock'. I began
to respect the rogue. Had I been placed as he was, I very much
doubt if I should have done so well.)

"An' if 'e's nothin' to say…?"

"We keep our eyes skinned," said Friar. "I know we're warm.
Any time now they're going to try and get out. They're going to
take a chance, Sloper: and that is where we shall come in."

"Or Boler."

"Boler be damned. The — is trailing us – it's all he can do.
We've lost him now; and as long as he doesn't find us, we can
count Boler out."

"Sez you," said Sloper. And then, "I don' like these three-
'anded games. Say you comes up with Mansel and takes the
stuff…an' then Boler steps out o' the laurels an' says ' 'Scuse
me'?"

"In that case Boler will meet it."

"Gawd," said Sloper. "An' 'alf the police be'ind 'im. I wish I
was back in London. An' you can 'ave Mayfair. Wappin' 'd do
me praoud."

"Don't be a fool," said Friar. "This is the biggest thing that
anyone's ever touched. No one has ever played for such stakes
before. Gems worth three or four million – whatever we like to
ask. No fences to take our winnings out of our mouths. And
Ferrers dare say nothing; for, if he does, he incriminates Mansel
and Chandos as well as himself – and the stuff goes back to
Austria, whence it came. I tell you – if it comes off, you can live
in Mayfair as I do…with half a million behind you, all to
yourself. South of France, if you like. I tell you, man, you'll be

rolling – for as long as you like to live. Well, that's worth working for – worth running every risk. Or is it? What d'you think?"

"Oh, I don' say, if it comes orf, it won' be jam. But – "

"But what?"

"You didn' ought to 'ave let that German in. I don' say that to Orris; but that's wot I know. Raoun' Mansel's neck, if you like: but the —'s raound ours. Look at them — police cars. Gives me the creeps each time I see one o' them. An' I 'aven' got over that do at Wagensburg. Bein' picked up like that, when I couldn't think straight. I'd like to know 'oo 'it me. I'd spoil 'is guts."

"Orris is late," said Friar, with his eyes on the road. "Where is the — waster?"

Be sure that was what I was thinking.

Since Sloper's appreciation of his colleague, I had been cursing my folly in letting Orris go. 'He won't go after his man. But point him out to him, and he'll never let go. And talk about deception...' Orris had been very clever. By being perfectly frank, he had run under my guard.

He had set a first-rate trap into which I had very nearly walked. Not that I had trusted the fellow: but I had underrated his loyalty to Friar. I had actually thought to buy this with fifty pounds. If Orris left the train before Salzburg...and managed to get a car...he could be here any minute. I could have done it – I should have... But it never entered my head that Orris would. And if he did, I was 'sunk'.

From Orris I turned to Friar. The man was on edge – of that there could be no doubt. I do not at all suggest that his nerve had gone: but he was apologetic – rather pleading his cause with Sloper than keeping his subordinate up to the bit. He knew, as Sloper knew, that the sands were running out – that unless a 'break' came quickly, the game was up.

I determined to give him his 'break'...

The road from Doris to Godel ran roughly from West to East. I lay to the North of that road, and the frontier, some eight miles distant, lay to the South. Twenty paces from the bridge towards Doris, a path was rising sharply into a wood.

Swiftly I pushed myself back, till I was abreast of Bell.

"You will move up," I breathed, "and watch that ditch. Friar and Sloper are there, and they're waiting for Orris to come. I'm coming, instead. And I'm going to draw them off. The moment they're gone you will take their place in the ditch; and when Orris comes, as I have a feeling he will, pull him in and hold him, until I return."

With that, I crawled to the right, until it was safe to rise: and then I ran, bent double, over the fields. When I was well out of sight, I turned to the left. And then I was through the hedge and was padding down the road towards Godel, with, if I am to be honest, my heart in my mouth.

I dared do no more than walk briskly, for I had a part to play.

I must pretend to be on the way to our lair, in which we were holding the gems, from which we were proposing to leave for Italy. If this pretence deceived Friar, he would not hold me up, but would decide to follow and see where I went. Now he had but a very few seconds to make up his mind. His instinct would be to stop me – I was a bird in the hand: but a moment's reflection would show him that, if he could successfully follow, he stood to gain far more than two birds in the bush.

I confess I did not enjoy the part of a bird in the hand. If Friar decided to take me, I should be badly placed. If he decided to follow, rather than lose me, the man would certainly fire – and a man whose back is turned, is a very fair mark. But I felt that Orris was coming, and if that was so, there was no other course to take.

One piece of luck I had, and that came in the shape of a van that was pelting along from Godel, before I had reached the path. At once I dived for the ditch on my right-hand side – and so assured Friar that I could not afford to be seen. When it was gone, I emerged and walked on till I came to the path. There I hung on my heel for a moment, to glance up and down the road. And then I took the path boldly, trying my best to believe that I was halfway home.

I dared not go too fast, for I had to allow them good hope of keeping me always in view: of the line the path took I had not the faintest idea, but even if it came to an end, I must by no means falter, for Friar must believe I was taking a way that I knew: most important – and trying – of all, I must never look back, to see if my ruse had borne and was bearing fruit. Suddenly I knew that it had, for one or the other slipped as he left the road.

And here a new fear beset me. This was that Friar or Sloper would stumble or make some such noise as I could not pretend not to hear. In such a case, I must either leap for coven or, if there was no cover, take to my heels – and hope very hard that Friar would miss his man.

However, all went well.

The path, to my great relief, was by no means straight, but bent to right and to left and, after some sixty paces, began to rise. Up it went, over a shoulder, and down to a tumbling stream: and then it crossed a meadow and entered the rising woods.

I knew they were still behind me, for my ears are country trained, and now and again I heard one of them put a foot wrong and strike a stone with his shoe: and since we had gone near a mile and they must be getting tired, I felt that the time was coming when I should give them the slip. The question was how to do it; for all might well be lost, unless they went on, supposing that I was ahead.

And then Fate played into my hands.

As I was approaching a bend, a peasant, with an axe on his shoulder, came striding round. I gave him good day and stopped him.

"Listen, my friend," I said. "My servants are coming behind me. Their names are Carson and Bell." The man repeated the names, which were easy to learn. "When you meet them, tell them to be as quick as they can, because the weather is fine and I wish to be gone."

"I will do your bidding, sir. But servants are all the same. I am my own master, and time is money to me: but the servant draws the same wages, whether he hastens or no."

We laughed, and I gave him money and told him to drink my health. Then I passed round the bend and, leaving the path, darted into the forest and lay down behind a beech. Almost at once I heard the peasant's voice…

Friar's German was said to be poor, but I like to think that he recognized 'Carson' and 'Bell'. Be that as it may, after, perhaps, ninety seconds, he and Sloper came hurriedly round the bend, stooping and peering as they did so, breathing hard and simply streaming with sweat. When they saw that the next reach was empty, they shambled into a run…

When they were out of sight, I took again to the path and made my way back to the road.

For what it was worth, I seemed to have won that trick.

As I left the path for the road, Bell's head rose out of the ditch thirty paces away.

As I came up –

"You were right, sir," he said: "I've got him. But when he saw me, he turned nasty, and I had to lay him out."

"So much the better," said I, getting into the ditch. "And how did it happen, Bell?"

"I moved up as you told me, sir, as soon as you'd gone. Friar an' Sloper was arguing about Orris. Friar was cursing his soul: but Sloper wouldn't have that. If Orris was late, he said, it meant he was on to something. An' then they saw you…

Bell paused and drew in his breath.

"I thought you were for it, sir. Friar had his pistol out before I could think. They never breathed a whisper – I think they was holding their breath. An' when you turned off up the path, you took them both by surprise. An' then they fell over themselves to follow you up. The noise they made – I thought you must 'ave heard them…

"An' at once I whips over that gate an' takes their place in the ditch.

"Eight to ten minutes later a van comes blinding along, claps on its brakes an' fetches up on the bridge. An' Orris climbs out of the cab, gives some notes to the driver an' then stands back. The van goes on towards Godel, and Orris watches it go. Then he swings round on his heel and makes for the ditch. As he comes up to the edge,

" 'Come on in, Orris,' I says; 'I'm waiting for you.' When he hears my voice, he's just struck all of a heap: didn' seem able to move; so I reaches out for his ankle an' pulls him down. An' then he goes mad: gets up an' goes for me, shouting an' cursing an' swearing – you never see such a show. So I puts him out, sir: it seemed the easiest way."

I nodded.

"I'll say he's a trier," I said. "It must have been gall and wormwood when you rose up."

"I think it did hit him hard, sir. He'd dropped fifty quid to get you. An' then he meets it again."

I parted the bracken and took a look at the rogue.

I felt suddenly sorry for Orris – a something pathetic figure, flat on his back. His face was pinched and dirty and travel-stained: he looked undernourished, and one of his knees was drawn up.

"He's a better man than Punter," I said. "He doesn't throw in his hand. And so he's a blasted nuisance, which Punter never was. What on earth shall we do with him, Bell?"

"We can't hardly bump him off, sir."

"No, we can't," I said. "It wouldn't be fair. He's only done his duty – and done it well. If something Sloper said hadn't opened my eyes, by God, he'd have torn it, Bell. We should have split on Orris, and that's the truth."

"I wondered what made you act, sir. It never entered my head that Orris would try and make it."

"Nor mine," said I. "I never dreamed it was in him. But that is Orris, Bell. A very valuable man. And now we must get out of here, in case the others come back."

Beneath our ministration, Orris was soon on his feet: but all his fight was gone, and he took the orders I gave him without a word. I led the way out of the ditch and, presently, off the road and over a gate; and the rogue, with Bell behind him, went like a lamb.

I headed across the country, bearing North; but I did not know the region or what we were going to find. After a full three miles, we came to a little rise which was hiding the lie of the land on its farther side. But I judged there was water there, and that was what I desired.

I told the others to stop and breasted the rise alone.

Below lay grass-grown cross roads, whose fingerpost was rotten and leaning, soon to come down: all about was a pleasant commonage – close cropped turf, bestrewn with a parcel of rocks. One road led over a bridge, beneath which the ghost of a river was making its silent way. In the winter, no doubt, this was a notable stream, but now there was little water – no more than ten or twelve inches, it seemed to me.

After a careful look, I returned to Orris and Bell.

"Bind his wrists, Bell," I said.

Bell took a cord from his pocket and bound them behind the man's back.

"And now his eyes."

" 'Ere," cried Orris, in protest.

"It's all night," I said. "I'm not going to kill you yet."

"Gawd 'elp," said Orris.

"It's up to you."

In silence his eyes were bound.

"And now follow me."

With Bell's hand fast on his collar, Orris stumbled along. I led the way round the crest and down to the roads. I took the one which ran East and over the bridge. As I have said, the water was making no sound, and, since the road was metalled, Orris cannot have known that he was crossing a bridge. So for another half mile. And there was a billet lying in the midst of the way – a log of wood, which had fallen off a waggon and been let lie.

I signed to Bell to steer Orris towards this obstruction...

Of course he stumbled and fell, and, because his hands were tied, he could not save himself, but rolled all over the road.

The shock apart, I fear that he hurt himself, for the flood of rebuke which he addressed to Bell was quite unprintable. And I confess with shame that, long before he had done, Bell was shaking with laughter and tears of mirth were running upon my cheeks. Indeed, it was most unfair: but it had to be done.

I picked up the billet and laid it down in the ditch. Then we pulled the man up to his feet and – of course unknown to Orris – began to retrace our steps. One minute later, perhaps, we left the road and made our way back to the water over the turf.

We guided him into the water, which shocked him as much as his fall; then we urged him up the opposite bank. And under a spreading beech tree he came to his journey's end.

"Go over him, Bell."

All the man had was his passport, in which was my cheque, and Austrian money amounting to seven pounds.

Orris was pleading.

"Don' take my passport, sir. I wanna get out o' this country. I'm through wiv Friar."

"Give them to me," I said. "And put your coat over his head."

"I can't see a thing, sir."

I put my cheque into my pocket.

"I don't think you can," I said: "but I want to be sure."

Orris' head was shrouded, as are those of men accused, to embarrass photographers.

I walked to a boulder some forty paces away. Putting forth all my strength, I managed to roll it aside. I laid the passport and money in the form which the stone had made. Then I rolled back the boulder, so that it lay as before. After that, I inspected the signpost. To snap this off short required no effort at all…

I made my way back to the beech tree and spoke to Bell.

"All right. Uncover his head and let him sit down."

With that, I sat down myself and lighted a cigarette.

"Can I 'ave my passport, sir?"

"You can," I said, "if you like to look for it. It's within fifty paces of where you're sitting now. For that, I give you my word. But you'll have to look very hard."

"You ain't put it in the water, 'ave you?"

"No. But if you don't want to look, you can always go to the Consul and – "

"No — fear," said Orris. "Wivin fifty yards?"

"Yes."

"You'll free me 'an's an' me eyes, sir?"

"No. That will be your affair. If you get down to it, it shouldn't take very long. And, with luck, some peasant may pass."

"Gawd 'elp," said Orris. "I don' want no — peasan's — round. An' supposin' they fin' my passport?"

"I don't think they will," I said. "It isn't too easy to see, and they don't know it's there."

" —," said Orris. "But wot about this bandidge? Mr Bell will want 'is ankerchief beck."

"I'll give him another," I said, and got to my feet.

"Now, listen 'ere, sir," said Orris. "If you'll unbandidge me eyes…"

And that was as much as I heard, for Bell and I were moving over the turf.

Three minutes later we stood upon the top of the rise. Orris, still blindfold, was making frantic efforts to get to his feet.

As we made our way back to Godel –

"I think," I said, "that we can write Orris off. He doesn't know where he is: he will think that Godel lies on the further side of that stream: the signpost is out of action: and if he desires his passport, I don't think he'll come across it for quite a long time."

"He won't budge without it, sir. You never heard what he said when you took it away. It's his – sort of talisman, sir."

"Not a bad talisman, either – for people like that. And now we must hurry, Bell. We've both got to have some breakfast, and you've got to have some sleep."

By noon that day the troupe was ready to move.

The waggon had been carefully loaded, so that such stuff as would be required at the inn could be removed and replaced without disturbing the rest of the stock-in-trade. As soon as the performance was over, the troupe and waggon would leave for the frontier-post. This was six miles from Godel. It seemed that by seven o'clock the cavalcade would be moving in Italy.

I had arranged with Colette that Bell and I should leave the troupe at the inn. I proposed to repair to the dell in which she and Jasper had found me the week before. There Bell and I would lie low: and then, when dusk had come in, we would take the smugglers' way.

The troupe would stay for that and the following nights by a hamlet called Jade. This I soon found on my map. So far as I could make out, Bell and I could be with them by eight o'clock.

"So have our tent pitched," I said, "for we shall be tired."

"I do not like it, Adam. What would Eve say?"

"Eve would say nothing at all, for she is a dutiful wife."

Colette set her chin in the air.

"I think she would say a great deal. Supposing you were to fall foul of a frontier-guard. I am told that they fire at sight."

"Let us hope that they do not see me. And do you want me stopped at a frontier-post?"

"Ah, no. I could not bear it."

"Then let me go my way – and breakfast with you tomorrow at eight o'clock."

"Who is this man to stop you? This dirt of a Boche?"

"Who, indeed?" said I. "Yet Austria does as he asks."

"I am ashamed of my country – to use an Englishman so. What is he like, this filth?"

"He is big and square-headed, as many of his countrymen are. His mouth is grim and brutal; his eyes seem to be afire. But he is a coward, Colette."

"As most of his countrymen are."

"Not all, Colette. Some have a fanatic courage."

"Say 'machine-made'."

"I think you are right," I said. "It is not natural. But he has not that. He would stamp on a creature he knew was weaker than he: but if a man showed him the whip, he would turn and run."

"Such things are not fit to live."

"I must confess he'd be much improved by death."

"Please do not improve him, Adam."

"Not I," said I, laughing. "If I were to see him, Colette, it would, I assure you, be I that would turn and run."

"I am glad to hear it," she said. "All the same, I cannot see you in that role."

"I hope very much, my dear, you won't have the chance."

"Is he looking for you?"

"That is the order which he has given your police."

Colette clapped a hand to her mouth.

"A policeman was here this morning – a plain-clothes man."

"Whilst I was out?"

She nodded.

"How do you know he was a policeman?"

"I knew when I saw him. You cannot mistake the breed."

"Did he ask any questions?"

"No: but he watched us, Adam. We had not long finished breakfast and Odin was washing up. And then he walked back to Godel."

"What could be better?" I said. "The inspection has taken place; but, happily, Bell and I were not on parade."

"For me," said Colette, gravely, "it was the finger of God."

"I think so, too. Be sure, I am very grateful."

"But what have you done, Adam?"

"I told you – I have given offence."

She looked at me very hard.

"Very well. I will ask no more. If I see his like again, I will tell you at once."

"If you please, Colette. I must not be taken now. Once I am clear of the inn – "

"My God, this accursed performance! No finger of God is there. And you are the very one that has brought it about. It is the masque, Adam dear, that has won us the invitation to play at the inn."

I smiled.

"To which you subscribe, Colette. I am not wholly to blame."

"Yes, yes. Of course I subscribe. But never before have I played as I play with you. If I am good, it is you that have made me so."

"Don't be absurd, Colette. I cannot act, and you know it. I am not drunk, like Ulysses – that I confess. But I can only smile and hold up my weights."

"I know. That is all you do. But you have a way no actor could ever capture. You are the real thing, Adam. And that is why you have gone to the hearts of these clowns… and why I have risen to heights I never knew I could reach." I began to laugh. "And what are you laughing for?"

"I wonder what you would say – to a friend of mine. He is a king among men. And if he were to play my part – well, the world would come running to see him for twenty miles round."

"Is it he who is coming to meet you?"

"In Italy? No. At least, I don't think he is. But I should like you to meet him, for he is the finest gentleman that I have ever known. As for him who will meet me in Italy, perhaps he will

151

join the troupe for two or three nights. He can sing and play like an angel – and make you die of laughing. He and Jasper together will bring down the house."

"And do we not bring down the house, when you lift me on high?"

"We do more than bring down the house. We bring unheard of requests to perform at a house of call."

Colette made a *moue*.

"We will talk again," she announced, "when we are in Italy."

The host of The Vat of Melody treated us well.

We were given an excellent lunch, and three changing rooms were provided close to the bar. These gave to a passage from which we could gain the terrace on which we were to perform.

For luncheon, the inn was full. Some were chance customers: most were the *bourgeois* of Godel, come to see from the stalls the troupe of which they had heard. Wise in his generation, the innkeeper did good business that Thursday afternoon.

Jasper and I shared one of the changing rooms, and there, by Bell's direction, the weights were put. This was natural enough: but I must confess I was glad to have them under my eyes.

Now, no stage was even used, but we had a three sided frame in which curtains were hung. The centre side faced the audience: the sides to the right and left were furnished with wings. The whole was extremely simple and weighed very light; but it was well contrived, for, while we were thus enabled to move and have our being 'behind the scenes', entrances and exits could be theatrically made – and our audiences liked the effect, which was, of course, more important than that which is afforded by an alfresco performance with no apparatus at all. The terrace just permitted our frame to go up – to the great content of Jasper, as of myself, for if someone should appear in the audience whom I did not wish to see, the contrivance would give me a chance to make good my escape.

But no such unwelcome spectator put his spoon into the dish. Bell was without the inn, ready to hasten to warn me of any untoward approach; but my scene with Colette was concluded, and he never came. Indeed, he was retrieving the weights and I was changing my clothes, before I heard the voice of Diana Revoke.

"Have you a bedroom here, where I can powder my nose?"

I sat very still.

This could mean only one thing – that Boler was here.

The thing that I had been dreading had come to pass.

And then Diana was gone – upstairs, no doubt, to some bedroom upon the first floor.

I slid into my trousers and coat…

Bell's head appeared.

"May we come in, sir? I've got the stretcher outside."

I beckoned him to come close, and he shut the door.

"Miss Revoke's in the inn," I said. "I've just heard her voice. And I think that where she is, the Boche will be. Get the weights into this room and then fade away. Go down in the cellars, or something. But I must get out. I shall go straight to the dell: but you must see the weights on the waggon, before you leave. If the Boche is still here, on no account help to load them, but see it done. Watch from a window, for instance. The moment you've seen them on, get out and follow me. And now bring the stretcher in."

As Bell and a scullion set down the last two weights, I stepped out into the passage and hastened towards the terrace from which I had come. I was hoping to see Colette, to say that the Boche was here and that I must be gone. But I was just too late, for Jasper was supervising the taking down of the frame, and Colette was not to be seen. I supposed that she had finished her rounds, given her collection to Jasper and gone to change. Lest Jasper should see me, I drew back into the passage and thought very hard.

I could hardly seek Colette, for she was sharing a room with the other girls: and so I must leave her to draw her own conclusions – which, should she set eyes upon Boler, were sure to be sound. All, therefore, I had to do was to leave the inn. All.

I knew the layout roughly. One of the doors in the passage gave to a private bar; a second door from the bar gave to the entrance hall. But I did not fancy the bar, still less the entrance hall.

I should make one thing clear. Diana, the Boche and the police were the people I hoped to avoid: but, beside the host and his servants, anyone who had seen the performance would know me for 'the strong man'. I should, therefore, attract attention; and attention always breeds talk. If this came to the ears of the Boche, the man might begin to ask questions; and if he did – well, before two minutes were out, the truth would be in his hands.

To reach the back door, I must either pass through the hall or travel the length of the terrace, for all to see. And the dining-room gave to the terrace: the day being fine and hot, its two french windows were open as wide as could be. If Diana and Boler had decided to break their fast...

I decided to leave by the bar.

I could not see through the keyhole, for this was blocked: so, after straining my ears, I ventured to open the door. There were only two people there, and I knew them both. One of the two was Boler, and one was Colette.

Her back was flat against Boler, and both were facing my way. His right arm was round her neck and his right hand clapped over her mouth, the thumb pressed tight against her delicate nose. Her beautiful eyes were starting; she could, of course, make no sound: only her left nostril allowed her to breathe: and this his hand was obstructing.

She was struggling violently, but the German's left arm was about her, and so she was utterly powerless to deal with his brutal assault. On the floor was a broken plate, with notes and silver scattered about its remains.

Boler did not see me, because his face was deep in Colette's soft curls. From the tone of his muffled voice, he seemed to be mouthing endearments...

And then I had the beast by the neck.

At my touch he let go Colette, and the girl fell down on her knees and set her hands on the floor. The whole of her body was heaving, for, now she could breathe again, she was drawing deep breaths. It seemed that she had taken no hurt.

Boler's hands were trying to tear away mine. He was short of breath now, and, of course, he could make no sound. I had taken him from behind, as he had taken Colette; so he could not know who it was that was holding him fast.

Had we been in the greenwood, I would have choked the man – and have hoped that he would not be found for forty-eight hours. But I could not afford to do such a thing in the inn. Loathed as he was, wilful murder was something no police could ignore.

And then I saw the pier-glass. This was a heavy sheet, applied to the stout, stone wall.

I forced the brute to the mirror, and let him gaze.

When he saw who it was that held him, the light of burning hatred flared in his starting eyes.

"Look on your own face," I said; "for, by God, when you see it next, it won't look the same."

Then, as a man puts the weight, I put his face to the wall beside the pier-glass – with all my might.

As he slumped to the ground and fell backward, I saw I had kept my word. His nose no longer projected, his teeth were gone, and where his face had been, a bloated mask of crimson was forming before my eyes. And a hole in this was screaming...

I picked up Colette and ran back out of the bar.

As I shut the door behind us –

"That's my gentleman fiend," I said. "At least, it was. And now I must go, Colette, as quick as I can."

With the tears running down her face, she flung her arms round my neck. "Adam, Adam."

I set my cheek against hers.

"Don't cry, sweetheart. Forget it. He's out of the running now. Did anyone see you together?"

She shook her head.

"Then, you know nothing about it. Oh, damn – there's your money there. You must say that he tried to kiss you, you dropped your money and ran. Stick to that, Colette. Go and tell Jasper so, by way of a start. Remember, that is *all* that happened and *all* you know."

"I will, I will. You can trust me."

"I know I can." I loosed her hands and kissed them. "And now I must go. See you tomorrow, my beauty."

Colette raised a tearstained face.

"God keep you safe, dear Adam, and – and thank you so very much."

I whipped back into the bar. This was natural enough, for the other door was open and people were pouring in. So I just made one of a crowd. About Boler was pandemonium. The German himself was still screaming, to beat the band. Some woman was in hysterics and was adding her yells to his. The host was demanding a doctor with all his might – I could not see him or Boler, because of the press.

I pretended to peer for a moment, just for the look of the thing. Then I went on and out of the other door.

As I entered the hall, I found myself face to face with Diana Revoke.

"Richard!"

"Thank God," said I. "Where's Mansel?"

Diana stared.

"How should I know? Oh, my God, that screaming... Whatever's the matter here?"

"A man in a fit, or something. I couldn't see." I drew her away from the door. "But this is vital, Diana. D'you mean you haven't seen Mansel? Didn't you get his letter, telling you where to go?" Wide eyed, she shook her head. I smothered an oath. "And you were to have gone between us. I've haunted Doris and Godel for twenty-four hours."

"Can't I go between you now?"

"I think you must try," I said. "But he may be gone."

"Where should I have met him, Richard?"

"At crossroads two miles beyond Villach – the Salzburg road. But you were to have met him on Tuesday."

"I'll go there at once."

"He won't be there before dark. And you'd better be careful, Diana. If the Boche has stopped that letter, he may be there, instead."

"I'll be careful, Richard. What do I say?"

"Say I'm in touch with Friar and I've lost the Boche."

"And you'll wait here?"

"I must, until you get back."

"Well, I shouldn't wait in this inn. I'll tell you why. You haven't lost the Boche, Richard. His car's outside."

"Good God."

"Get out and come back when it's dark. I'll be as quick as I can. I ought to be here by midnight."

"Not here, if the Boche is here. There's a bridge a mile towards Doris, with half its parapet gone. I'll be there from ten o'clock on. By the way, what's your car?"

"A – a Packard. My cousin's down in the village, changing a wheel."

(I thought that was very quick.)

"Is your cousin discreet, Diana?"

The lady smiled.

"Better than that. He's a perfect — fool. And he wants to marry me."

I took her hand in mine and looked into her eyes.

"In that case," said I, "he can't be a — fool."

As I put her hand to my lips, her fingers closed upon mine.

"Take care of yourself, Richard."

I smiled.

I'll do my best."

And then I was gone.

And as I went, I wondered whether so many falsehoods had ever been bandied in such a short space of time.

With the tail of my eye, I saw the German's car. It would be some time, I reflected, before he drove her again.

I deliberately turned to the East, for I had no doubt that Diana was watching which way I took: but, when I was out of sight, I took to the woods and turned back; and after a stroll of two hours, I came to the dell.

The hour was six o'clock, and Bell was sitting beside me, grimly reporting what he had seen and heard.

"Of course I heard the screams, sir. An' I couldn't think what they meant. But I was down in the cellars and too well placed to leave. There's a hatch to put barrels through: this wasn't properly shut, and I could see everything.

"I saw you leave the inn; and that surprised me a lot, for I quite thought you were gone. An' then I knew that the screams were to do with you. An' then, without any warning, the shrieks began… An' that was Miss Revoke: there's no mistaking her voice. So then I did go back…

"I suppose you'd call it hysterics. She didn' see me, of course, for I took care to keep behind. But Boler was in her arms, and her hair was all over his face. So I didn't see that till later. She was fairly howling German, and whenever she cried your name, she spat on the floor. An' Boler was yelling blue murder, because, when she held him to her, she shook him up. An' then he goes for her an' catches her one in the face. An', if you'll believe me, sir, she strikes him back. An', after all, he hadn't a face to strike. It made me think of dogs that'll go for a dog that's hurt."

Bell stopped, to draw in his breath.

"I'll say you know how to hit, sir. There was his head, of course; but I give you my word, at first I thought it was the other way round. I thought it was the back of his head that you'd done in. An' then I saw the end of his tie...

"Well, after she's struck him, they actually has a scrap. It wasn't human, sir...An' people has to pull them apart."

"Not human, but German," I murmured. And then, "Go on."

"An' then she says, 'Are you sure it was Chandos?' she says. Well, he can't speak his words, but when she says that, he very nearly goes mad. He sits up an' beats the floor and keeps trying to shout your name. An' then a doctor arrives...

"I thought I'd better go then, so I slipped back to the cellar and watched from there. Almost as soon as I got there, Miss Revoke comes out an' gets into Boler's car. I suppose she was going for medicine – I never saw her again.

"Very soon after she'd gone, I saw the waggon loaded. Miss Colette was there, to see the weights go on. She looked very pale, and Mr Jasper came out and put his arm round her shoulders, as though to comfort her. He looked very grave and kept frowning, which isn't like him. And then the waggon goes off and they followed behind.

"Well, I was ready to go, when I heard a car coming from Doris. Up it comes to the inn, and out gets Herr Kerrelin. The landlord comes out at a run – I think he thought it was Miss Revoke come back. When he sees it isn't, he bows an' makes to usher him in.

"Mr Kerrelin's no fool, sir. Quick as a flash, 'Who were you expecting?' he says. So the landlord says there's a German lying half dead an' somebody's gone to the chemist's to get what the doctor needs. 'A German?' says Kerrelin, frowning, an' walks straight into the inn. After, perhaps, one minute, out he comes again, with the landlord behind. 'This is not for me,' he says.

'Report to your constable. A German has been assaulted. Well, what of that? This is not Germany – yet.' An' the landlord begins to laugh. 'If you ask me,' he says, 'he kissed the strong man's girl.' 'No doubt,' says Kerrelin. 'An' the strong man kissed him back.' Laugh, sir? You should have seen them...I had to laugh myself. An' then Kerrelin gets in his car and off he goes.

"Well, I saw no use in waiting – I'd seen enough. So I watches my chance and then slips out of the house."

"Good for you, Bell," I said. "Our luck's still holding – I never saw such a thing. First Friar, and then Boler. And, by the grace of God, we've been able to fix them both."

"By the grace of God, sir," said Bell. "I've seen you take some risks, but I thought you were dead this morning, when you came down that road. For twenty-five paces Friar was covering you – and I was just going to kill him, when you turned off. I didn't dare wait no longer, because of the look on his face."

Half an hour before sunset, we ventured to leave the dell.

I would have left earlier, but for the awkward chance that our movements might be observed by some patrol. For frontiers are patrolled in a casual way; and if a guard sees a man who is moving towards a frontier late in the afternoon, he will do his best to stop him or have him stopped. And I desired no brush with the frontier-guards. But patrols come in at dusk.

Using the greatest caution, we crossed the road and made at once for the beechwood in which I had taken cover the week before: there I picked up my line, and, after waiting until the sun was down, we set out to gain the water which we were to cross. The more the light failed, the faster we dared to go, for, were I to miss the place at which we could cross the water, we might well have to wait until dawn could put me right. But after an hour and three quarters – of very hard going and much anxiety – we were standing beside the torrent, by which I had stood before, and there was the beech beyond it, looming against the stars.

Two minutes later, I had my hand on the line...

I cannot pretend that I enjoyed the crossing.

The rope was stout and was knotted, to make it easy to hold: but the sound and fury of the water seemed to be greater by night, and I had no idea at all of our landing place. But it was worse for Bell, for I had seen by daylight what we must do. There was about the business no danger, for, if one failed to land, it was nothing to climb the rope and come down by the tree: but the uproar, the thrust and ferment of the water – a race of black and silver surging across our path, and the curtain of darkness, masking the solid comfort of earth and sky – these things disguised the venture, to make it hideous.

But, as is so often the way, the crossing which seemed so dreadful was easily made.

I landed perfectly, swung the rope into the darkness and waited for Bell. As he arrived, I caught him and set him down, but I think that he could have landed without my help.

Then I climbed into the beech tree and put the rope back on the bough, so that no one – not even a smuggler – should know that a man had gone by.

From then on our way was easy, though something tedious. Except from a distance, I had not surveyed our route: but from time to time I consulted the compass I had, and after three hours I was sure that we were in Italy.

We rested then, till the dawn began to come up. Then we pushed forward briskly, always down the valleys which I had marked. And so, about seven o'clock, we found ourselves on a ridge which commanded a little hamlet in the Italian style.

It seemed best to avoid the village, and so we did: but later we struck the road and began to make good time; with the happy result that about a quarter to eight we rounded a corner to see a crest ahead and Colette sitting there in the sunlight, busily darning what seemed to be one of my socks.

She looked up to see us coming, dropped her work and came running with outstretched arms. I caught and held her. Then I put her up on my shoulder, as I was accustomed to do when we were playing our parts.

"Adam, Adam – and Bell who shares your secrets, though I may not. I knew you would come, of course, because you are a man of your word, but I am very glad to see you again. Your tent is all ready and breakfast is waiting for you. Was it – very difficult?"

"No," said I. "It was easy – and that's the truth."

Bell, the silent, gave tongue.

"It wasn't easy, sir. You make things seem easy, the way you handle them."

"Damn it, Bell," said I, "we've had much harder times."

"That's very true, sir. We have. And I know you've an eye to mountains. But to come all those miles in the dark, an' never put a foot wrong…"

"I agree with Bell," said Colette. "But, most of all, I am very happy to see you safe and sound. Our voyage was less successful. Three miles from the frontier-post, the waggon broke down. The rear axle went. You never saw such a thing. But Jasper was marvellous. 'Unload the waggon,' he cries, 'while I seek a smith.' And he sends me off to the post to tell them that we are delayed. The guards will not listen to me, so I return. There is the smith at work, by the side of the way; so Jasper comes with me to the frontier-post. Very soon he has the guards laughing. And when the waggon arrives, although it is after the time, they let it go through. So all is very well. But we come to Jade so late that we cannot pitch the camp, but sleep in the inn. And now, my dear, I come to the tragedy. When that half-wit, Odin, loaded the waggon again, the one thing he forgot was your precious weights. I had seen them set to one side – not laid with the other stuff, because they were yours. And, since I am with Jasper, Odin, that king of fools, must leave them behind. But Jasper has gone to get them. The waggon, of course, is with him. And Odin, too."

"How – how long will they be?" I said – and hardly knew my own voice.

"They should be back," said Colette, "by half past ten."

In fact they were back by nine – without the weights. The guards had made it clean that, while they were free to pass in, they would not be free to pass out. In a word, the frontier was closed, and Austria could not be quitted without a special pass. To *bona fide* travellers, this would be issued at Villach, or any principal town. When Jasper had asked why this ban had been suddenly set, the sergeant had frowned. 'The police are no fools,' he said. 'The last time they took this action, a car was found with its spare tyres filled with gold.'

6

The Hard Way

Of such is the way of Fortune.

Throughout our enterprise, the dame had smiled upon us again and again. On the seventh day of June Mansel and I had entered Austria: and we had reached Palin's inn at nine o'clock that night. Had we reached it but four hours later, the chamber would have been empty and I should never have had a tale to tell. At twelve o'clock one night, the Boche had visited Hohenems, search warrant in hand: had he come the night before, he would have caught us red-handed, moving the gems. Had Orris not disobeyed orders and shown a light, and had I not been passing at that very time, there can, I think, be no doubt that Friar would have got us down. Then I had met with Jasper and so found a way in a million to get the gems out. And now a careless fool had cast the whole of our winnings into the draught.

Little wonder I felt very tired. I believe and shall always maintain that Jasper's dreadful report took a month from my life. It meant that the hunt was up. A very little deduction, and the police would identify me as Jasper's 'strong man'. And Orris, long ago free, would report to Friar. And Friar would know in a flash that the gems were within the weights. And the weights were at his disposal – as at that of the police...

"You have eaten nothing," said Colette, with her eyes on my face.

"I am not hungry," I said. "But I want to talk to you." I got to my feet. "I like the look of those lynchets: and there we shall not be disturbed."

We were upon the outskirts of Jade, and a road wound up to another, smaller hamlet some three miles off. And beside the road were lynchets – a very charming feature, as lynchets always are.

I led the way to the nearest: there I took my seat and lighted a cigarette.

"Listen, Colette," said I, "and I'll tell you a tale."

"A true tale, Adam?"

"Most true. I shall exaggerate nothing – you have my word for that."

"Proceed, please," said Colette.

"An Englishman, whom I know, has a castle in Austria. He and his beautiful wife have lived there for several years. But now the Boche is coming and so he must go. In that castle he had a treasure of very great price. It was beyond all value – and nobody knew of it. It was a treasure of jewels, the like of which the world has never seen: but, more than that, it was historical. And the Englishman felt very strongly that such a treasure as that should not be left for the Boche. He desired to take it to England and to give it to a famous museum, because then it would be safe and could be admired for ever by high and low. Well, that was all right: but because of its very great value, he would not have been permitted to take it away. Austria would have stopped him from taking it out."

"And saved it for the Boche," said Colette.

"Exactly," said I. "Which was more than my friend could bear. And so he asked me to help him to get it out. Well, I was very happy to do so. And that was why I came to Austria. And I could have done it, Colette, without any fuss. But I had a piece of bad luck. A thief – a brilliant thief, had heard of those gems.

And just when I had arrived, he made an attempt to steal them. I managed to spoil his game, and then he offered to do a deal with me. I think, perhaps, you can guess what my answer was. 'Very well,' he said. 'If you won't deal with me I'll go to the Boche.' And the Boche was in charge of the police. I told him to go – and be damned. And so he did."

"He went to the Boche?"

"He did. And the Boche was on to me, as a dog on a rat. Well, I got the gems out of the castle, and then I was stuck. For the police had been warned to watch the frontier-posts. And I dared not carry the gems. I was ready to cross the frontier – perhaps, by a smuggler's path. But bear the gems, I dared not – they were too valuable. And so I sought for a way. And then you and Jasper came and showed me the way."

"We showed you the way?" said Colette.

"You showed me the way. I took out the sand and packed the gems in the weights."

"God Almighty," breathed Colette, and put her hands to her head.

"That was why I would not tell you my secret. Because, if I had done so, you would have been scared to death. And now the weights are in Austria, lying by the side of some road. Millions of pounds lie within them. And I am here. Do you wonder I ate no breakfast? And they are not mine, Colette. They do not belong to me. I was doing this for a friend. They are his – and were to be England's. And now I have let the two down."

"I think," said Colette, "I think I am going to be sick."

"That," said I, "would be useless. Describe, instead, the spot where you left the weights."

"I had them put off the road, by the side of a wood. There was a wayside crucifix: we were the far side of that – the frontier side. And there was a row of poplars a little lower down."

"Going towards the frontier, a crucifix, then the weights, and then a row of poplars... Is that what you mean?"

"That is correct," said Colette. "And all on the right as you go. Not three miles from the frontier, for we had passed the stone. But why must you know, Adam? You cannot go back."

"I shall go back tonight," said I. "What else can I do?"

Colette was down on her knees.

"Adam, I beseech you, see reason. Because of me, you have broken the Boche in pieces. I saw what I saw. And then you fled – and came out. I have been beside myself the whole of last night. But now you are safe. To go back would be sheer madness. The district will be alive with nothing but police. You are the one man on earth who cannot go back."

"Yet must I do it," I said. "I cannot leave those gems by the side of the way."

"Jasper will go and collect them and presently get his pass out."

"And have the weights searched at the Customs… Besides, by now I am known for Jasper's 'strong man'. No, no, I alone can do it. And I am going to do it. I shall return tonight, lie up tomorrow, and come back tomorrow night. I cannot bring the weights, for they would be far too heavy to bear by the smuggler's way. But I can carry their contents, and so I will."

"You will be taken, Adam. You have not a chance."

"I've an excellent chance, Colette. But, chance or no, my dear, I am going back. Those gems are in my charge. If they were in yours, would you leave them…by the side of the road?"

"The fool!" screamed Colette. "The fool to have left the weights behind!"

"That is the way of a fool. They do incredible things. Fools have made history, Colette. Lost battles, brought empires down, because they are fools. But they will always be with us, so long as the world goes round. The fool in his folly, Colette, has wrought more havoc than any evil man. They mean no ill; and so we do not suspect them, as we suspect a knave. And therein lies their power to bring all our plans to naught. But what is the use of talking? The thing is done. Odin has played the fool: and

167

I have got to go back, to make his folly good." Colette cupped her face in her palms.

"I cannot bear it, Adam. For my sake, you put forth your strength – and took away from the Boche the semblance of man. And since he commands the police – "

"My dear," said I, "he'd been looking for me for days."

"I do not care. The fire, perhaps, was there. But you poured fuel upon it, because he was ill-treating me. Had you not interfered, he would never have known you were there. And now the whole district is roused. You cannot go back, Adam dear. It would be – suicide."

"I am going tonight, Colette."

"In that case I shall come with you, to show you the spot."

I shook my head.

"You are very sweet, Colette. But the way I go is a way no woman can take."

"You will take Bell?"

I shook my head.

"Bell will want to come, but this is a one-man job."

The truth was I dared not take Bell, in case I did not come back.

"So you mean to go back alone to a land which has closed its frontiers for fear that you should escape."

I smiled.

"Some years ago I did that – and here I am."

"Did you go back alone?"

"No," I said, "I admit I was not alone. But I had far more to do, and that wasn't a one-man job. But let that go. Your strong man is out of the bill, until you can get the weights. And so he is free for the moment to – go on leave. That is what I am going to do. But I shall be back on Sunday. And then I will eat such a breakfast as never was eaten before."

"What time shall you leave?" said Colette.

"About sundown."

"Very well. I will have some food ready for you to take."

"Not too much, Colette. I'll make up when I get back."

"And wine?"

I shook my head.

"Water will do for me. There are plenty of springs."

"Very well." She hesitated. "May I tell Jasper – what you have told me?"

"Yes," I said. "And don't let him go for the weights until I return."

"He will not go till the frontier is open again."

"Which means you will stay here," I said. "I had not thought about that, but my wits are confused."

"We must have the weights," said Colette. "To replace them would be very costly – more than we can afford. When I think of all that money spilt on the floor... People had been very generous. There must have been more than three pounds."

"You will allow me the honour to make that my affair. Let us call it five pounds. I would have given fifty to put the Boche where he belonged. And then you gave me my chance."

"Jasper would not hear of it, Adam. When I told him what you had done, he said the good God had sent you 'to save Colette'. I know he has said nothing yet: but that is because he cannot trust himself. He is afraid of tears and, when he tries to thank you, he knows that he will break down."

"Tell him I did what I did to please myself. The Boche had laid hands on my sweet. And whoever does that offends me – and pays the price."

Colette had her eyes on the ground.

"I told you," she said, "I liked great gentlemen."

With that, she was gone.

Later I spoke with Bell.

"I must go and get them, Bell: but then you knew that."

"Yes, sir. When shall we start?"

"I can't afford to take you. I must have someone outside in case I get stuck."

"I'd – rather come with you, sir."

"I know you would. I shall miss you. It can't be helped. If I am not back by Monday, wire to Captain Mansel, saying I'm overdue."

"To London, sir?"

"That's right. He'll know what action to take. And now we must summon Mr Palin. I'll write out a wire in a minute, for you to send. You must meet him and put him wise. Present him to Jasper and see that he sleeps in my bed. I'm sure he'll go very well."

"Not with Miss Colette, sir."

"Which is absurd – he's my friend. And do what you can for her: she's rather upset. I'd better take a kit-bag, so empty one. And don't forget the key, to unfasten the plates."

"Very good, sir. You're – set on going?"

"What else can I do?"

"I – don't like your going alone, sir."

I laughed.

"You never do, Bell. But I always come back."

"You will look out for Friar, sir?"

"I certainly will," I said.

"He'll shoot at sight – Friar will, sir. Don't forget that."

"I won't forget – I promise: if the fellow runs into me, I'll put him down."

I rested for most of that day: but at six o'clock that evening Jasper came to my tent.

"Well, my friend," said I; "and where have you been all day?"

Jasper folded his hands.

"You have a proverb, sir, saying 'Motley's the only wear'. For me, that is very true. I have no other suit. Yet there are times when I cannot wear my motley: and then I am ashamed of my nakedness. Today has been one of those times. But now, for very shame, I have come to you; for I cannot let you go off, until I have said my say. God alone can reward you for what you did yesterday. You not only pulled the dog off, but you broke the dog in pieces for what he had done. I saw him, and I am content. And I spoke with the doctor later – I wished to savour his fate. And the doctor said that, though the man will recover, his visage will be so shocking that he must live in private and cannot go out and about. And so my Colette, my darling, and all his other victims are now avenged. And how have we paid our debt? By leaving behind your weights – the tools with which you have added cubits to our stature…in which you had hidden a treasure beyond all price. That, then, is our return for what you have done. You counted upon us to help you, and you had every right. Of course you did not tell us, for, had we known, we should have been frightened to death. But you relied upon us. 'My weights,' you said, 'that Bell has taken such care of, upon which my performance depends…be sure they will bring my weights with them, though they bring nothing else.' And then…we left them behind…by the side of the way." He put a hand to his head. "I knew, of course, that you had not joined us for nothing. Gentlemen such as you do not join strolling players because the strolling players suggest that they should. I knew that in some way or other this strange association would serve your turn. But that did not concern me, for, once you had passed your word, I knew you would give full measure – and so, indeed, you have. No man was ever so generous, so handsome in all he did. Well, there we are. You have kept your side of the bargain with all your might: you have saved and avenged Colette: and, in return, we have struck you a mortal blow."

"Jasper, Jasper," I cried, "I cannot sit still and let you talk in this way. No one could ever contend that the fault was yours. I do not even blame Odin. Odin is one of those fools that now and again do something to break the heart. They have no brains, but they are not idiotic, and so we use them for duties which do not require them to think. As such, they are very useful – Odin is an excellent cook. But now and again they do the unpredictable thing. Sometimes it does not matter: sometimes it does. But whether or no it matters, it is nobody's fault – not even Odin's, for that is the way he is made. So, my good friend, you must not blame yourself. I do not blame myself, though, if it was anyone's fault, then it must have been mine: but I dared not stay with the waggon because of the police – as well as of some others whose brains are extremely quick. Once they knew me for your 'strong man', they would have guessed at once that hidden within the weights were the gems they sought. So I had to let the weights go and take a chance...

"Well, it didn't come off, Jasper. Perhaps I should have told you; but ignorance is the best armour in such a matter as this. Had I told you the truth, you would have cared for the weights, but, when you came to the Customs, your heart would have been in your mouth. And Customs are trained to observe uneasiness. Still, I should have done better. And now I must return to repair my mistake."

Jasper put his hands to his head.

"You trusted us," he wailed, "and we have betrayed your trust. And now you are going back to the hornets' nest you have roused. Had you not been leaving the country, you would not have broken the Boche. And now you are going back to a danger more lively and pressing than that from which you escaped."

"Nevertheless, I must go."

"Say rather 'I shall go', sir, for few men would. The chestnuts are not yours – to pull out of the fire. But you belong to the class that will do for a friend what you would not do for yourself. And I hear you will go alone. I do not like that – I do not like it at all. Four eyes are better than two, in a matter of life and death. Then, again, you must rest a little between your moves: and, if there are two, one can always watch, while the other sleeps. Were I a younger man, I would go myself. Nothing on earth, sir, would stop me. But I am no longer young. Although you may not think it, I am near sixty-five, and I could not do the two journeys – that I know. And so I should hamper you. But I have found a young lad, who is very eager and willing to be your *aide de camp*. The idea of crossing the frontier appeals to him; and with my life I will answer for his entire devotion in this your enterprise." Before I could protest, he went on. "I do not expect you to take him on what I may say. I have, of course, told him nothing about the gems. But he will meet you at sundown a mile from here. He can walk with you for a little towards the path you will take, and you can talk with him and see what you think. I have told him your decision is final – that if you decline his company, he must accept your ruling without demur. But I hope that you will take him – with all my heart. I mean that – with all my heart. For, if he is of some service, I shall have contributed something towards repairing the evil which Odin has done."

I rose and put out my hand.

"You're the best of good fellows, Jasper, and if I don't take the lad, you must not think me ungracious or heedless of what you have done. But this will be a perilous business, and I am accustomed to danger, but he is not. The police are out to stop me – perhaps to arrest me now. And there are others, Jasper, desperate men, one of whom has done murder to help him to get these gems. More than once, already, I've spoiled their game, and if I should clash with them, it mayn't be too good."

"I will answer for his courage," said Jasper.

"Of that, I am sure. But a man requires more than courage, to deal with people like that. Besides, if there is to be trouble, I cannot have him involved. Still, I might take him with me and leave him beside the path. Anyway, we will see. I'll size him up, Jasper – I promise you that: and if I think he'll help me, I'll take him along."

With my hand in his, Jasper looked me full in the eyes.

"I hope, sir, that you will take him – with all my heart."

Then he wished me good luck and said he should look for my coming and other things. Finally, he bowed himself out, and I called for Bell. And with his faithful help, I made ready to take a journey from which, if I am to be honest, I doubted that I should come back.

There was nothing at all in my favour, but much against the issue I so much desired. Could I have waited a week, the flurry would have died down: but neither the police nor Friar could be sure I was over the border, and so for the next two days they would be scouring the district with all their might. Once it was officially known, the police could not ignore the assault on the Boche: he had, of course, denounced me, and they would be bound to arrest me for that, if for nothing else. And Orris would by now have reported, and Friar would have the truth in his hands. Could I have waited, I say, police and Friar might well have gone empty away. But I could not afford to wait. Anyone finding the weights would see that they were of some value, although they might not know what purpose they served. A peasant, for instance, would certainly fetch his tumbril and take them away. A passing gypsy would heave them into his van. If Friar were to stumble upon them…

I looked at Bell.

"Miss Colette," I said, "was going to put up some food."

"It's in the kit-bag, sir, with the key and a change of socks. You won't take anything else, sir."

I shook my head.

"I must travel as light as I can. Where's Miss Colette?"

"She's gone on to talk to the lad, sir. She'll wait with him till you come."

I wrinkled my nose.

"Mr Jasper means very well, but I don't fancy a pupil in this particular case."

"I – wish you'd take me, sir."

"I can't, and you know it, Bell. I've got to leave you here in case I get stuck."

"Then I hope you'll take the lad, sir. Mr Jasper wouldn't recommend him, if he – "

"Mr Jasper's a man of peace. But we are accustomed to violence – to matters of life and death. Mr Jasper has no idea of the way I may have to deal with the chances I've got to take."

"The lad can watch while you rest, sir."

I shrugged my shoulders.

"I'll look him over, Bell: but he'll have to be out of the ruck if he's going with me." I passed to the mouth of the tent and looked to the West. "I'd better be off now. The sun's going down."

In silence, Bell picked up the kit-bag and walked with me to the stream which bordered our camp.

As we came to a little footbridge –

"Give me the doings," I said. "I'll go on alone."

In silence, Bell gave me the kit-bag. Then he stood to one side and took off his hat.

"God keep you, sir," he said quietly.

I put out my hand for his.

"I'll come back, Bell," I said. "Somehow I always do."

With his hand in mine –

"I know you will, sir," said Bell. And again, as though in defiance, "I *know* you will."

I smiled and nodded.

"Till Sunday morning, Bell."

Then I passed on to the footbridge and up to the road beyond.

More than a mile had gone by, and I was beginning to hope that the lad had thought better of his bargain, when I saw a figure ahead, on a ridge by the side of the way. And as I drew nearer, I saw it was that of a youth. His back was turned towards me, and he was standing square, regarding the set of sun. I could not see Colette, but she might have been sitting below him, just out of sight. Be that as it might, I felt that this was the lad whom Jasper and Bell were so anxious that I should take. And then I was sure it was he, for he was clad in the Austrian national dress.

All of a sudden he turned, as though to look for me: and when he saw me coming, he flung up his arms – a pleasant, welcoming gesture, that argued an eager heart. So he stood for a moment against the red of the sky, and I remember thinking how striking a figure he cut. Then he came running towards me, and, after a little, I saw that it was Colette.

At this, I stood still in my tracks: and when she was ten feet from me, she did the same. Then she put her hands on her hips and looked at me.

That she made a splendid picture, I must allow. Her feathered hat was cocked, and her snow-white shirt and handsome, sleeveless jacket became her perfectly: her shorts, her footless stockings and stout, black brogues, all fitted her very well: but the air with which she wore them, her eager and gallant demeanour kindled the heart.

So for a short half minute. Then she swept off her hat and bowed, and her curls fell about her face.

"Will you take the lad, sir?" she said.

I remembered Bell's insistence and how Jasper had begged me to do so 'with all his heart'.

"I suppose I shall have to," I said.

She pitched her hat over her shoulder and flung herself into my arms.

"Adam, Adam, you never thought it was me."

"How should I, Colette? I take people at their word."

"We arranged it together, Jasper and Bell and I. You see we were all agreed that you must not go alone. And Jasper was too old, and Bell you had ordered to stay, so that left me. And we had the dress – I have often worn it before. I did mean to cut off my hair, but Bell said you would not like that, so I let it be." Here she recovered her hat and turned her back on me. "So now you must put it up. Just pile it up on my head, and I'll put on the hat."

Helplessly, I did as she said.

"And now we must be going." She took my arm. "We can talk as we go. I will be very obedient – I promise you that. I will do all that you tell me – except that I will not leave you by day or night. And you will be glad of me. Think – I can take you straight to the spot where the weights were left. I can watch while you rest and can serve you in many ways. Bell has told and has taught me the things I can do. I know the touch that will wake you and how you always prefer to drink from a glass – I have one there, in my pouch that is lying by the side of the way. And a sponge to wipe your face. You would not take these things, because you were one: but, now we are two, you shall have your luxuries."

"Colette," I said, "I think you are out of your mind, and so are Jasper and Bell. But I am glad that you are, and I am very happy that you are coming with me."

For a moment she made no answer.

Then –

"There is my pouch," she said, and whipped a little ahead, to pluck it out of a bush.

As I came up with her, I saw that her colour was high.

"I am glad you are glad," she said. "It is out of all order, of course, but I think that Eve would approve. If she truly loves you, she, too, would be glad that you should have someone beside you these coming hours."

"I tell you this, Colette, that Eve will never rest until she has seen and thanked you for what you have done."

"I need no thanks," said Colette. "I am pleasing myself. You see, I – like you, Adam; and when you – like a person you want to be with them and help them as best you can. I am very fond of you, Adam. Our lives are very different: mine does not lead me to meet – great gentlemen. And – "

"Colette, I beg you – "

" – now, by chance, I have met one. Oh, do not shake your head. I know what I know. Had we never met, and had you happened to lunch at The Vat of Melody yesterday afternoon, you would have smiled and thanked me and put a note in my plate…and then have gone out to your car and never have thought again of the girl with the strolling players who made the round of the guests. But, as it is, you have walked into my life... Very soon now, you will walk out of it again. And one day I shall marry – a nephew of Jasper's, perhaps, on his mother's side. He is a clerk in Venice. Or else, perhaps, the son of some innkeeper. Be sure I shall have my chances. But always I shall remember what he will never know – that once upon a time a great gentleman was my familiar friend and that I was his squire in a matter of life and death."

"My sweet Colette," I said, "for God's sake, don't dress this up. Nothing at all may happen, except a stolen march. There may be a sordid squabble in which, to save my own, I have to take a man's life. Such things are not romantic. The lust for gold is always an ugly thing. And the things it breeds are hideous. The police are out for these gems, because the German wants them. They are not his, and he has no right to them: but he is a German, and Germans must have what they want. The others are out for the gems, because they covet the money the gems will bring. The gems are not theirs, and they have no right to them. But that does not matter to them, because they are thieves. Already they have done murder, to help them to their desires. Those are the people whom I am up against. The police will behave correctly – of that I am sure: but they are out to take me for what I have done and for what I am trying to do. The others will go all lengths: if they can kill me, they will. So in this adventure of ours will be no romance. Only fatigue and danger and, if it should come to a showdown, jungle law."

Colette threw up her head.

"You cannot see the romance, for it is locked in my breast. It is more precious to me than the gems you are going to fetch. It is a cordial, my dear, and when I am old and tired, it will always warm my heart."

"Colette," I said, "you're hopeless. I believe you could weave a romance about changing a wheel."

"That would depend," said Colette, "upon who was driving the car."

We laughed together at that. Then we quickened our pace, for the shadows were closing in.

It goes, of course, without saying that I was more than uneasy about the arrangement to which I had now subscribed. I had not argued the point, for things had gone too far. All unknown to me, the plot had been hatched and measures had been taken to carry it out. Colette had approached Bell and Jasper, and they had approved her plan – and had led me up to the water which I was to drink. And now I had drunk it: Colette was coming with me, for all I knew, to battle and murder and sudden death. Had I ordered her back, I doubt if she would have gone: indeed, I am sure she would have followed – or, rather, have tried to follow, keeping out of my sight. But she was so eager and glowing, so instant that I should take her that, as I have shown already, I threw in my hand and let her have her way. To withstand so handsome an instinct is very hard. Still, I was far from easy. Colette was the picture of health and was very strong: but the journey across the frontier was no child's play. The crossing of the water alone was a most unpleasant ordeal. But, quite apart from that, the going was very hard, and she would be very tired when we came to the other side. Yet, to rest there was out of the question. It was my hope to reach the roads by dawn and, before the world was stirring, to find the weights. Once their precious burden was in my bag, I could think about taking my rest. Then I should have to decide where I could best lie up until dusk came in. But, until I had found the weights and secured the gems, I dared not waste a moment – *I could not rest*. To carry this first objective was well within my power; but I am a very strong man and have learned to endure. Whether Colette could do it, I dared not think.

I declined to look beyond the recovery of the gems. That was the point for which I was going to ride. The future could care for itself. For, once they were in my bag, if I were taken, then I should be taken dead.

As we left the road for a valley –

"How," said Colette, "are you so sure of your way? When all is said and done, you have only taken it once. And then it was light."

"It's a matter of practice," I said. "I wasn't always so good. But this is very easy, for there is the line of the mountains against the sky. In five minutes we shall strike water, and that will lead us along for two or three miles."

And so it did. But the going was very hard and we were moving uphill. Except here and there, we could not walk side by side, but Colette moved steadily behind me, keeping the pace I set.

After an hour we rested, but not for long. I spread the slack of my bag for her to sit upon and then lay down beside her upon our ghost of a path. We did not speak, but I saw Colette look about her, slowly turning her head, now regarding the heaven, now listening, all the time drawing deep breaths. Then her hand stole into mine and held it tight. There was no need of words, for I knew how she felt.

I have seen many beautiful nights, but I cannot remember one when the senses were so much enriched. The sky was blue-black velvet, pricked with a glory of brilliants, to feast the eye. All about us the mountains were lifting their aged heads, to make of the sable horizon a very lovely erasement such as no herald on earth could ever devise. We might have been sitting in some theatre, built for a race of giants, regarding a stage hung above us, on which a million worlds were playing their dazzling parts. Many waters made us music, and since, with the daylight, all other sound had died, a background of absolute silence rendered their dulcet notes. The gallantry of a torrent, the lisp of a baby brook, the steady rush of deep water, the gurgle of welling springs – all were there to be heard, and an ear accustomed to Nature could pick the instruments out. And the air was fragrancy – fresh and clean and vital, rich with a bouquet no wine can ever deliver, the breath of hanging forests and the humour of mountain lawns.

A star fell, and Colette caught my hand to her heart…

We rested for just ten minutes. Then I got to my feet, and, putting paradise behind us, we took up a march which allowed no contemplation; for though the heaven was as lovely and the chorus of the waters as rich, all my powers were directed to picking and stealing my way, and I moved through the wonder about us oblivious to everything else.

What hour it was when we came to the barrier torrent, I cannot say; but I know it was later than I had hoped to be there.

From this side, for some strange reason, its vehemence seemed more fearful, its threat more sinister. This may have been because there were fewer rocks, and the speed and might of the race, darker almost than the darkness, argued the awful way of the waters under the earth.

I put an arm round Colette and held her close.

"We shall cross this together, great heart. You will be on my back with your arms round my neck."

The girl put a hand to her throat.

"We have to cross this, Adam?"

"Yes, Colette. And, believe me, it's nothing at all. You wait here and watch me."

With that, I climbed into the beech, and very soon I was back with the rope in my hands.

"You see?" I said. "With a run, this will carry us over, as if we were on a trapeze. We shan't even get wet, my dear. But when we land, be careful that I don't fall upon you. When I say 'Down!', let go, and you'll fall very soft."

"I see," said Colette, quietly. "When you say 'Down!' "

"That's right, my sweet. I've done it already, you know, and so has Bell. It looks much worse than it is."

"I am not afraid," said Colette. "I should be, if I were alone. I should be terrified. But – I am not alone: and so I am not afraid. Shall we go now, Adam dear?"

"On to my back," I said, stooping…

She was very light, but, of course, I could not hold her, because I needed both hands to hold our weight to the rope. What would happen if I failed to land us and we must climb up to the tree, I dared not think.

"Lock your arms round my neck," I said, "and whatever happens, Colette, you must not let go."

"Is that too tight, Adam?"

"Lord, no," said I. "And dig in your knees, as though you were riding a horse."

I felt her grip my loins.

I reached as high as I could: then I laid hold like grim death, took my run and launched us over the flood.

I suppose two seconds went by before we had crossed, but, to tell the truth, it seemed much longer than that.

Then –

"Down!" I croaked.

The arms and knees fell away, and I let myself go…

I sat up with the rope in my hands and the sweat running into my eyes. Then Colette's arms went about me and her cheek was pressed against mine.

"Adam, Adam," she cried, "I should not have come. No man can make such an effort and be the same."

I wrung the sweat from my brow.

"I'm quite all right, my beauty. It wasn't your weight – you weigh nothing: and I was glad to have you upon my back. But there was just one moment at which we had to alight. And only one. Still, that's behind us now: and when we do it again, we shall be coming back."

Then I made fast the rope to the staple. This, in such a way that if any smuggler came to the opposite side, I will lay any money that smuggler went empty away. Perhaps this was not quite fair; but the rope was our way of escape.

And then we rested a little, on the bank of the savage water, hand in hand, like two children who have come safe out of some pass.

The dawn was up, before we came to the road. At once we turned to the right, making good pace along it for nearly a mile. Then we turned to the left, and forty minutes later we turned to the right again. We were now between Doris and Godel, on the road I had reason to know. This was the way to the frontier, by which, some seven miles on, the weights had been left.

Never shall I forget those seven miles.

To hasten was, quite frankly, beyond our power; for we had been on our feet for more than ten hours. How Colette covered this lap, I do not know: I could not afford to spare her, for every minute was precious – and we were behind our time. The way became more dangerous with every second that passed; but take to the woods, I dared not, for, had our way not been smooth, our progress would have dropped to a crawl. And yet the road was deadly – a neverending series of reaches, with, once in a while, a milestone, whose legend broke the heart. Ten miles to the frontier...and, after a long time, nine...then eight...then seven...then six... Six miles, still to the frontier, which meant we had three to go.

The road did not run through Godel, but passed it by: only, The Vat of Melody stood by the side of our way.

But I was ready for that.

Five hundred yards from the inn, there was, I knew, a footpath which left the road, for I had crossed it on Thursday, when I had left the inn. This joined another footpath which I had actually used: and the latter led back to the road, perhaps a mile to the East. By making this painful detour, we could avoid the inn; but it added much to the distance we had to cover, and though its surface was good, this did not, of course, compare with that of the smooth highway.

As we came back to the road, I shot a glance at my watch – a quarter to eight.

Colette looked pale and drawn, but her head was high. It tore my heart to drive her, but what could I do? I had to get on. Had I proposed to leave her, she would have laughed in my face. After all, she was there to show me the spot where the weights had been left.

To add to our grievous burden, traffic began to share the road with us: motor traffic, I mean, for I had no fear of the carts. Of these we had passed six or eight, but the peasants had done no more than give us good day. Nor had I much fear of the lorry: but when I heard a car coming, I swung Colette into the bracken beside the way. And there we lay down together until the car had gone by. This must have happened twelve times in the last three miles; and every time we lay down, it cost us the world to rise.

Indeed, it was past nine o'clock, when I felt a touch on my arm and Colette breathed "*There*!"

"Where, exactly?" I said.

"Just before we come to the barn on the opposite side of the road. There is a little hollow, above and beyond the ditch."

I liked the look of the spot, for it lay upon the edge of a wood. The boughs, indeed, stretched out to the road itself: and the undergrowth was thick and would harbour us very well. More. From my point of view, it made a most excellent cache: and I felt like forgiving Odin his great delinquency. 'Out of sight, out of mind,' says the proverb. And if they were out of his sight, then were they out of the sight of everyone else.

I almost broke into a run…

I had still thirty paces to go, when I saw the marks on either side of the ditch. The soil was moist, and the verdure was crushed and trampled…and the end of a bough had been broken and left to hang its gay head…

I think that my heart turned over within my breast.

Then I perceived that Odin and such as had helped him must have left marks behind them when they had bestowed the boxes containing the weights: for it could have been no child's play to get them over the ditch. That, then, was the explanation. And so I breathed again. Still, I was not too easy. If I could observe their traces, then so could other eyes.

And so, no doubt, they had. For when I had leaped the ditch, I saw that the hollow was empty and that the weights were gone.

7

Two's Company

To be honest, I cannot remember the next few moments of time. The shock, I suppose, has occasioned a blank in my memory. But I know I was sitting down, with my head in my hands, while Colette was lying beside me, face downward in the hollow, an arm across her eyes, sobbing and sobbing, as though her heart would break.

I have suffered heavier blows. But, perhaps because of the effort which we had made, perhaps because the gems were not mine, but Ferrers', life seemed to have lost its savour. If I had felt tired before, I now felt utterly finished, unfit to lift a hand. Indeed, there was no health in me – and that is the truth. But some wise man has said that there is in every being one more ounce of resistance than he himself thinks there is. And when I saw Colette lying there, worn out, forlorn and weeping, I set about comforting her without thinking what I did. And this, as I shall show, was the saving of me.

I picked her up and held her close in my arms.

"You mustn't cry, Colette. Because the weights are gone, we mustn't give up. They probably aren't very far. We must put our minds to the business of getting them back. For all I know, they may be inside that barn. I don't think the police have found them, for if they had, they would have left a man here."

"It – may – be – the – others," she said.

"It may be – anyone. But, just because they're not here, I'm not going to throw in my hand. We're going to sit here and breakfast. And then I shall leave you here and have a look round. Don't say that you will come with me, because I have made up my mind. You are too tired to help me in any search. But when you have rested awhile, your strength will come back. And then you shall help me, my pretty, in all that I do."

To that she made no answer, and, after a moment, I saw that she was asleep. As gently as I could, I laid her down. Then I got to my feet, picked her up and carried her a few paces into the wood. There, in a fold of the ground, was a bed of leaves; and since I could do no better, I laid her on that.

She made a pathetic picture, pale and wan, still drawing tremulous breaths. Her hat had fallen off, and her tumbled curls declared her a weary Rosalind. But sleep was what she needed, and that she had. When she awoke, she would be herself again.

I opened my kit-bag and set some food beside her. Then I returned to the hollow to break my fast, for from there I could watch the road, for what that was worth.

Little enough, perhaps; but something had to be done. If there was no work for my hands, there was work for my eyes and my feet. I must watch and search – and use what wits I had. just because the hollow was empty, was I to sit still? And then slink back to Jade, with my tail between my legs? Mansel would not have done that, and neither would I.

So long as it was not the police that had found and taken the weights, a chance remained of tracing them – very slender, perhaps, but still a chance. I decided to assume it was Friar. Once Orris had joined his master and made his report, Friar would know at once that the gems were within the weights. He would, therefore, follow the troupe, which meant he would take the same road, keeping his eyes about him, for all he was worth. Now I found it unlikely that the weights had been out of sight. The boxes had been laid to one side, and the hollow had been convenient, because it had made a ledge on the sloping ground. The idea of concealment had entered nobody's head. The probability was that the boxes could be seen from the road – by a man who was using his eyes. So Friar might well have seen them, and, just because he was Friar, instead of an ordinary man, have stopped the car and gone back...to see what the boxes held... (I did not think this was likely. Indeed, I did not think it was Friar that had taken the weights. But I had to make bricks somehow, and since I had no straw, I had to use meaner stuff.) Now if Friar had found the weights, what would he do? At once, I saw that he would contrive to get them into the barn. This was rising some twenty paces ahead, on the opposite side of the road. With the police all over the place, he would not want to carry them in the car. But the barn offered just the cover he had to have. There he could open the weights and make assurance sure. In other words, it made a retiring room. While I ate, I made up my mind that, before I did anything else, I would visit the barn.

And if it was not Friar that had taken the weights...

In that case, it was probably some peasant, using a horse driven cart. Such a man would be walking along, before or behind or beside his vehicle. Even if he was upon it, his pace would be slow enough to allow him to notice the weights. No man in a car or a lorry was likely to see the things. His eyes would be on the road, because of his speed. But the peasant had time to look about him. He was, no doubt, in the habit of using this road, and so the slightest excrescence upon the familiar scene –

Here Friar came out of the barn and stepped to the edge of the road. He stood, looking hard towards Godel, as though for one he expected to come that way. Then, as though in impatience, he savaged his chin. And then he turned on his heel and re-entered the barn. Had he looked across the road, he must, I think, have seen me – or seen that someone was there. But he had eyes for nothing but the road that ran to the West.

The sight of the man revived me as nothing else could have done. My heart leaped up and my weariness fell away, for now I knew that the gems were under my hand. I had only to cross the road, to pick them up. In fact, Friar had done me a service; for the weights were far better with him than lying by the side of the road: then, again, he had carried them into cover, which I should have had to do, before I unscrewed the plates.

I knew for what Friar was waiting. He was awaiting a tool with which to open the weights. Orris or Sloper had taken the car to Godel, there to procure a key to unscrew the plates. This might have to be forged. It was simple enough to make, and if Sloper had the dimensions, twenty minutes or less would do the trick. But it would almost certainly have to be made; for while the nose of a spanner would, I think, have loosened them four days ago, once I had packed the weights I had screwed the plates into place with all my might. And so Friar was waiting on Orris...or Sloper...or both his men. And I was here, in the greenwood, unknown to anyone.

Before I did anything else, I went to look at Colette. But she was still sleeping like the dead. Praying that she would sleep on, I took out my pistol and put off the safety catch. Then I slid it into my pocket and set out to cross the road.

This I did a hundred yards on, towards the frontier, for Friar might have had a peephole for all I knew. Then I came carefully back and up to the barn.

This was some sixty feet long by thirty wide. It was roughly built of stone and was heavily thatched. There was a substantial gap between the top of the walls and the roof itself, but, though this was admitting the air, the eaves of the thatch were long, and I knew that within the barn the light would be dim indeed. And Friar's eyes would be used to such a half-light: but mine would not.

Now Friar had appeared from the opposite side of the barn, using a grass-grown track which led to the road. It was, therefore, manifest that the great door was upon that side: so I stole round the back of the barn, to see if I could conveniently enter that way.

It is obvious, of course, that I held one very good card – namely, the fact that Friar did not know I was here: and since Friar could handle a pistol, but I could not, to throw away that card would have been the act of a fool. I do not mean that I am a very bad shot, but I am not quick on the trigger, as some men are. And Friar was in the first class, for the shot he had fired at Mansel was what is called 'a snap-shot'; yet his aim had been deadly, and if Mansel had not read his movement, he must have been killed.

One leaf of the door was open – wide enough for a man to pass in and out. But I dared not pass that way, while Friar was within; for the sunshine was now very gay and must have been lighting the barn through the open door: the slightest obstruction, therefore, was bound to catch anyone's eye – and Friar was impatiently waiting for such an obstruction to come.

Now the last thing I wanted was that Sloper or Orris should arrive. And one or both might any minute drive up. So I began to study the walls of the barn, to see if some tree would bring me up to the gap which lay between them and the thatch. This I did from behind an oak, in case Friar should emerge, and since I could see no tree that would help me at all, I was about to retire to the end of the barn, when Friar, swearing under his breath, swung out of the door and started along the track, to peer down the road.

Happily, I was all ready. Whilst his back was turned and before he had reached the road, I had whipped between the leaves of the door and out of his sight.

At once I closed my eyes, for, as I had known it would be, the light in the barn was dim. When I opened them after ten seconds, I saw very well.

To the right of the door, loose mounds of hay were filling about a third of the barn: to the left, a cart and two waggons had all that side to themselves. Only a ladder was lying against the wall. At the foot of the piles of hay were lying the weights: each had been turned on its side, to expose its plate; but all the plates were in place and, apparently, had not been moved. This suggested that I had guessed right – that Friar had sent for a tool: then I saw a screwdriver there and a pair of pliers, which told me that he had been trying to take out the plates. The boxes I could not see, but I had no doubt that they were within the hay.

Whilst I was observing these things, my ears were pricked for the warning of Friar's return, for I knew I must deal with him before the others returned. Once I had dealt with Friar, the rest would be easy enough. As like as not, I should be gone with the gems, before Sloper and Orris came back.

Without thinking, I took my stand behind the leaf that was shut, with my pistol clubbed in my hand, for, if I could help it, I did not want to fire.

And then I heard the sound of a car...

That it was coming from Godel I knew in a flash: but the road was open to all, and it might have been anyone's car. But somehow I knew it was not. I knew it was Friar's car...and that Sloper and Orris were in it, bearing the tool that was needed to open the weights.

And so it was.

It overran the barn, and I heard Friar howl imprecations before it had stopped. Then I heard the reverse gear engaged, and somebody bringing her back. Then I heard Friar's excited questions and Sloper reply, "OK". Then came hurried footsteps, followed by the slam of a door.

I had already decided to stay where I was.

Friar was my meat. Once he was out of the way, to deal with the others should not be very hard.

The man came in panting – of such is the lust for gold.

As he entered, I struck him behind the ear – a hammer blow; and he crumpled and fell face downward, with the instrument which he had sent for fast in his hand.

For a moment I strained my ears. Then I picked him up and heaved him into the waggon, standing six feet away.

As I stood again to the door –

" 'Arf a mo," said Orris. "An' wot would you say that was?"

"Wot was?" said Sloper.

"Sort o' rattle," said Orris. "Like somethin' fallin' down."

Be sure I was cursing myself. To be honest, I had made sure that Orris and Sloper would bring the car up to the door. With the police at full stretch, to leave it out on the road was the act of a fool. But one, of course, could have moved it, while the other made for the barn. And now, as luck would have it, both had left the car and made straight for the barn.

The two were listening intently – of that I could have no doubt.

Then –

"Imaginin' things," said Sloper. " 'E's gettin' down to them weights."

"I don't 'ear him at it," said Orris.

Sloper lifted his voice.

"You all right, sir?" he cried.

I whipped out of cover and faced them.

"Friar's had it," I said: "and I'm out for blood this morning, so don't you move."

Their four eyes fast on my pistol, the two stood as still as stone.

"Lock your fingers behind your heads."

They did so without a word.

"Now turn your backs on me."

With my left hand, I took their arms and pitched them, one after the other, into the barn.

It had been in my mind to march them back to the car, to order them into their seats, to take my place in the back and then to force them to drive the car into the barn. Had I not been alone, this would have been easy enough. But, after a moment's reflection, because they were two to one, I knew that I must not risk their failure to play my game. I believe that they would have played it, for when there is sitting behind you the man who has killed your chief, it takes considerable courage to take any action of which he will disapprove. But such a manoeuvre was offering too many chances... Once the engine was running, if one of the two were to thrust the gear into reverse, it would certainly cost him his life, but I might be injured before I could leave the car. Or there might be arms in the car, of which I did not know. And there were other objections, which must be manifest. So, with the greatest reluctance, I made up my mind that the car must stay where it was. If the police were to pass and see it, my race was run. But, placed as I was, I dared not try to move it...

I should, of course, have struck down either one or both of the rogues: and had I not been so weary, I think my brain would have shown me that, whether I liked it or no, the thing must be done. But, when you have made a prisoner, your instinct is to use him as prisoners should be used and not to offer him violence unless he seeks to escape. And instinct is always active, although the brain may be dead.

Be that as it may, I bade Orris stand fast and Sloper open the leaves of the door of the barn, for I needed plenty of light, if I was to watch two such men. And when the leaves were open, I marched them in.

"You see that ladder there? Go and pick it up... Now carry it past the door and mount it against the wall."

After a ludicrous struggle, they did as I said.

Now the top of the wall was some twenty feet above ground; and, to my relief, the ladder was slightly longer than that. This meant I could send them to sit on the top of the wall; for, once the ladder was gone, they could not descend. Perhaps that is saying too much, for any man could have got down: but his movements would have had to be slow and cautiously made, unless, of course, he was willing to risk his neck. And I did not think Sloper or Orris belonged to that reckless class.

Indeed, when I ordered them up, there was the deuce of a scene, which, had I not been so pressed, I should have enjoyed.

"Wot, up there?" protested Sloper. "Oh, be yer age."

"Sloper," I said, "I'm wasting no time on you. If you're not on that wall in one minute, you'll follow your master home."

Sloper looked at me very hard. Then he looked up the ladder and covered his eyes. And then he took a deep breath and went straight up.

As he climbed on to the wall –

"Move along to make room for Orris."

Sloper crawled to the right.

"I can' do it, sir," whimpered Orris. "I 'aven't no 'ead for 'eights."

I cursed him on to the rungs.

When he was halfway up, he said he could go no further. The man was certainly trembling in every limb. But I had no time to spare, for any moment a peasant might enter the barn.

"You'd better make it," I said, "lest a worse thing befall."

"I tell you, I can't, sir. When I was seving – "

I fired just below his feet, and ten seconds later Orris was up on the wall. But the courage which fear had lent him was spent once he was up; and he dared not sit down, as had Sloper, but crouched on his hands and knees, shaking all over, as though his last hour was at hand.

I thrust the ladder sideways, so that it fell: then I recovered my bag and made for the weights.

I laid my pistol down and took out the opening bar.

Then I looked up at the rogues.

"I've too much to do," I said, "to watch you the whole of the time: but two or three times a minute, I shall look up. If, when I look up, I observe that either of you has moved, I shall immediately shoot him. And this will be all the warning he's going to get."

Neither made any answer, but Sloper moistened his lips.

The transfer of the gems took longer than I had expected, for I had to be very careful that none escaped. I had not the time to count them, but I made quite sure that each of the weights was empty, before I laid it aside. I put the gems into the bag with what care I could, praying that the wool about each would keep it from injury. Then I tied the bag tight above them, so that they could not shift, and I tied its neck again, in case they did. Once in the bag, they did not weigh a great deal – less, I should say, than ten pounds, but I cannot be sure.

I screwed back the plates and pitched the weights, now empty, into the hay. It went to my heart to leave them, for Jasper's sake: but I knew that we could not be burdened with things of that bulk. Before we were back at Jade, the gems would weigh heavy enough.

I tested the knots on the bag and, taking up my pistol, I got to my feet. I sought for and found the pistols which I had thrown into the barn and slid them, one after the other, into my coat.

Then I addressed the rogues.

"Don't move just yet," I said, "for I'm coming back. I shall be less than one minute. And anyone not in his place will meet it good and proper – be sure of that."

With that, I stepped to the door…

I need hardly say that I did not intend to return, but I did not wish them to see the way I took. Not that there was much chance of their doing that, for, so far as I could see, a man could only descend by reaching a leaf of the door; and that would be none too pleasant and would cost him a lot of skin. Still, Sloper could have done it in half a minute of time, for he was eight feet from the doorway – and less than that.

Just before I stepped out of the barn, I hung on my heel and leaned out, to be sure that the coast was clear.

In that instant I was aware of some danger behind: my eyes or my ears may have warned me – of that I cannot be sure. But I know that I flung myself forward…

So Sloper missed me…and met the iron ground with a sickening thud.

He made a frantic effort to rise, but his back was plainly broken and almost at once he collapsed.

I glanced at Orris, still crouching upon the wall. Then I turned Sloper over, ran for an armful of hay and set this beneath his head.

"You're a brave man, Sloper," I said.

His eyes never opened: his lips parted a little, but that was all.

" 'Ad to try," he murmured, "coz you done the guvnor in. Call it the ole school tie. 'E was a — all right; but 'e was good to me." He opened his eyes there, and, though, I think, he saw nothing, they roved to and fro. "You 'aven't no water, 'ave you? I think I've broken me beck."

"I'll get some," I said. "Have you got a cup in the car?"

"Cubby-'ole," he murmured.

I threw a long look at Orris, still crouching on the top of the wall and staring down over his shoulder with horror inhabiting his eyes.

Then I put up my pistol, seized the kit-bag and hurried out of the barn.

I knew where there was a rill. Eighty yards off, perhaps, on the other side of the road.

Taking a glass from the car, I ran there as fast as I could; but I had to come back more slowly, for fear of spilling the water which I had won.

Whilst I was going and coming, no traffic passed, and all I saw was a waggon a great way off.

Sloper was as I had left him, but when I looked for Orris, Orris was gone.

I looked round and smothered an oath.

Then I kneeled down beside Sloper and lifted his head.

After all, the man was dying – and dying hard.

He managed to drink a little.

"Nice an' cole," he breathed, "but I can' do any more." I laid back his head: then I soused my handkerchief and wiped the sweat from his face. "You're a good bloke, you are, sir. But Orris is dirt. Beat it, 'e 'as. I'll say 'e can put on an act. 'E 'ad me on."

"How did he get down, Sloper?"

"Run along the wall an' jump in the 'ay. An' you gorn ter get me water. No ole school tie about 'im. Gawd, I'm goin' swimy."

He lay like dead for a moment. Then a terrible spasm convulsed his frame.

As I wiped his face and throat –

"Orris," he panted. " 'E's spiteful. 'E'll try to get you, sir."

"Is he armed?" said I.

"Not if you got his rod. But…'e's a trier…Orris."

"Thank you, Sloper. Don't try and talk any more. I'm sorry about Mr Friar, but I knew it was him or me."

"I'll say it was. 'E meant to 'ave them jools."

Again he seemed to collapse. Indeed, his breath was so low that I thought he was gone. Then, as though with an effort, he opened his glazing eyes.

"Primrose 'Ill," be murmured. "Used to play there, as a kid. Roll on the green grass, while me sister spooned. I 'member…one arter…noon…"

The babble faded and died. And half a minute later, Sloper was dead.

So a faithful servant died as did Shakespeare's Falstaff, a good many years before.

I picked his body up and laid it down in the hay. Then I stepped to the waggon and looked at Friar. He was dead, too. I suppose I had cracked his skull. I searched him, found two pistols and took them away.

Then I left the barn – I confess with my chin on my shoulder, for Orris was yet alive and was out of the bag.

' 'E'll try to get you, sir.'

Well, there was nothing for it. He'd have to try.

I was now much in need of rest; but this I dared not take, until Colette was refreshed. Besides, I must find some spot where I could get my back to a wall.

But first I must do my best to give Orris the slip.

Where the man might be lurking, I had no idea: but I did not believe he could move in the country as I could and I had a very good hope of throwing him off.

With this intent, I passed round the back of the barn. Then I set off towards the frontier, moving beside the road. After covering nearly a mile, I came to a little culvert, allowing a little stream to pass beneath the highway. At once I turned to the left, as though seeking a bridge, and then, behind the cover of bracken, dropped into the bed of the brook. Bent double, I made my way back and, passing under the culvert, clambered up into the woods on the farther side of the road.

Here I lay down, to survey the way I had come. But though I waited ten minutes, I saw no sign of Orris and, except for cars on the road, no movement at all.

Cautiously, I made my way back to where I had left Colette.

As I went, I glanced at my watch – twenty minutes past ten.

Colette was still fast asleep on her bed of leaves, and the food I had set beside her had not been touched.

Though it went to my heart to wake her, I knew we must leave the immediate neighbourhood – not only because of Orris, but in case the bodies of Friar and Sloper were found; for if hue and cry were raised, the woods about the barn would be the first to be searched. We must, therefore, make for some spot on the way to the smuggler's path – if possible, fairly high up, from which we could see about us, yet not be seen.

Then, again, I had to get rid of the pistols which I had won; for I was festooned with the things, which, for one thing, weighed a great deal and, for another, could bear grave witness against me, if I should fall foul of the police. Yet I dared not cast them away, in case Orris should be behind me and pick one up. I could have removed their clips, but, for all I knew, he had a spare clip upon him, and I had no mind to arm my enemy. A torrent was what I needed: for there I could sink them so fast that neither Orris nor anyone else would ever see them again.

Here, perhaps, I should make it quite clear that the fact that Orris was at large hung like some dreadful millstone about my neck. I was, frankly, terribly tired. Thursday had been a hard day, and so had the following night. The rest I had had on Friday had been very poor. Because I was so much concerned, I had hardly slept at all; and, though the repose had refreshed me, I would not have chosen to make such a journey that night. My encounter with Friar and his men had summoned what must have been almost the last reserves I had and whilst I was prepared to go on until I felt it was safe to, so to speak, put up my feet, to be always upon the *qui vive* added very much to a burden which was already as heavy as any that I have borne.

Still, there was nothing for it. Our wonderful luck had returned – for it was a most merciful chance that Friar, and not some peasant, had found the weights. Had some peasant carried them off, albeit in innocence, I cannot think when I should have run them to earth, for, until I had had some rest, to tramp from farm to farm would have been beyond my power. Our run of good fortune was back, and I was not going to break it, so long as I could stand up. Once I was back at Jade, I could sleep for a week.

Taking comfort from this reflection, I took Colette's little hand and put it up to my lips. But that was no good at all. I had to ruffle her curls, before she would open her eyes.

As she started up –

"It's long past ten, my dear. We've got to get on."

Colette clapped a hand to her brow.

"And I was to watch while you slept! Adam, Adam, why did you not leave me behind?" Her eye caught the meagre ration which I had laid out. "You, who are unfit to stand up, have been watching and waiting on me. If ever a trust was betrayed!"

"Come, come, Colette. Had I had need of you, I should have seen that you watched. But I had no need of you, and so it was best you should sleep; for very soon now you must watch, while I take my rest."

Colette put a hand to her head.

"I cannot remember. Why had you no need of me?"

"Because I had work to do. I had to recover the weights."

Colette stared.

"That's right. The weights were gone. And you have been looking for them. I could have helped you there."

"I found them, my dear. And I have the gems here, in my bag."

"Adam!"

"I can hardly believe it myself, but there they are. But since I must hold what I have, I want you to eat your breakfast and then strike out with me for the smuggler's path. I don't want to go so far: but we must get away from here. We must find some fold in the hills in which we can pass the day – one of us keeping watch, while the other sleeps. I think there are many such places, where we can lie safe. But the sooner we find one, the better – for that, you must take my word. You shall know everything later: but now I want to get on."

Colette stood up at once.

"I will break my fast there," she said, and picked up the food.

"Eat a little now," I said. " It will give you strength."

She shook her head.

"My appetite will be the better, when we are safe."

She thrust the scraps into her pouch. I threw a look over my shoulder and pointed the way.

"Make for that stricken tree: I'll follow behind."

So began an excursion which lasted for nearly three hours. For most of that time we had to make our own path: for all of that time I had to keep our direction, carry those cursed pistols and look behind.

And then at last, I saw, a long way below us, the road which presently ran between the dell I had found and the smuggler's path: and fifty feet up was a little grass covered lip which argued a dip or hollow upon its farther side.

I should, I know, have approached this by a circuitous. route. But I was at the end of my tether, and that is the truth. My steps had become uncertain, my legs were trembling beneath me of sheer fatigue.

How I covered those fifty feet, I shall never know; but, close upon the heels of Colette, I stumbled over the lip, to sink down in a little aerie, which in its shape resembled a gravy-well.

Colette was kneeling beside me, with fear in her beautiful eyes.

"Adam, Adam darling, you look so ill."

"I'm done, my sweet. I shall have to doze for a little. There is where you come in. Will you watch while I rest?"

"You know I will. But – "

"In half an hour," I said, "I shall be myself again. It must not be more than that. Unstrap my watch." She took my watch from my wrist. "In half an hour from now, I have a duty to do. It will not take very long, and then I will rest again. But I charge you, Colette, to wake me in half an hour."

"It will break my heart," she said, "but I will do as you say."

"Watch well, Colette, especially the way we have come. If you see any sort of movement, rouse me at once. I do not want to be taken, now I have got so far."

"If," said Colette, "we are taken, it will not be because I have slept at my post."

I smiled and nodded. Then I pillowed my head on the kit-bag and fell asleep.

As, I suppose, was natural, my half hour seemed to be gone as soon as it had begun; indeed, when Colette touched my shoulder, my hand went at once to my pistol, because I imagined she had ill news to report. Then she showed me my watch, and I saw it was a quarter to two.

Still, my sleep had refreshed me and now I felt more than able to do what I had to do. This was to find some water in which I could sink the firearms belonging to Friar and his men. The duty was such as had to be properly done; for Orris unarmed was a nuisance, but Orris armed could make an end of me before I knew he was there.

I was sorely tempted to leave Colette in the aerie against my return, and, but for Orris, I would have: but, though I was ready to swear that we had left him behind, I dared not take the risk of exposing Colette to the mercy of such a man. And, of course, being very tired, we had made poor time from the barn; but Orris was fresh.

Colette had returned to her post and was looking out.

She was lying flat, as a soldier lies upon the range, with her eyes just above the lip; and her head was slowly moving, which showed she was sweeping the ground upon every side. Such devotion to duty touched me, as nothing else could have done, for, though she was out of her depth and though she was mad to know how I had recovered the gems, she had put away childish things. She had her orders, and that was enough for her. Later on, perhaps: but now she was on parade. Few girls, I think, would have observed such discipline.

"Don't move, Colette, but listen to what I am going to say. Directly south-west there's a ridge, about twenty-five paces away. I'm going to look over that. Don't call if you see any movement, but come to me."

"Very well, Adam," she said.

Laden with kit-bag and pistols – I dared leave neither behind – I clambered up to the ridge, there to lie down. As I had hoped it would, this commanded the country for two or three miles, and I very soon saw the wink of tumbling water, further and lower than I liked it, but not too far. Listening intently, I thought I could hear its song. And then I knew that the water which I could hear must be closer than that. Studying the lie of the land, I judged that there was a valley I could not see, not very much more than a quarter of a mile away: if I was right, and there was a torrent within it, this should be a vigorous head of water, that, but for the valley that kept it, would be declaring its presence with a much louder voice.

(That in fact I was right does me no credit at all, for I am well used to mountains and know and love the order in which hills stand: I can read the hang of their forests, the course which their waters take; and when a page of that lovely book is hidden, I am able to guess its contents more surely than other men. I have not the gift of tongues, but the speech and language of Nature has always appealed to me: and perhaps because I have always sat at her feet, I have come to learn it a little, so that I can interpret some of her simpler ways. Then, again, my wife has taught me: and she can commune with Nature, can talk with birds and with beasts and set them at ease, can stand in a wood blindfold and name the trees about her by hearing the answer their branches give to the wind.)

I made my way back to the aerie and bade Colette come with me.

Within ten minutes of time we had struck a sturdy stream, which was pounding out of the mountains with all the time-honoured flourish that tumbling water is always so proud to wear. And there, while Colette kept watch, I committed to its charge first the rounds and then the pistols to which they belonged. Then I soused my head and drank and rinsed my arms and my hands – and never found water more grateful in all my life. Then I watched while Colette made her toilet, if you can give it that name. To be honest, I think you can, for, when she came to my side and smiled into my eyes, I saw that fountains still practised their ancient art. Her lovely face was painted, her beautiful head was tired, for her colour was high and her hair was powdered with little brilliants of water that rendered the glory of the sunshine with all their might.

"You must be a nymph," I said.

"Like Eve?"

"That's right. Eve is a nymph. I found her up in the mountains and carried her off."

"Am I to believe you, Adam?"

"Ask her, when you meet her, and she will confirm what I say. She mayn't admit she's a nymph, but I think she is."

"I shall know if she is: for if she is just a woman she will not like me."

"Why d'you say that, Colette?"

"Because I have had her husband all to myself. If I had a hump on my back, she would not mind. But I have no hump on my back and I am in love with you."

"Colette, for God's sake – "

"She is not like you, for you are very simple. She will know, the moment she sees my face. And if she is all you say, she will put her arms about me and love me for loving you. But if she is just a woman, I shall be hateful in her sight."

I put a hand to my head.

"Is that why you came?" I said.

"Of course, my dear. When you were to run into danger, how could I stay behind? But I am not going to trespass – I know my place. And it would do no good, for Eve has all your heart. I hope very much you will kiss me, when we have made our landfall and all is well: but I know that it will mean nothing, because, if Eve were here, I should not exist."

I took her face in my hands and kissed her eyes and her lips.

"You will always exist," I said, "for so long as I live. It is perfectly true that Jenny has all my heart: but I am not made of stone, and when a great lady does me such honour as this – "

"But I am not a great lady."

"You are one of the greatest ladies that I have ever known."

She did not speak, but she put her arms round my neck and pressed her cheek tight against mine. Then she threw back her head and smiled.

"Do you wonder that I love you?" she said.

"Yes," I said. "I find it remarkable."

And there something made me look round.

At the head of the miniature valley, I saw a bough spring into place.

Quick as a flash, I fired. And then I was climbing the bank as fast as I could. But when I was up, there was no sign of any man. Searching the spot at which I had seen the movement, I found a mark that might have been made by a heel: but though I sought high and low, Orris, if it was he, had made himself scarce. Of course, the roar of the water swallowed the sound of any hasty retreat, and the neighbourhood offered good cover on every side.

I turned to Colette, who had followed as fast as she could.

"This is a nuisance," I said. "I think I know who it was, and if I am right, he's unarmed. For all that, he is a trier, as I have reason to know. If we are careful, I don't see what he can do: but it means that we can't let up, as we did just now." Looking round, I fingered my chin. "I had meant to go back to where I had my sleep: but I think he must know that place, and so we had better go on. If we can find a spot overlooking the smuggler's path, we can take it in turns to rest until dusk comes in. And then, though he's trailed us so far, we should be able to lose him for good and all."

I think my decision was good, but I made it heavily; for I was still terribly tired, and I had promised myself that, when we got back to our aerie – but ten minutes' walk – I should sleep for another hour, before relieving Colette. And now we must struggle on, till we found a new resting place.

And there I saw that Colette looked very much shaken…

I put my arm about her and made her sit down.

"I told you, my sweet, that the way I was going was one that no woman should take."

Colette put a hand to her head.

"I am very sorry," she said. "I shall not do it again. I have seen shots fired at a fair, but never in an endeavour to kill a man."

Lamely enough –

"I didn't kill him," I said.

"I know. I wish you had. You were terribly quick."

I smiled.

"Had it been Mansel," I said, "he would have fired before the bough had stopped moving – and got his man."

Colette sighed.

"First Palin, then Mansel," she said. "I am tired of these paragons. I think you do very well. In any event, you do well enough for me."

"I think," I said, "I think you are better now. If so, let us get on: for we must, both of us, rest before we set out for Jade."

Colette got to her feet.

"You made me cross, and so you made me better: I cannot bear that you should diminish yourself. I sleep like the dead, and wake – to find that, while I was sleeping, you have recovered the gems. The quest was to me quite hopeless. It was because it was hopeless that I, the weaker vessel, could not go on. The shock turned my blood to water. I just collapsed. But you went on – and achieved the impossible thing. How many hours have you slept since Wednesday night? And today is Saturday. And still you are up and doing – and ready to cross the frontier, torrent and all. Such endurance is supernatural: only the greatest heart could so overcome the flesh. Yet, Palin and Mansel are very much finer than you. The one will make me laugh – "

"So he will," I said, doggedly.

Colette stamped her foot.

"I have no desire," she said, "to be made to laugh."

"You'll fall for Mansel," I said. "You see if you don't. For there is about him a royalty that nobody can deny."

Colette kissed her hand and put it up to my lips.

"Perhaps. But I shall not love him." She looked round. "Let us go on. I want you to take your rest."

An hour and more went by before we had found a spot which I could approve. Though not as good as the aerie, it did very well. Two miles ahead I could see the smuggler's way, and there was a cliff behind us, to cover our rear. And box bushes, growing about it, gave cover enough.

As we threw ourselves down –

"Listen, my lady," I said. "It is nearly half past three, and, now that I see the way, I do not think we need move until half past eight. That gives us five hours. I think I must sleep for one hour. Then you will sleep for two. Then I shall sleep for two more. And then we will leave. Will you promise upon your honour to wake me at half past four?"

"On one condition, I give you my word," said Colette. "That is that at half past four you tell me something that I should like to know."

"Why what is that, Colette?"

"Have you to ask, Adam?"

"You must tell me," I said, "for I am too tired to think."

Colette put her head on one side.

"You must forgive me," she said. "I am not like Bell. I am sure Bell asks no questions. But I should like to know how you came by the gems."

I closed my eyes.

"By God, Colette, I'm sorry."

She was on her knees and had caught my hand to her breast.

"Adam, dear, you are used to working with men. And while deeds have to be done, men have no time for words. When the action is over, then they will talk. But I am a woman, Adam. And I will wager that Eve would have asked before now."

I began to laugh…

But before I could start my tale, she had moved to a boulder which lay at the foot of the cliff. Sitting there, she could see about us: yet, because of the box, she could hardly be seen. I watched her steadily searching the neighbouring mountainside. Then I took off my wristwatch and rose and put it into her hand.

"At half past four," I said.

"O man of few words," she said, "at half past four."

"O martinet," said I, "at five and twenty to five."

She did not look at me, but a smile stole into her face. Then, once again, I laid my head down on my kit-bag and fell asleep.

It was five o'clock, and I was keeping watch. Colette was lying beside me, fast asleep.

My tale had been told in some detail, whilst we were breaking our fast: and now at last I was able to think things over, measure our chances and generally look ahead.

We had been very fortunate so far, for we had been moving in country near enough to the border to claim the casual attention of frontier-guards. Yet we had met no one at all, and, if we had been observed, we had not been approached. Then, again, we had reached a point from which, in less than an hour, we could strike the smuggler's way, and if we did not move until the shadows were falling, the odds against some encounter were long, indeed.

Three things only concerned me.

The first was that, though we were resting, we were extremely tired. How many miles lay before us, I neither knew nor cared: I knew that we could cover them somehow – if all went well. But when a path is so rough as not to deserve that name, when it is strewn with boulders and crossed by mountain streams…when you are moving in darkness and, though you carry a torch, you must on no account use it to guide your steps…and when you are almost too tired to lift up your feet…then it is easy to stumble, to wrench or sprain an ankle or even to break a leg. I did not think it likely that I should do such a thing; but Colette was not used, as I was, to journeys like this, and her legs were very slender and were not furnished, as mine were, with tendons like steel.

The second was the barrier water.

We had crossed this without any fuss the night before: but then we were fresh. Colette's weight had been nothing, and she had done all that I asked her and done it well. But now we were very tired…and there were the gems to be carried…and the landing was not so easy upon the opposite side. And if I should bungle the business and fail to land, I was not at all sure that I should have the strength to climb the dangling rope and so gain the bough. (I have already shown that, though he hung in mid-air, a man had only to climb to the branch to which the rope was made fast: then he could climb down the tree, which grew upon the Italian side of the flood.) Then and there I decided that, for that sinister passage, Colette must bear the gems. The bag could be tied to her neck and could rest on her back. Then, if I failed to land, by standing upon my shoulders, she should, I thought, be able to reach the bough, so that, though I could not follow, the gems would be saved.

And the third of the things was Orris.

I had no doubt at all that it was he that had peered from the head of the little valley in which we had stood: and I was surprised and dismayed that such a man should have managed, in country so much against him, to cling to our heels. If he had got so far, it seemed extremely unlikely that we had shaken him off: and if I was right in this, he would assuredly follow us down to the smuggler's way. It would be dark by then, but the night would favour Orris as much as it favoured us, for, while it would be harder to see us, he could approach much closer without being seen. Over all, I had a feeling that I had not done with the man. Since I was armed and weighed far more than he did, he would not be wise to attack: but the battle is not always to the strong, and Fortune will smile upon the man who 'will never let go'.

There was nothing to be done, I decided, but to lay a trap for Orris and pray that he would walk in. When you wish to tackle a man who is following you, you turn a corner and stop and wait for him to come round. That is, of course, elementary. Now in the ordinary way, Orris was far too skilful to enter a trap like that: but across the smuggler's way, there was running a minor torrent, none too easy to cross. There were, I daresay, a score of ways across it, but I had found only one which was close to the path. And this must be carefully taken, because the water was rough. If then we took this way – and turned aside in the bushes upon the opposite side, Orris, if he was behind us, must surely walk into my arms. For men of his sort dislike a noisy water, although, as a rule, its bark is worse than its bite.

Of such were my reflections that beautiful summer evening, while sunshine and shadow fought for the everlasting hills. Foot by foot, the former receded, and the exquisite peace of sundown covered the great retreat. The breeze hauled down its flag: sounds I had not been aware of stole on the air; and the cool of the valleys about us rose up in a cloud of fragrance no eye could see, refreshing my tired senses and lacing, as with a cordial, each breath I drew.

'Now came still Evening on...'

I woke Colette, as I had sworn to wake her, just short of seven o'clock: but I had no desire to sleep, so the two of us watched together until it was nearly eight.

With her head against my shoulder –

"It is nearly time," said Colette. "I cannot see forty paces: and when I cannot see twenty, we must be gone."

I put an arm about her.

"Yes, my gallant Colette, it is nearly time."

"You have won your match," she said. "I think you will always win; for no one and nothing can stand against the force of your will."

"I have had many failures, Colette; and I am not home yet."

"You may call them failures, though I do not think most people would. You see, I know you, Adam. There is no cunning in you, although you are very wise: but there is within you a drive, the like of which I have never imagined before. When the wind was against us at Godel, you took charge – and raised the big tent in its teeth in ten minutes of time. It is that determination that forces the hand of Fortune, whether she will or no. And so we shall cross the frontier, bearing the gems...the gems which are a nonsuch...which the Boche and Friar and all the police in the country were out to take. But you will carry them out, as you meant to do. And tomorrow evening I shall not sit by your side...with your strong arm about me and my head against your breast. We are alone now, and so we can do as we please. There is no one to watch or whisper, because I have lost my heart."

I took a deep breath.

"Do you want to distress me, Colette? I am a most ordinary man, but I belong to a world that you do not know. If you were to enter that world, you would take it by storm – a thing I have never done and could never do. You would be the rage, Colette. You would have so many suitors, you would not know which to choose. And then I should lose my stature, and you would find me a very ordinary man."

"Did Eve do that?" said Colette.

I swallowed.

"I don't think she ever found me anything else."

"Shall we say she was easily pleased?"

"That goes without saying," I said.

"Then we shall get on together, for so am I."

"I cannot argue," I said. "I never could. I only feed my opponent, as you can see. But I can make a plain statement, and here it is. During this venture of ours, you have been my rod and my staff. I could not have done, without you, what I have done. Now Bell has often been my rod and my staff. But you have been more than that. A great deal more. Twenty-four hours ago, when you came running towards me, my heart leaped up. When I wake, to meet your smile, I feel a new man. The sight of you, moving before me, makes me less tired. And when I hold you like this, the courage that is within you seems to flow into my veins. From first to last, Colette, you have been the light of my eyes."

Colette made no answer, but only sat very still.

When at last I turned to regard her, I saw that tears were trickling upon her cheeks.

"Colette, my beauty!"

She hid her face in my jacket and spoke very low.

"I am – very – happy, my darling. A spring in my heart has broken, that I never knew was there. Your 'plain statement' has set it running; and now, though my body may age, my heart will be always young."

With my eyes on the fading landscape, I sat very still, holding her close and feeling as feels a rich man who, in some game of hazard, has won from his poor opponent all that he had.

Nearly five hours had gone by and I could hear the roar of the torrent, a quarter of a mile ahead.

So far all had gone well.

Colette had never faltered, and, though I found the gems heavy – a signal, if ever there was one, that I was upon my last legs – the cool, night air, inspired with the generous virtue of countless springs, had been the saving of me. Tired as I was, I felt fresher than I had felt all day, because, I suppose, my blood was fortified.

One mercy we had been vouchsafed – Orris was gone. To this I could not swear, for I had not killed the man nor had I seen him die. But two miles back I had set my trap for him, and, though I had waited five minutes, he had not appeared. This was a great relief, for up to then I had walked with my chin on my shoulder, in case of accidents. But now it seemed clear that we could dismiss the spectre which had been lurking behind us for so many hours.

I touched Colette on her shoulder.

As she turned –

"Five minutes' rest." I said.

We turned aside and sat down.

"You can hear the water, Colette?"

"Yes, Adam."

"When we come to cross it, I want you to wear the gems. I will fasten the cord round your neck and bind the bag to your back. So you will have your arms free. When we are over the torrent, then I will take them again."

Her hand stole into mine.

"Of course I will bear them, Adam: but why do you wish me to?"

"In case I should fail to land. Then, when the rope stops swinging, we shall be hanging directly over the water, beneath a great bough. I do not think it will happen; but, if it should, when I jerk my head – for of course we cannot talk – you must lay hold of the rope, mount on my shoulders and clamber on to the bough. Move along it at once, until you come to the trunk. There you can wait for me or slip down to the ground."

"I see," said Colette. "And you?"

"Once your weight is gone, I shall follow you up. But this is only in case I should fail to land."

"You might have failed to land when we crossed before. But you gave me no such instructions before we crossed."

"I know. I should have done so. But now we have the gems with us, and we must take no risks."

"I see," said Colette, again. "And you will follow me up?"

"That's right."

"And if you have not the strength to climb the rope?"

I laughed.

"Of course I shall have the strength. It's only about six feet; and I shall be up on the bough before you have reached the trunk."

Colette held my hand very tight.

"Listen, my very dear. Let us cross the water in turn. I will go first, if you like. But for you to support us both is a fearful strain. And if you should fail to land...and, when the rope has stopped swinging, I am to stand upon your shoulders, as though upon the rung of a ladder, to reach the bough...I know you are very strong, but that is to ask too much of any man. You will see me up, I know: but supposing, after that, your tired arms cannot hoist you on to the bough..."

I shook my head.

"My sweet, I cannot let you cross that water alone. But I will meet you half way. Instead of clasping my neck, you shall lay hold of the rope before we take off. That will relieve me a lot. In any event, your weight is nothing at all, and I am so glad to carry 'the light of my eyes'."

Colette caught my hand to her lips.

After a moment –

"I will do as you say," she said. "I will not fail you, my dear."

And then we were moving again. Of instinct, I looked behind, but nothing blotted the darkness, which was not Stygian. Though there was no moon, the stars were very bright, and I could tell substance from shadow five or six paces away.

So we came to the savage water that barred our way.

At once I sought for the staple, to find the rope safe and sound. Having made sure, I left it; for I did not want to be hampered while I attired Colette. This was easy to do; but I had to open the kit-bag, to get at a length of cord. I did not pass the cord round her neck, for fear of embarrassing her, but over her shoulders, instead: then I crossed the ends on her chest and brought them back under her arms: then with four or five turns I bound the bag to her body, so that it could not move.

"Put up your arms, my beauty, and show me you're free to move."

She did as I said, bending forward and sideways and shaking herself. But the bag never moved.

"I shan't speak again, till we're over. But please hold on very tight, for the fairest of all the gems is not in the bag."

She made as though she would answer, but when I bent my head, I felt her lips on my cheek.

For a moment, I held her close.

Then I stepped to the staple and loosed the rope.

I have said that, attached to the rope, was a fishing line. Before I unfastened the former, I took two turns of the latter about my wrist. I did this more of instinct than of intelligence, for the fishing line was also attached to the staple, and, had I let the rope go, I had but to pick up the line to pull it in. But, because I was so weary, I did as I did.

When I got back to Colette, she had put off her brogues and, tying them by their laces, had hung them about her neck. It was too late to protest, but I knew she had done it to spare me, in case she must mount upon my shoulders, to make her way into the tree.

And then, for the first time, I looked at that thirsty water, flowing out of and into the darkness and raging for a turbulent moment under our eyes. Savage, cold, ruthless, unearthly strong, though it did not seem to flaunt it, its power was manifest. The weight of a breaker is there for all to see – and the strength which it spends on some rock or the head of some pier. But the weight and fury of the torrent was more restrained and seemed to swallow resistance, punishing all obstruction, forcing narrows with a grim, overbearing thrust and reducing to the rank of pebbles the boulders that littered its bed.

Well, I had beaten it twice, and I would beat it again.

I turned to measure my distance.

Then I laid hold of the rope and signed to Colette.

In a trice she was on my back and, stretching up her arms, had grasped the rope above the grip of my hands.

I turned to smile into her eyes, and she bent her head.

I moved back as far as I could...

Then I hurled myself forward, with all my might.

And, as I launched us, somebody 'tackled' me low...

I knew, of course, who it was. What I shall never know is how, for all those miles, he had clung to our heels, not once declaring his presence, never approaching too close, nor falling too far behind, avoiding the trap I had set and sinking his very existence, until at last he had made me drop my guard. For that was what Orris had done. Had I looked over my shoulder before I took off, he must either have stayed in the shadows or launched his attack while my feet were still on the ground. But I did not look over my shoulder and so I played into his hands.

I sometimes think that he must have been able to see, as cats are said to be able, as well by night as by day: which would resolve the riddle, for the blind would then have been leading a rogue with the gift of sight.

Be that as it may, at the most perilous moment, Orris had struck.

He had, of course, surveyed our preparations – had watched me attire Colette and then unfasten the rope. Till then he had not perceived how we were proposing to cross so important a stream. But when, with Colette on my back, I laid hold of the rope, he saw, I suppose, in a flash not only how we were to cross, but that, once we had left the bank, he would see us no more.

And so he dropped his mask and flung himself upon me, to spoil our game.

By the mercy of God, he moved one instant too late to reach Colette, but he caught me about the thighs, and the three of us swung together over the flood.

The strain upon my arms was awful, but somehow I kept my hold; and, because of the drag on the rope at the moment of taking off, we hardly passed the dead centre and came to rest almost at once.

I jerked my head to the left.

At once Colette drew herself up…Then her knees were upon my shoulders…and then her feet…

For a moment she seemed to be groping…

And then she gave a light spring and I knew she was up on the bough.

At once I lashed out at Orris, as best I could. I dared not relax my grip, which was failing fast, but I kicked and squirmed like a madman, to shake him off. But he only clung the closer, using his nails on my flesh as the claws of a beast – a behaviour, I fancy, dictated as much by fear as by malice, for the torrent threatened much more than a watery grave.

So we fought this desperate battle, both very badly placed; for if he won, we should, both of us, die together a very unpleasant death; but if I won, I should not have the strength left to climb the rope and so should lose my life a few moments later than he.

And then he ended the matter by sinking his teeth in my leg.

I can only suppose that this was a dying gesture – the impulse of the jackal to mutilate the being he cannot kill. Be that as it may, it enraged me as nothing else he had done, and since I had no hope left, I determined to send him to hell before the torrent below us should rob me of my clear right.

I took my right hand from the rope and felt for and found his throat. And then I tore him off me and shook him with all my might. Then I dragged his face up to mine and looked into his eyes, to meet the bright stare of horror, with which such beings greet death. So for one last moment. Then my left hand gave in, and, thrusting Orris before me, I fell down into the race.

In that instant he must have died, for the force of the water slammed us against a boulder as though we were lay-figures or baulks of wood. But though my breath was taken, I was not hurt, for Orris' body was my buffer and took the shock. Then the water swept me sideways to jam me in the jaws of a chasm between two rocks: but, though I was bruised and shaken, my head was above the flood. Till then I had not thought to make any effort at all to save my life: I had never dreamed I could live in such water as that: but now, although I was in a straitjacket, I was not dead. I could neither see nor hear, and the movement and the bellow about me bade fair to disorder my wits. I was fast in a welter of tumult, such as I never conceived, that overwhelmed mind and body – a blinding, deafening volume of merciless force that was holding my frame in a vice and was viciously lashing my face, which was looking upstream. But it was not injuring me, and, so far as I could judge, I was still unhurt. Still, if I was to go on living, I knew I must leave the water as quickly as ever I could, for, for one thing, the turmoil and uproar would very soon steal my brain and, for another, the water was very cold; and once my limbs were numbed, I could never emerge alive.

And then I remembered the rope…

(This shows, I think, how dazed and shaken I was, for I had entirely forgotten the obvious and only thing which could at all avail me to save my life.)

The question was how to regain it. And then I remembered the line of which I had taken two turns about my wrist. I recalled that this had been taut, when I was still in mid-air; it was just possible, therefore, that it was still in place.

Such was the pressure of the water, it took me all I knew to bring my right hand over to meet my left, when at once this encountered the line, still fast to my wrist.

A few moments later, I had the rope in my hands.

This I drew gradually tight, hauling it in against the will of the torrent, which seemed to be doing its best to tear it away. Then I pulled myself up a little out of the pounding flood, till my neck was clear of the water and so I could turn my head. I could still see next to nothing, because of the spray, but I did make out that the rock on my right, that is to say, towards the Italian side, was higher than that on my left. If, then, I could get below it, I might find a little shelter – if you can give it that name; for the rock, being high, would receive the full force of the water, but, I, being under its lee, should only receive the inrush from either side.

I had no means of knowing whether the length of the rope would allow me to make this move: but I knew that, if I stayed where I was, I must surely die, and since, as I saw it, there was no better move which I could endeavour to make, I hauled myself slowly forward, trying to bear to the right.

It was the hardest labour, and more than once I very near threw in my hand, for I was breasting a savage, relentless force, to which flesh and blood were playthings, which frowned upon obstruction, which seemed determined to tear the rope from my grasp; for the thrash of the rope's end behind me was unbelievable.

The critical moment would come, when I was free of the chasm in the jaws of which I had stuck, for then the race would sweep my legs from beneath me and do its very utmost to carry me off. Indeed, I had small hope of reaching my rock, for only the current itself could carry me there.

As I had foreseen, when I pulled myself clear of the cleft, my legs were swept from beneath me before I could think, but thrusting out my left leg, I encountered an edge of rock, and that enabled me to bear to the right. Paying out a little rope, I found myself lying across the jaws of the chasm in which I had lately been held, with my shoulders against the rock I was trying to reach: but the pressure upon my stomach was painfully high and I knew I must move or perish before many moments had passed. In desperation, I took my right hand from the rope, and sought for some handhold by which I could drag myself on. This I found almost at once, for my fingers encountered a crevice which seemed to be full of slime. I instantly dragged myself forward, taking, as I did so, a fearful punishment; for the water was actually breaking about my head and, if my left hand had slipped, my skull would at once have been fractured against the rock. And then I was clear of the chasm and was lying against my rock, with my right foot braced against something – I know not what, and, to my great relief, with both hands again on the rope.

I pulled myself up a little and tried to take stock: for my strength was nearly gone, and I knew if I made one mistake, it would be my last. And then I saw that the sloping top of my rock was hardly awash. Perhaps two inches of water were flowing over its head, which meant I could stand upon it, provided I had my rope.

Once again I took my right hand away from the rope and, throwing up my right arm, found the edge of the rock with my armpit and strove to heave myself up; but the gesture had cost me the little foothold I had and the water seized my legs and pinned and drove them against the side of the rock. Since this had been worn away, I seemed to be in a fair way to be broken in two, for my body was being bent sideways into a bow, but I had enough sense to pay out a little rope, and a moment later had both my arms on the rock. So some of the strain was gone, and, though my body was still bent into a bow, at least I was not being tortured, for now my legs were directly beneath my arms. But my back was now being pounded as never before. It seemed as though tons of water were falling upon my spine – and not continuously, but with shock upon shock, for that is the way of a torrent, if it is heavy enough, as any man who has watched one will readily testify.

I think it goes without saying that only a man of iron could endure for long such terrible punishment, and once again in my life I proved the truth of the adage that out of the eater will sometimes come forth meat. Driven to desperation, I made such an effort as I never made before. With both my hands on the rope, I bent my elbows and hoisted my body up: then somehow I bent my knees, and a moment later I was swept on to the rock.

And there I lay, all asprawl, with shallow water about me, flowing as fast as it could, but with a force that was insignificant. Still, when I dropped my head, it ran into my mouth; so I heaved on my faithful rope until I was sitting up with my back to the stream. And then, at last, I relaxed, with the rope lying over my shoulder tight in my hands, drawing deep, sobbing breaths, as a man that has run himself out.

Although this escape from death has taken some time to tell, I very much doubt if more than two minutes went by between the end of Orris and my coming out of the storm. At the time, it seemed longer than that...it seemed a century. But that is always the way, when you walk with Death.

How long I sat upon that rock, I have no idea; but I was so much exhausted that I was half way to stupor, when something that was not water struck me upon my left cheek.

At once I roused myself and looked to the left; and there, ten paces away, was standing Colette. I could see the white of her shirt and after a little I made out the white of her face.

This brought me back to my senses. I might be out of the pit, but I was not out of the wood. And I had to get out of the wood...and back to Jade.

To be perfectly frank, I had forgotten Colette and the gems and everything. But when a man fights for his life, he can think about little else, and in this particular conflict I had been matched against no ordinary foe.

I lifted an arm, in the hope that she would see it. Then I turned to the business of reaching the bank.

I will not set down in detail how I achieved this end, for it cannot be of much interest and it would take too long. Enough that it was not easy, that, being very tired, right at the last, I stumbled and must have lost my race, had not Colette had the wit to see the help I needed and to thrust it into my hands.

I was only four feet from the bank and I still had my rope. Had this been attached to the bank, and not to the tree, by hauling upon it I could have pulled myself in: but when I hauled upon it, I pulled myself upstream and away from the bank. In an effort to counter this trend, I took a false step, and I had to throw out my right hand to save myself from falling against a rock. And then I was off my balance and could not get my right hand back to the rope. And there I hung, with the water, now only waist deep, swirling and gobbling about me and putting such a drag on the half of my body it had that the muscles of my left arm were cracking beneath the strain.

And then twigs brushed my face…

Colette had bent down a sapling and guided it into my arms. I clutched it with my right hand…

Its trunk was slender enough, but its roots were firm, and they and my rope, between them, held me safe. So for perhaps two minutes. Then another sapling came down, and on that was lying the cord with which I had bound the kit-bag upon Colette's back. This she had doubled twice over, and when I pulled upon it, I knew it was fast to some tree.

So I came out of the water and on to dry land.

Now whether or no I fainted, I cannot say; but the next thing that I remember is that I was stripped to the waist and Colette was kneeling across me, chafing my chest and my sides.

I had not the strength to sit up, but I cried her name.

She lowered her face to mine.

"Better, my darling?"

"The gems," I said. "Where are they?"

"The cursed things," said Colette, "are lying beside your head."

I began to laugh, and Colette returned to her labour, jerking out speech as she worked.

"Are you surprised that I hate them? They almost cost you your life. What are they all beside one hair of your head? You risk your life ten times over to get them as far as this: and then, when your strength has failed, you give them to me to carry – and let your life go. Because He loves you, the good God gave it back. It is either that, or you are a demi-god; for Hercules himself could hardly have fought that water and won his match. And if he had, he would have done thirteen labours, instead of twelve."

Here I begged her to stop her work on my chest and ribs: for her indignation was venting itself on my skin, and, indeed, I was very much better and almost fit to proceed.

As I sat up –

"But for Colette," I said, "neither I nor the gems would be here. I do not think that we should have got so far. But we should have got no further – and that's God's truth. And now, my beauty, I think that we should get on. We are still in the danger zone, and we do not want to be taken upon the last lap."

Colette was wringing the water out of my shirt.

"You cannot wear this, Adam."

I took it out of her hand.

"It will soon get dry," I said. "And I would sooner wear it than carry it on my back."

I shall never know how we covered those last few miles, for I was half dead and Colette could hardly stand up. With my arm about her shoulders, I shambled along somehow, the kit-bag bound to my back. Now and again we stopped for five minutes or so, but only where I could lean against a rock or a tree: for I dared not sit down, for fear that, if I did, I should be unable to rise.

We were, of course, a long way behind our time, and the sun was up before we had left the valleys and reached the region no frontier-guards patrol. But, perhaps because it was Sunday, we were not stopped or fired on, although I think that a smuggler would have had his heart in his mouth.

It was very near half past six when I saw three figures ahead.

"It's Jasper and Bell," shrieked Colette. "And another I do not know."

"Try Andrew Palin," I croaked – and there my legs gave way, and I fell down on the ground.

Colette was down on her knees.

"Adam, Adam, my darling."

"It's quite all right, my beauty. It's when you see help is at hand that your muscles give way." I threw a glance over my shoulder. "Kiss me quickly, great heart, for they wouldn't understand."

Colette threw her arms about me and held me tight. Then she bent her head and kissed me upon the lips.

"Light of my eyes," I murmured…

When the three came over the ridge, I was asleep in her arms.

Bell was kneeling beside me, shaking my arm.

"Miss Colette says you're all right, sir, but I've never seen you so pale."

"I'm quite all right, Bell. But I'm devilish tired."

Palin was kneeling upon the opposite side.

"You don't look too good, Chandos. You're sure you're not hurt?"

I raised myself on an elbow.

"Look here," I said, laughing; "this isn't holy ground. And I'm not going to die just yet. I'll say I'm tired. And, like the sainted Paul, I have fought with beasts."

"I do hope you did murder," said Palin. "Just for the look of the thing. It makes it so much more romantic."

"I did Friar in," I said, laughing. "But that was an execution – he wasn't fair to Goat."

"Most unfair," said Palin. "In fact, he was more than unfair. He was almost rude. And you were rude back. What a very beautiful thought!"

"That'll do," said I. "You were asking after my health. Let me say, once for all, that I am organically sound. But see to Colette, will you? But for her, I shouldn't be here. And that's God's truth. But she can hardly stand up, and she doesn't weigh very much. D'you think you could carry her, Palin? I'd do it, if I was able – and she deserves the best."

"Consider it done," said Palin, and got to his feet.

"You take the kit-bag, Bell, and hitch it on to your back."

As he was doing my bidding –

"And Orris, sir?" said Bell.

"I – contributed to his death…but he almost got me, Bell. Sloper was dead right. I tore him off me at last, but he never let go."

Bell was nodding his head.

"I was always afraid of him, sir. He had a look of Casemate about him. An' all day yesterday I couldn't get him out of my mind."

"You're perfectly right," I said. "He had a look of Casemate. So history repeats herself, for they both of them got a long way – and both of them failed."

Casemate was a mean fellow – an underling rogue: but that Mansel is living today was not his fault.

And then came Jasper.

With my hand in his –

"Well, Jasper," I said. "You would have me take the lad."

"I am proud that you did so, sir."

"When you answered for his courage, you were on very sure ground. He has one of the greatest hearts that I have ever known. He has been my rod and my staff. Had I not taken him with me, I must have lost my life."

Tears began to trickle down Jasper's cheeks.

"I have no words," he said simply. "My cup is full."

A few moments later, our strange procession took shape. First Palin, with Colette in his arms. Then myself, between Bell and Jasper, an arm about either's neck. And Bell was bearing the kit-bag upon his back.

I held the party back, for, though I did my best, I could hardly move my legs and kept on falling asleep. Indeed, I shall never know how we got as far as we did, before Palin and Bell and Jasper came into view; for Colette and I had come to the end of our tether some time before that: but each, I think, was reluctant to let the other down.

So we came back to Jade, at about a quarter past ten…of a lovely summer morning…just as the bells were knolling the peasants to church.

8

Present Laughter

When I woke, I was in my tent, and Colette was sitting still, with her eyes on my face.

"Hullo, my sweet," I said. "And how do you feel?"

"I am only just up," she said, "and I am perfectly well. But how are you, my darling? You do not look as you did at The Vat of Melody."

"I'm quite all right," I said. "But I think I shall always be tired for the rest of my life. Send me Bell, will you, sweetheart? And come back in half an hour."

"I'm here, sir," said Bell, from behind me. "You're sure you're all night?"

"As good as new, Bell. Did I look very bad?"

Bell spoke between his teeth.

"Never again, sir," he said. "I'll never let you out of my sight."

"Never again," I said. "I promise you that. By the way, are the gems all right?"

"Under that blanket, sir."

Whilst I was making my toilet, Palin arrived.

"If the half," he said, "of what Colette says is true, I ought to have left my shoes outside your tent."

Razor in hand –

"I'll overlook it," I said. "And what do you know?"

"No more than you do," said Palin, "and probably not as much. A wire went off to Mansel at midday yesterday. 'All well', it said, as arranged. It seemed an understatement, but let that go."

"Yesterday?" said I. "What day is it now?"

"It's just four o'clock on Monday afternoon. You're sure you're all right, Chandos? You look fine-drawn."

"Sound as a bell," I said. "I'm only tired."

"Breakfast?"

I wrinkled my nose.

"Not very much. A cup of coffee, perhaps, and a piece of toast. My appetite will return, but it will have to be lured."

Colette, of course, brought me my breakfast and made me eat. But once I was bathed and shaved, I felt a new man.

As I lighted a cigarette –

"Tell me your story, Colette. You know what happened to me; but – "

"I have no idea," screamed Colette, "what happened to you. In an effort to emulate Bell, I have waited till now to be told. And the effort has told upon me. I know you fell into the water, from which, against all reason, you came out alive. But I do not know why you fell in or why the rope only took us halfway across."

"D'you mean," I said, "you don't know why I failed to land?"

"How should I, Adam dearest? I know that the rope stopped swinging almost at once. And so I did as you said and climbed into the tree. When you did not follow, I tried to take hold of the rope, but this was in the grip of the water and you did not seem to be there. I nearly fainted then, but somehow or other I made my way down the trunk and so to the ground. I was standing by the side of the torrent – I think I was crying your name, when out of the boiling water I saw an animal climbing on to a rock. I thought that it was a seal, for it had the look of a seal: only it moved so slowly, as though it was very tired. And then I knew it was you.

"I watched you climb on to the rock: and there you sat down, with the water racing about you, and sank your head on your chest. I was sure that you had been injured – I had no doubt. I cried, but you could not hear me, and, after a minute or two, you began to sway. This terrified me, so I ran for something to throw. I found a piece of stick, and I threw it and saw you wave. And then, a long time after, I saw you close to the bank."

"And brought me ashore, great heart – God save your pretty face."

Colette blew me a kiss. Then –

"And now please tell me, Adam, why you fell down."

"When I left the bank," I said, "I was carrying you on my back and Orris about my legs."

Colette's eyes widened in horror.

"Orris," she breathed. "It was Orris?"

"We were hanging, all three together, over the stream."

Colette shut her eyes.

"God in heaven," she breathed. "And you held on until I was up in the tree." She opened her eyes. "Did you kill the vermin, Adam?"

"I had to do with his death."

Shortly I told her what happened from the time when I left the bank to the time when I reached the rock. As I made an end –

"You must hand it to Orris," I said. "He knew how to do his stuff."

"I hand him nothing, Adam. Orris was only a jackal. The whole of that day he never dared to attack. But when you were badly placed, he summoned up courage to run between your legs."

She may on may not have been right. I cannot pretend to say. I think it is clear that Orris' hatred of me overruled his desire for the gems. If it comes to that, it also overruled his desire to live; for he must have known that to cast me into that water would cost him his life. Yet, he did as he did. And, as I told Colette, you must give the devil his due. For his job was to bring me down – and he very near did.

Had the weights been there, I could not have appeared that night. But Colette appeared, as usual, and Palin, as I had predicted, far more than took my place. He could speak and sing Italian and was an immense success; his improvised scene with Colette took the house by storm, and when Jasper and he were together, I nearly died of laughing, although I could understand but a quarter of what was said.

He was a great acquisition, as I had known he would be: and I think he enjoyed every moment, for he was a showman born. That he should fall for Colette was natural enough: and, though she did not accept them, she did not reject his addresses out of hand. This, frankly, did my heart good, for Andrew Palin was one of the very best: and he used Colette as he used Olivia Ferrers, which shows, I think, that he found her a lady of high degree.

And so she was. Many a time I have wondered who was her sire. She did not know: she scarcely remembered her mother. She had no name but Colette. I sometimes think that Jasper worshipped her mother, who died of love for somebody greater than he. But that is pure speculation; for Colette knew nothing at all, and Jasper never talked.

We passed from Jade to Gala, from Gala to Eglantine. Each time we moved, I sent a note to Mansel, c/o The Heart of Gold. And then, on a Saturday evening, a week to the hour since I had sat watching the sunset above the smuggler's way, I looked up to see him standing in the mouth of my tent.

"Oh, very good," said I. "Very good, indeed."

"All well, William?"

I glanced at the blanket beside me.

"They're under that. Bell and Palin and I take it in turns to sit here. I'm growing used to them now, but I shan't be sorry to get them off my hands."

"You took them out of the weights?"

I began to laugh.

"Yes," I said. "I took them out of the weights. And now sit down, for I'm going to tell you a tale that will take a month from your life."

Mansel sat down, smiling.

"You never cabled till Sunday. That told me that someone or something had put a spoke in your wheel."

I told him my tale.

When I came to Odin's lapse, he covered his face with his hands.

"Not a month," he said. "A year. Even though all is well, it makes me feel weak at the knees."

"I don't believe I'll ever be quite the same."

"I know," said Mansel. "I've had some. Such things are bad for the soul. Never mind. Let me have Act Two."

By the time my tale was done, the performance was about to begin, so Bell and Carson took over, and Mansel and I went to sit at the back of 'the house'. And when the show was over, I introduced Mansel to Jasper and then to Colette.

Mansel bowed to Colette. Then he took her small hand and put it up to his lips.

"I'm not going to thank you," he said. "One doesn't thank great ladies for being themselves. But I'm very glad you were there. Apart from the fact that I value William's life, to have you beside him must have meant everything."

Colette dropped her eyes, and the colour came into her face.

As once before, I picked her up and set her down on my shoulder.

"That is how," I said, "she deserved to come home."

"I deserve nothing," said Colette. "I found it a great adventure. And I would do it with Adam all over again."

"But not with me," said Mansel.

Colette's fingers gripped my shoulder.

"Only with Adam," she said. "Others might have got there: but Adam's the only man who could have got back."

Mansel smiled up at her. Then he put up his arms and lifted her down. On her way to the ground he held her, so that her pretty face was level with his.

"We've a bond in common," he said.

Colette looked him full in the eyes. Then she said something to him which I could not hear. And Mansel nodded and set her cheek against his…

At supper I sat, as usual, on Jasper's left; and Colette between Palin and me. But Mansel would not sit upon Jasper's right. Instead, he took his seat with the smaller fry, whom he had put at their ease before one minute was out. And before the end of supper, Odin was actually standing behind his seat, with an eye to his plate and his glass, which, so far as I know, he never had done before. But that was always the way, for Mansel induced a very respectful devotion wherever he went. His manner was very easy and his address superb: but his powerful personality seemed to warm people's hearts. Strangers would do for him what they would not do for friends; and yet he never cajoled them or 'played them up'. He was always perfectly natural in all that he said and did, but he had that indefinable presence which very few are born with and none can ever acquire.

It was past eleven o'clock when we bade the others good night, and Mansel, Palin and I repaired to my tent. And while Mansel told his tale, Carson and Bell were moving in the shadows outside.

"From what you tell me, William, the efforts I made to divert attention from you were of little avail. I fancy the truth is this – that the Boche, being well aware of his own incompetence, determined, as children do, to follow a better man. The police had their hand upon Friar. The latter had taken them straight to Wagensburg. Very well. Friar should lead them again, and when he had run us to earth, the Boche would come in. His hold upon Friar appears to have been rather loose, but I think it unlikely that he could have left the district, unless he had done as you did and forced the frontier. And that is a thing that Friar could never have done. He would never have tried to do it, for thieves have other ways of getting their booty out.

"My efforts, however, attracted attention to me; and the Customs were up on their toes when I came to the German border, *en route* for France. That was last Thursday week, as we had arranged. On one excuse or another they held me for forty-eight hours. The Rolls was pushed into a shed, coachbuilders were summoned, and there, before my eyes, her body was stripped. Upholstery and trimming – off they came, to Carson's distraction, as you may well believe. And then the rules came out. Amid intense excitement, the secret locker was found: but when they opened this, it was full of spares. That was a nasty knock, but they wouldn't let go. They took the tyres off the wheels, and when they drew blank there, they took off the petrol tank and opened that. They then declared their intention of taking the gearbox down, but I suggested they drained it and looked inside.

" 'Sir,' said the wallah-in-chief, 'will you swear that that box is empty?'

" 'Certainly not,' said I. 'It's full of gears and oil.'

" 'But nothing else?'

" 'You'd much better look,' said I. 'You don't seem to like my word.'

"At that, they threw in their hand. And gave the coachbuilders orders to put things back. All things considered, I think they did very well, but I never got off until Saturday afternoon.

"I wasn't troubled again. Probably word had gone through that I wasn't worth powder and shot. So I came to Strasburg on Sunday.

"It was a nasty jar to find no cable from you, and I don't mind admitting I passed a sleepless night. I decided to wait until midday on Monday. If your wire hadn't come by then, I should have to go back. And then, on Monday morning, your wire arrived.

"I left Carson to bring the Rolls and took to the air...

"The first thing I did was to get hold of George St Olave. He is one of the Standing Committee, controlling all museums and things like that. And George is a very live wire. When he'd heard what I had to say, he sent for some keeper or other who knows about precious stones. And there our luck came in, for, by the grace of God, the keeper had been overseas and had seen the breviary of Pope Alexander the Sixth. And in that is the Pope's own list of these fabulous gems. When I told him the collection was intact and was waiting to come to England, he damned near died. And when I said that I'd seen them and helped to put them up, he kept on walking round me, as if I wasn't real.

" 'But,' he kept saying, 'the thing's incredible.'

" 'I know it is,' said I. 'The brutal fact remains that I have driven hundreds of miles with those gems in the boot of my car. And now please tell me this – does England want them or not? If she wants them, she has them for nothing. If she doesn't want them, they go to the USA – where they will be sold.' " He looked at George.

" 'We've *got* to have them,' he said.

" 'Then no funny business,' said I. 'We've got them as far as Trieste. But Austria's after them, and so is Germany. Any moment now Italy may sit up, and they're on her soil. To be frank, we've got a long way: but this is where you come in, and unless you come in damned quick, you'll lose the lot.'

" 'What d'you suggest?' they said.

" 'A private yacht,' said I. 'Gammon's is in commission, I happen to know. If you tell him the truth, I'm sure that he will lend her. She's got to be at Trieste as soon as ever she can. And when she's there, the Captain must take my orders, because it is up to me to get the gems on board. And when we get to England, the Customs must let us alone. If you can't arrange that, I won't play.'

233

"'I'll see to that,' says George.

" 'Two things more.' I laid your two passports down. 'Those men have risked their lives to get the gems over the border and into Italy. I want diplomatic visas for both – and I want them in twenty-four hours. Unless and until I get them, I will not leave for Trieste.'

" 'I'll do it somehow,' says George. 'To Cleveland Row?'

" 'Yes, please. And the other thing is this. The yacht must carry a passenger out to Trieste. It will bring back four or more: but it must take one out.'

" 'That's easy,' said George. 'I take it you don't want Gammon.'

" 'Not on your life,' said I. 'Nor any of Gammon's friends. This is a hush-hush job, for which perhaps Gammon might get a CMG'

"George smothered a grin.

" 'And what about you?' he said.

" 'We don't want anything. Our names must not appear. But Ferrers should have a peerage. It isn't every day that a fellow forgoes twenty million, for England's sake.'

" 'He can have what he likes,' said George. 'I'll guarantee that.'

"Well, it wasn't all so easy – I mean, it took time. But the passports reached me on Thursday – here they are – and the yacht weighed anchor on Friday, complete with passenger."

"And who is that?" said I.

"Not even to you," said Mansel; by which I knew it was someone from Scotland Yard. "The yacht should be at Trieste tomorrow week. Till then, we must watch and pray – and take what precautions we can, in case of accidents."

On Monday the tents were struck and we moved to the skirts of Trieste.

This was not what Jasper had meant to do, for he had proposed to move south, till he came to Padua. But the troupe had no engagements, and Palin was very much better than any strong man. Since the weights were gone, Jasper was only too thankful to have his help, and, had he said that he wished to make for Milan, *en route* for the South of France, I am sure that Jasper would have at once agreed. For Palin had made up his mind to stay with the troupe. The life was to his liking, to play and sing to an audience afforded him great delight, and he had already produced a very much better masque – a very charming trifle, which would have been well received on the London stage. The music was all his own, as, indeed, was the whole production, and Jasper, an artist himself, was quite overcome by its manifest excellence. Finally, Palin had fallen flat for Colette.

Still his duty to the Ferrers came first. Neither Mansel nor I could return to Austria: but Palin could return – and the Ferrers were anxiously waiting for news which we dared not write. So Mansel and I arranged that the troupe should be our guests for the next ten days. Colette and Jasper would stay at The Heart of Gold, and the others would rest at an inn which Jasper knew. By that time, all being well, the yacht would be ready to sail again for England and Palin should have returned from his visit to Hohenems. We had a battle with Jasper, before we could gain his consent to do as we wished: but we had our way in the end, and on the Tuesday evening the four of us were installed at The Heart of Gold and Palin was on his way back, through France, to Austria.

On Wednesday morning I took Colette to the shops and made her choose silk and satin and frocks to wear: and while we were so engaged, Mansel was procuring a car. And so, for the next few days, we spent a riotous time, seeing the sights and driving about the country and dining out and dancing until the sky was pale – for Mansel had brought my luggage as far as Trieste. These ways were such as Colette had never known, and it gave me infinite pleasure to introduce them to her. She was so radiantly happy for all to see, for each experience was new –

and yet she met it as though to the manner born. Anyone must have been proud to be her squire, for, while she was lovely to look at, her eager and artless manner seemed to inspire affection wherever she went. To see his darling so happy lifted up Jasper's heart, and though, except by day, he would not go out, he had to hear in the morning all she had seen and done the night before. And then he would come and thank me, with tears in his eyes…

And all this time the gems lay under our hand, yet out of sight. Our rooms at The Heart of Gold stood about a little courtyard. This, we four and the servants had to ourselves. In its midst was an ancient well, no longer used. It was a pretty relic of other days; and since there was water there, but ten feet down, the ferns about it prospered, because, I suppose, of the moisture that rose from below. Examining this by night, we saw that a line of dogs was running down the wall of the well: this made, of course, a primitive ladder, by which a man could easily go up and down. Indeed, I have seen many safes which were less convenient; for, though it was not barred, very few men, I think, would have suspected the duty we made it do.

Though I think it was heavy enough, we weighted the kit-bag further and lowered it into the well: then I went down, while Mansel lighted my steps, and fastened the cord to a dog which was under water and so out of sight. We did not leave matters there, and someone was always on duty, by day and night: but since we were six in number, this was easy enough.

And then, on Monday morning, a wireless message arrived, to say that the yacht would arrive on the following day.

The telegram was delivered, as we were about to set out.

"Today?" said Colette, quickly.

"No," said Mansel, "tomorrow. During the afternoon. I hope very much that you'll sleep aboard that night."

"Me sleep aboard?"

"I hope so. You see, we shan't sail for more than twenty-four hours. And Bell will go aboard with you and stay till we come."

"You want me out of the way."

"No, we don't, sweetheart. It's just that I think you'll enjoy it. She's one of the finest yachts that's ever been built."

"I'd rather stay here with you."

"On Wednesday morning, we shall be with you again. And then I'll lay you tell me that I was right."

"Very well," sighed Colette.

What was in Mansel's mind, I had no idea: but he had said nothing so far of getting the gems to the yacht, and I supposed it had something to do with that. For myself, I could not think how we were to climb this fence, for the quays were alive with Customs officials and police. My passport and that of Bell bore diplomatic visas; but that was to quash an objection, if it were made, that they were out of order – for, of course, they should have been stamped at some frontier-post. Though such visas allowed us to take our baggage *unopened* out of Italy, to count upon such a privilege would have been most unwise; for if Italy had but an inkling of what was afoot, she would not stand upon convention or hesitate to ignore international courtesy.

But Mansel kept his counsel. All he asked me to do was to bear a note to the Captain as soon as the yacht had berthed, to stay aboard until Bell arrived with Colette, and then to return at once to The Heart of Gold.

But all of this was for Tuesday. So far as we were concerned, the morrow could care for itself.

The dance music faded and died, and Colette led the way to our table, close to the edge of the terrace commanding the open sea.

Instead of sitting down, she passed to the parapet, laying her palms upon the stone and looking down on the garden which sloped to the water's edge.

The night was flawless, and our surroundings superb. A monstrous moon was making her ancient magic by land and sea: there ran the traditional path across the waters, a quivering sash of silver, old as the hills themselves, and yet, as ever, beyond the reach of art: the terraced garden was a mystery of spires and bastions of shadow, of shafts and badges of light, of the fretful lace of branches, printed upon the flags, of the plume of a playing fountain, seemingly hung upon the air – for the basin was out of sight, and all that the eye could see was the head of the gallant flourish, rising and falling and dancing, to round the miracle. Except for a wandering zephyr, all the winds were still, and the regular breathing of Ocean was all the sound there was – stertorous breathing, perhaps, but even enough, the gentle crush of the breakers...and then the snore of the drawback before she expired again.

"Must we go yet, Adam?"

"No, my sweet. We can stay for as long as you please."

"Then let us go down to the garden..."

Together we passed down the steps and into the shadowy acre of make-believe, and there Colette took my arm, "because," she said, "there is no one to see us now."

For a little we strolled in silence. Then we came to the court of the fountain, and there we sat down.

"Adam, dear, I have had a letter from Andrew. He will be back on Wednesday. And he has asked me, Adam, to be his wife."

"I am very glad, my beauty. I thought he would. He is the best of good fellows, and, as his wife, you will take your rightful place."

"But I am not in love with him, Adam. I am in love with you."

I put my arm about her and held her close.

"You are not in love with me, sweetheart: you are in love with an image which you have set up. You found a strong man in the greenwood, and because he was not of your world you rated him high. Then he came to live with the troupe, and you liked his ways. Then he pulled you out of a jam – at The Vat of Melody. And then you and he together looked Death in the eyes. And, because your heart is generous, you love such a stable-companion – as he loves you. In my sight, Colette, the hairs of your head are numbered. But, though we love one another, we are not in love. And you will come to love Andrew as you would never love me. You two have so much in common, and, though, perhaps, I am stronger, he is the better man."

"Have you done?" said Colette.

"Oh, hell," said I, and put a hand to my head.

Colette looked up at me, smiling.

"You see," she said, "how very simple you are. You do not know yourself. But I do know you, my darling. You have the heart of a lion and the way of a little child. Perhaps I have a weakness for lions, but I can tell you this – that I would give dinner and dance, this lovely dress and the pride of being with you, this pretty garden which seems like Paradise...I say I would give it all to be moving once more with you on the smuggler's way. Never mind. Shall I marry him, Adam?"

"If you do, my sweet, I'm sure that you'll get full measure, and no man on earth can offer you more than that."

"I wish Eve was here," said Colette.

"Why d'you say that?" I said.

"Because I should like to ask her. I think she'd know. You see, we've something in common – we both like lions."

I felt I had shot my bolt.

"As soon as the gems are in England, I'll bring her out."

Colette shook her head.

"I cannot keep him waiting like that. And if I marry him, then he will have all my heart. But a little bit of my heart will not be there. Eve will have that in her keeping, to add to hers. Just a very little bit, Adam...about the size of...a keepsake..."

"Colette, Colette, I have nothing to give you back." Colette looked up at me, and I saw the tears on her cheeks. Then she put up her arms and took my face in her hands. "Nothing to give me back." She sighed. "My lion is very simple and cannot see the nose in front of his face."

"Indeed, he can," said I. "It's a very beautiful nose. But I think I like the mouth best."

Colette gave a sob of delight and threw her arms round my neck.

It was nearly three when we came to The Heart of Gold.

As I kissed her fingertips –

"*Qui va là?*" said a voice.

We stared at each other in silence.

Then came a chuckle of laughter – a gross, Rabelaisian chuckle that made my hackles rise.

"*Bon appétit,*" said the voice, and laughed again.

"By God, it's a parrot," I said, and then I heard Mansel laughing...

As we came to his door, his light went up.

"Yes," he said, "it's a parrot. There he is. He has very strong views about ladies who dance their stockings down."

"Please observe," said Colette, "that mine are in place."

"You must show them to the parrot," said Mansel. " He is the censor, not I."

Colette dropped the bird a curtsey.

"*Regardez, Monsieur,*" she said.

The parrot's reply was quite unprintable.

I was still laughing, when Mansel covered its cage.

"This is too much," said Colette. "I shall go to bed. But why a parrot that does not know how to behave?"

"I'll tell you on Wednesday, sweetheart."

Colette blew us each a kiss and danced out of the room.

The yacht, a most beautiful ship, anchored at half past one on the following afternoon, and, about a quarter past two, her pinnace left for the quay. For that I can vouch, for I was awaiting the pinnace, to go aboard. And very selfconscious I felt, for I had the parrot with me, and the shocking things it was saying were making the Customs Officers hold their sides. When I tried to quiet it, it bit me – an ugly gash, at which everyone laughed the louder, and I had to laugh myself. But I was cursing Mansel under my breath.

Never could I remember when he had been so cryptic, yet so precise.

I was to take the parrot and go aboard, bearing a note addressed to 'The Passenger'. When I asked the latter's name, "I can't tell you that," he said, "but I'm sure you'll get on all right." "Can I talk to him?" I said. "You can say what you like," said Mansel, "but only behind closed doors. The Captain's not in on this; but the passenger is." "Am I under his orders," I said. "I wouldn't say that," said Mansel: "but you must be very civil. These VIPs expect a certain deference."

At half past four the pinnace would return to the quay, to bring aboard Colette, escorted by Bell. ("You'll introduce Colette to the VIP. The latter will wish to thank her for all she has done.")

And at five o'clock I was to leave the yacht and return to The Heart of Gold.

The parrot, God be praised, was to stay on the yacht.

The pinnace was coming now, so I picked up the battered cage and went down the steps.

Then one of her crew was ashore and was holding her close to the stone.

"Mr Chandos?" said the jolly faced coxswain.

"That's right. Take this bird, will you? He's going aboard."

"*Mais comme il est —*," yelled the parrot. Before this gratuitous insult, the coxswain recoiled, and a roar of laughter behind me showed that intelligent anticipation was among the attributes of the Customs of Trieste.

The coxswain looked at me.

"I 'ope 'e don' talk no English."

I looked at him.

"The French he affects," I said, "seems to be understood."

The coxswain shrugged his shoulders.

"One picks things up, sir," he said.

"Well, pick up that cage," said I. "And take care he doesn't get you."

"He'd better try," said the coxswain. He seized the cage and set it down on a thwart. "Gorblime, if 'e ain' done it." He held up a welling thumb. "Jus' look at that. Stuck his 'ead through the bars."

At this new misadventure, the glee of the Customs Officers knew no bounds. Dignity went to the winds, and two of them clasped one another in paroxysms of mirth. It was, I confess, the richest comedy, and had I been but an onlooker, I should have died of laughter to see such sport. But as being in charge of the parrot, I could not savour the salt; and when I remembered Mansel, I felt quite mutinous.

"I'm very sorry," I said. "The brute isn't mine: if it was, I'd open that door and let it go home."

"Wouldn' 'ave to open the door, sir."

This was true. Had anyone squeezed its prison, the parrot would have gone free. And the cage was none too big. But so degraded a bird deserved to be meanly lodged.

I stepped aboard the pinnace and took my seat.

As was to be expected, the pinnace was very well found, and it had an elaborate awning against the power of the sun. Since I was on the port side, I hardly saw the yacht until, after five or six minutes, there was her accommodation ladder approaching our starboard beam.

As I got to my feet –

"Shall I send the bird up, sir?"

"Please. And see that he doesn't get out. He isn't mine."

The parrot made an extremely vulgar noise.

I swung myself on to the ladder and, naturally, lifted my eyes…

Then a hand went up to my head, for Jenny, my blessed darling, was standing at the head of the steps.

I forgot the parrot and Mansel: I forgot Colette and the gems. I had thought that she was in Wiltshire…had sent her a little letter only the day before. And now here she was at Trieste, looking 'a million dollars' in blue and white, with Sarah, her maid, behind her, smiling all over her face.

And then she was in my arms…and the world about us was void, and Time was standing still.

Sitting at ease in a most luxurious stateroom, I told my darling all that there was to tell. And Jenny sat and listened, with one of my hands in hers and stars in her lovely eyes.

An excellent lunch was served, but we let it go. But Sarah brought a tankard and set it down by my side.

When at last I had done –

"Colette," said Jenny. "I want to see her so much. I want to thank Colette for taking my place."

"She could never do that, my darling."

"I think she did terribly well. And of course she's in love with you, William. Why shouldn't she be?"

"She isn't, Jenny darling. If she had seen Palin first – "

"I haven't seen Palin," said Jenny. "But if he compares with you, he must be a hell of a man."

"Oh, I give up," said I. "You're two of a kind. Just because I can bend an iron bar – "

"I don't think it's that," said Jenny. "I don't quite know what it is. Jonathan's greater than you, but I always loved you best."

"Listen, my blessed darling. I want you to understand this – that more than once I have had to make love to Colette. It wasn't hard, for she is so very sweet: but I had to make love to her, because I could not send such a great-heart empty away."

"I couldn't have borne it if you had. She did what she did out of love: it would have been cruel, my darling, to give her nothing back. I am so rich, William, so very rich. Do you think that I can spare nothing to a girl who has comforted you?"

I picked my wife up in my arms.

"Jenny, there's no one like you in all the world."

"I love to hear you say that."

"No one like you, my darling – and that's the truth."

I kissed her and set her down...

Then we read Mansel's letter, which was, as always, very much to the point.

Jenny sweetheart,

Tomorrow at ten o'clock, you and Colette will come ashore with Bell. Bell will carry the parrot, which, I think perhaps you'll agree, should have a new cage. William will be on the quay and will take you off to buy one, before you do anything else. Then he'll bring you back to our inn. And there you will meet Jasper, whom I know you will like very much. I'm very sorry the parrot is so outspoken: I think perhaps you can reform him, given time.

With all my love,

Tuesday   *Jonathan.*

Time was now getting on, so I found an officer and asked that the pinnace might leave at half past four.

"To pick up my servant, Bell, who is bringing my luggage aboard. And he'll have a lady with him. I'm going ashore at five, but they're going to spend the night."

"That's all right, Mr Chandos. I'll see to everything."

It was a quarter past five before the pinnace returned, but Colette and Bell and my luggage were all aboard.

As he stepped on to the ladder, Bell's eyes met mine...

Wondering what was afoot, I greeted Colette.

"Come, my beauty," I said. "Before I go, you must meet the passenger."

"Oh, I'm nervous, Adam. I wish you could stay on the yacht." She stopped and stood looking round. "What a lovely hall, Adam. I never knew they had halls on board a ship."

"Nor did I, my dear. I tell you, she's opened my eyes."

I led her straight to the stateroom, and opened the door.

Jenny was standing beyond, on the private deck.

"Jenny, this is Colette. Colette, this is Eve."

I heard Colette catch her breath, and a hand went up to her mouth.

Then my wife stretched out her arms, with a glorious smile on her face.

Colette ran across the stateroom and caught Jenny's hands to her breast.

As Jenny stooped to kiss her, I shut the door.

Bell was waiting in the passage.

"Yes?" I said.

"They're on to something, sir. Had everything out of the cases and turned them inside out. Of course, I showed them the passports, but they only smiled. That's why we're so late – I had to repack in the shed."

I fingered my chin.

"And here's a show," I said slowly. "Oh, well, it can't be helped. I must get back to the inn as soon as I can. Look after Madam: you're under her orders now."

"Madam, sir? Not Mrs Chandos?"

Bell's honest face was alight, as I had not seen it for weeks.

"That's right," I said, smiling. "And Sarah's somewhere about. As I say, you're under her orders, but she is in your charge."

Mansel heard me out.

Then –

"I thought that might happen," he said. "It's all this cursed delay. If we could have had the yacht waiting, a week ago… Before the day is out, they'll be watching this house, Germany's split to Italy – two of a kind. Rather than let us have it, she's ready to share the loot. But we'll beat them yet, William. That's where the parrot comes in. Did he make any sort of impression?"

"Impression's too mild a term. Sensation might do. The Customs had the time of their lives. There were only two to start with, but when I left the quay, there were four or five. And all of them laughing their souls out. I admit it was most amusing – for everyone else. But I do dislike being embarrassed. If that bird was a human being, he'd be in jug."

"I'm sorry," said Mansel, laughing, "but you bear excellent news. I went to a lot of trouble to get that bird. I think you'll admit that he's quite exceptional. While you were squiring Colette, I was vetting parrots, until, at last, I found the bird I required. A foul-mouthed brute, whose enunciation was good. That bird, William, knows how to produce his voice."

"I'll give you that."

"And more than that – he's vicious."

"I'll give you that, too."

"Don't say he got you, William?" I held up my hand. "Did the Customs witness the outrage?"

"Of course they did. When he bit the coxswain, too, they nearly fell off the quay."

"God be praised," said Mansel. "I don't deserve such luck." He saw the look on my face and began to laugh. "And now you shall have the truth. When you hear it, I think you'll forgive me, for you have done so much better than you could ever have done if I had put you wise.

"Now what are we up against? We are very nearly home, and yet we stand in danger of losing everything. Something has been said, and the Customs are up on their toes. So we've got to distract the Customs – a difficult thing to do. And the very best way to distract is to attract the attention to something else. Now just because the parrot attracts their attention, they're not going to chalk our baggage without seeing what's inside. Parrot and baggage are two quite separate things. But if the parrot is making them split their sides, they may not look so hard at the parrot's cage.

"Tomorrow Jenny will purchase a nice new cage. I'll tell you where to take her and I will show you the cage which she is to buy. They're really beautiful cages – they've only got four left. I bought the fifth this morning – it's in my room.

"When Jenny has bought the cage, you will buy sand and seed and the parrot will enter in. And then you will all repair to The Heart of Gold. And while we are having a drink, Carson will effect the exchange. The parrot will leave his cage for the one I purchased this morning, and no one but we and the parrot will know that the change has been made. Jenny won't know and the police outside won't know – that the cage in which the bird comes to The Heart of Gold will not be the cage in which he returns to the yacht. Just to round the matter, *no one* will ever know… Last night I measured the depth of the water within the well. It's a little more than twelve feet. So when Carson has made the exchange, he will take Jenny's cage and drop it into the well.

"A feature of these cages is their most excellent trays. The ordinary tray is really little more than a flimsy sheet of tin. But this is a proper tray, with sides all round, an inch and a half in height. And it's very substantial, William. Then, again, the cage is capacious – twenty inches by twenty: that's pretty big. So the gems will go into the tray without any fuss. In fact, we shall have to pad them – I've plenty of cotton wool. And that we shall do tonight, while honest men are asleep. Now when they are all in the tray, and nice and tight, we shall turn the cage upside down and slide the tray back. Then Carson will carefully solder the tray into place – just along the edge at the bottom, so that it can't slip out. We shall then reverse the cage, which means that the gems will be resting upon its floor: and the tray, being upside down, will cover them up. In other words, the cage will have a false bottom, which we have contrived. Then the sand will go in, and if the Customs observe that the sand is unusually thick, then they're better men than I am, and that's God's truth."

Perhaps because I am not at all ingenious, I thought and shall always think that the plan which Mansel had laid was a very fine piece of work. Many perhaps could think of a better and simpler way of unloosing our Gordian knot: but two things must be borne in mind – first, that though the gems should come safely aboard the yacht, the crew of the yacht must never suspect their presence; and, secondly, that whatever plan we adopted *must not fail*. In other words, all possible risks must be foreseen and dealt with – by which I mean so much reduced that they ceased to deserve the name. For this was no ordinary smuggling of stockings or cigarettes: it was taking out of a country a wonder of all the world: and the stake was no fine – not even a prosecution…it was the loss to England of this astounding nonsuch, which now an English gentleman held in fee.

Indeed, as I see it, Mansel had left nothing to chance. By taking the parrot aboard, I had acquainted the Customs with that undesirable bird: they looked upon him with favour: he was for them a fellow of infinite jest. And they would be only too glad to see him again. What was more, they knew he was vicious, that he would be a brave man that laid hands on his cage. So, tomorrow, when he came off, he would be well received: and when he went back to the yacht, he would be an old friend. And it was so very natural that two tender hearted young ladies should buy him a nice new cage.

A knock at the door, and Carson entered the room.

"There's a plain-clothes man on the inn, sir."

"I thought that was coming," said Mansel. "It's just as well we're leaving. So long as he stays outside till tomorrow afternoon…"

By half past two the next morning, the gems were safe in the cage. Mansel and I did the business, while Carson watched the watcher and Jasper watched the courtyard.

Then we put sand in the cage, and water and seed in the bowls.

The cage was now very heavy – no doubt about that: but, since it was all of brass, it was very heavy to start with. For all that, I made up my mind that Bell and I, between us, must handle the thing, for the coxswain would surely exclaim when he felt the weight.

Then we put into the kit-bag what was left of the wool and the solder, as well as the soldering iron: and having restored its weights, we made its mouth fast and let it fall into the well.

Less than seven hours later, I drove to the quay. And, precisely at ten o'clock, the pinnace was at the steps.

The Customs were there to receive it – and had their reward.

Colette followed Jenny out. Then Bell stepped ashore with the parrot, looking unusually grim.

As he mounted the steps –

"*Vive la —,*" shrieked the parrot. "*Vive la —*"

The word which I have omitted is more than coarse. Never before, I should think, has so offensive a precept been so declared.

The Customs clasped one another and roared their delight.

Colette was shaking with laughter, but Jenny frowned.

As I put her hand to my lips –

"Darling," she said, "we can't go on like this. He must have another cage. This is no better than a hovel. I had him out this morning, and he was quite all right. But it's when he's in that cage that he says these dreadful things."

As though to confirm this conclusion, the parrot made the noise he had made the day before, on reaching the yacht. This was a new one on the Customs, who laughed so much and so long that I had to laugh myself.

"You see?" said Jenny. "We must get him out of that cage."

I took off my coat and threw it over the cage.

"Into the car, sweetheart. I think I know of a shop. We'll go there at once."

249

I drove, with Bell beside me, gingerly holding the parrot upon his knees. And twenty minutes later, the parrot had a new home.

The bird was so much overcome by his new estate that he wasted no time upon words, but clambered all over his residence, proving the swing and the bars and tasting the seed and the water and treading the sand.

"There you are," said Jenny. "What did I say?"

"You may be right, my darling. I'm not so sure. It's a nice, new home, and he isn't used to it yet. I think, when he's settled down, the power of speech may return."

"Anyway, it's worth it, to see the poor bird so pleased."

"There," said Colette, "I am with you. This passes his comprehension. It touches the heart to see his delight in that swing."

I confess I was bound to agree. The parrot's pleasure was pathetic. Gurgling with laughter, he pushed the swing to and fro; and then he clambered within it and crowed with delight. The cage, which had cost four pounds, was cheap at the price.

Then I drove to The Heart of Gold. And there were Mansel and Jasper, waiting to welcome us in.

It was a great reunion, for Mansel adored Jenny, and Jasper worshipped Colette. Colette presented Jasper, who bowed over Jenny's hand, but Jenny took his arm and made him walk with her while she spoke of Colette. What she said, I do not know, but Jasper's face was transfigured when they came back. Then we all sat down in the garden, and Mansel called for wine. And, as though to round our pleasure, a telegram came from Palin to say that he hoped to arrive that evening at nine o'clock.

"We shall be gone," said Mansel, "for we must be aboard by eight. But I'll leave a note for him."

"And so will I," said Jenny. "Give me some paper, William. I'll write it now."

And so she did, showing it to me as she wrote it and asking if I approved.

Dear Andrew,
I know you will make Colette happy. If you would like to make me happy, too, please bring her to stay at Maintenance very soon. I am very fond of her, and I think she is fond of me.

Our best love to you both,
Jenny Chandos.

Then she covered the letter and sealed it up.

Mansel glanced at his watch.

"It's now past twelve," he said, "and Jenny, Colette and Bell should be getting back. I want Jasper to see the yacht, and he's promised to go aboard at half past three. At five o'clock Colette and he will come off and will come back here. I'm sorry to be so dictatorial, but all our movements today must be made to time."

"Sir," said Jasper, "you command my great admiration. You have the brain and the way of a Chief of Staff."

Five minutes later we were again in the car. And Bell and the parrot with us.

It would not be true to say that when we reached the quay we were greeted with cheers; but the moment they saw the car, the Customs began to grin and one of them ran for the others who were in some shed.

The pinnace was at the steps, so we wasted no time. But the parrot was not the bird to let a good audience down. As I handed Jenny aboard –

"*Pas de* —!" he screamed. And then again, "*Pas de* —!"

The sentiment was laudable. Of that there can be no doubt. He who cries 'No nonsense!' deserves to be commended, rather than blamed. The trouble was that the word he used was not 'nonsense'. It was a word which Christians are not supposed to use – and to say that the Customs 'ate' it, is less than true.

It was his Parthian shaft. He had kept the good wine until now.

All the same, I was not ungrateful. The cage was a fearful weight – and the Customs were helpless for mirth.

Colette's face was flaming, and two red spots were burning in Jenny's cheeks.

As I handed the cage to Bell –

"You're a wicked bird," said Jenny. "You did it on purpose, because you knew they were waiting to hear what you'd say. Directly you get on board you're going to be covered up. And so you'll stay till tomorrow."

I must confess that the parrot looked something abashed. And then the pinnace went off, with its precious freight.

That summer afternoon was one of the very longest I ever knew.

When Jasper had left with Carson about a quarter past three, Time seemed to slow to a standstill, and more than once I thought that my watch had stopped. Of such is the hell of waiting, when you can do nothing else…when Time is arrayed against you, and can, if your enemy knows it, be used to bring you down.

It was oppressively hot, and Mansel and I sat out in the little courtyard, smoking and drinking beer and hardly exchanging a word. We were very nearly home. But I knew I should not be easy, until we were on the high seas. Neither would Mansel. Within the three-mile limit, the yacht could be stopped.

There was little enough to fear. We had flown the last of our fences and flown it well. And now we were in the straight. But we were not home. And Carson had lately reported that there were now two policemen watching the inn. It is when you are almost home that the slightest risk increases in menace and stature, and peril is magnified.

I was to go aboard first, for we did not know how much the Italians knew; and for us to be seen together might verify some report. So I was to take my leave, as soon as Colette and Jasper returned to The Heart of Gold.

And then, at last, some clock chimed a quarter past five.

"Any minute now," said Mansel. "You'll leave in a quarter of an hour. Send the pinnace for us at seven o'clock. We may be a little while, for they'll probably comb my baggage as they combed yours. But try not to worry, William. It's going to be quite all right."

"Those wallahs outside," I said. "When they see you leaving with luggage – "

"They won't," said Mansel. "I thought of that yesterday morning, before the police came on. While you were aboard, Carson took it off to the station and parked it there. And he's not coming back to the inn. When he's driven you down to the quay, he will return the car. And he will meet me at the station at six forty-five. From there we shall take a taxi down to the quay."

I sighed.

"Talk about staff work…You do deserve to win. If you're not aboard by eight, I shall come ashore."

Mansel set a hand on my shoulder.

"No, my faithful William. I had to leave you, and now you may have to leave me. Whether or no I'm on board, the yacht will weigh anchor at eight. Those are the Captain's orders, and he will carry them out. *And you must stay with the gems.* It's about a hundred to one that I shall fetch up. But, if I don't – well, they can do nothing to me. They *have* got something on you, for you have forced a frontier and flattened a Boche. But they have nothing on me. They can make me miss the boat, but that is all they can do. And if they do that – well, I shall be in England before you and shall come aboard at Fowey instead of Trieste."

And there Colette and Jasper came into the court.

"Come, Jasper," said Mansel, rising. "I want to talk to you."

As they left the courtyard, I turned to Colette.

"Well, my sweet, are you happy?"

253

"I have never been so happy in all my life. And I owe it all to you, Adam."

"Don't be absurd. You owe it all to yourself."

"I am not absurd," cried Colette. "Except that I found you, I have done nothing at all. But you have taken my hand and raised me to your estate. I know very well that I am a daw among peacocks – "

"Colette, my beauty, I cannot stay here and listen to talk like this. Please believe that it hurts me. And it is not fair to Andrew, who loves you so well. Think what you please of yourself, but remember this. Andrew Palin would never marry beneath him – he is not of that kind. You do not know who your father and mother were: but I think they must both be rejoicing to see their daughter taking her rightful place,"

Colette raised her eyes to mine: her lovely face was transfigured by some most powerful emotion, I could not share: her parted lips were trembling; her eyes were brimming with tears.

"I do not know which I love best – you, my darling, or Eve."

I drew her into my arms.

"I knew you two would get on."

"Adam, Adam, you never told me the half. I know I have named her rightly, for she belongs to Paradise, body and soul. Once you called me a nymph, but she is the goddess to whom the nymphs belong. We talked till two this morning, and all about you."

"My God," said I. "Were you stuck as fast as that?"

"Why not?" said Colette. "You are the biggest thing in both of our lives."

I held her off.

"Colette," I said, "you are going to marry Andrew – a very good friend of mine and one of the best of men. He will make you a splendid husband, and you will make him an equally splendid wife. When you know him as you know me, you will see the truth of my words. God forbid that you should endure together what you and I endured a fortnight or so ago. But together you will encounter the rough as well as the smooth: and it is sharing the rough that ties men and women together – ties them more tightly together than a lifetime of halcyon days."

"But I loved you before," said Colette. "That was why I went."

So much for my homily. But I never could argue with women – I have not the art.

I took a deep breath.

"I must be going, sweetheart. I think, perhaps, I shall see you before very long. And then you will be Mrs Palin, and – "

"No, no. Just Colette. And you will always be Adam: and Eve will always be Eve…She – she said I was to kiss you, my darling, with all her heart and mine."

I bent my head, and her arms went about my neck.

"Say it once more," she breathed: "once more, my very darling, and never again."

"Light of my eyes," I whispered, and wondered what I had done to be honoured like this.

Then I went off to find Jasper and bid that good man goodbye.

With my hand in his –

"It was a good day for us, sir, when we found you asleep in the greenwood a month ago."

I smiled.

"It was a good day for me."

"Of that, I am not so sure. Never mind. I want you to know precisely what you have done for me. You have reached me down the moon and have given it into my hands. I have never cried for it, sir: but I have longed for it for the last ten years – an idle thing to do, for strolling players have nothing to do with moons. And then you gave it to me. In a word, you have raised Colette to her proper place. I have no words to thank you – I know that you want no thanks. But now I can live and die happy, because I have seen my darling come by her own."

"Let us put it like this," said I. "No one of us three, by himself, could reach the moon. But I climbed on to your shoulders, and then Colette climbed up and stood upon mine. And so she was able to reach it and give it into your hands."

Twenty minutes later, I was again on board.

Jenny was standing beside me, and I was watching the quay with my binocular.

"There they are," I said. "The taxi's just come to rest…Mansel is paying the man, and the Customs are telling the porters to take the luggage away… They're taking it into a shed: Carson is going with it, and Mansel is strolling behind…They're out of sight now." I laid the binocular down. "I don't see how they can waste more than a quarter of an hour."

A slim arm slid within mine.

"Come and walk, my darling. It's better than standing here."

For twenty minutes we strolled the deck of the yacht and Jenny made me tell her some of my tale again. She found the scene in the barn as moving as any other – except of course, the battle I had with the torrent, to save my life. And I think, perhaps, she was right, for when I was in the barn, I was badly placed. Tired as I was, I had to work very hard and, while I was working, to watch two desperate men. The car was outside, to give our presence away. Any moment the police might have entered, and found me with the gems in my hands – and Friar lying dead in the waggon, for what that was worth. But the very finger of Fortune was on my shoulder that day.

"Poor Sloper," said Jenny. "I'm sorry he lost his life."

"So am I," said I. "He was a merry rogue; he was very decent to me; and he was faithful to death. But if he hadn't died and if he'd kept up with Orris, it's very much more than likely that they would have got me down."

"That's right. He had to die, if you were to live. But I'm glad you didn't do it. Just look at the lives, my darling, these gems have cost. Three, five years ago, and now four more. You know, it was a shame about Goat."

"My sweet," I said, "I couldn't agree with you more. Friar will not be forgiven for putting Goat down. Goat was in his service – and had no reason to think that his master was going to strike. It was a cold-blooded murder, done to suit Friar's convenience: and Friar thought no more of it than you or I would think of stopping a passing car, to ask for a lift."

"I'm glad he's dead," said Jenny.

"So am I. I'm sorry I had to do it, but he was a dangerous man. And did he want those gems? But his staff-work was very bad. That very first night he posted no sentinel. And Punter had told him and Palin had actually shown him what he was up against: yet he brought no planks or trestles to build a stage." I broke off, to glance at my watch. "My God, it's half past seven. They ought to be here by now."

I hastened to where I had laid the fieldglasses down.

These showed me the pinnace, waiting at the foot of the steps: but Mansel was not to be seen, and only one Customs Officer lounged on the quay.

Another ten minutes dragged by, while I kept using my glasses and laying them down: and Jenny stood beside me, her eyes on the distant quay.

"There's somebody coming, William."

Up went my glasses again.

It was Carson, shepherding the porters...

As the luggage went into the pinnace, Mansel appeared, with two or three uniformed Customs and one in plain clothes. As he came to the head of the steps, he said something which made them laugh. Then he raised his hat, and the others saluted him. Thirty seconds later, the pinnace had left the steps.

Mansel came aboard at exactly twelve minutes to eight. Three minutes later, the pinnace was being shipped; and before eight bells had been struck, the yacht was under way.

"It wasn't too bad," said Mansel. "Perhaps I should say that it wouldn't have been too bad, if it hadn't been perfectly clear that they were playing for time. I think they were expecting instructions… So they went through my stuff as slowly as ever they could. I stood it as long as I dared. Then I threw the cards on the table. 'You're wasting time,' I said, 'and you know it as well as I. If you have orders to detain me, say so and let me see them. If – ' They declared that they had no such orders. 'Then chalk my baggage,' I said, 'and let me go.' They looked to their chief for instructions. The latter glanced at his watch: then he shrugged his shoulders and nodded his head. And that is as much as I know. But I don't mind admitting, William, that the sooner we leave the three-mile limit behind, the better pleased I shall be."

"Does the Captain know?"

Mansel nodded.

"In his orders," he said. " 'Once under way, you will leave the three-mile limit as soon as ever you can.' "

"I'm no sailor," I said. "Will ten minutes bring us clear?"

"I don't know," said Mansel. "Anything doing on the quay?"

Jenny had my binocular up to her eyes.

"Two men are talking to the plain-clothes Customs man."

"That's the head wallah," said Mansel.

"They all seem rather excited – they keep on lifting their arms. There's somebody running now… It's another Customs man… He's speaking to the head wallah… And now they're both running off the way he came."

"Telephone call for a monkey. That's what he was waiting for."

There was a little silence.

Then –

"What's the procedure," I said, "for stopping a ship?"

"I've no idea," said Mansel. "Wireless, I suppose, from some superintendent or other. Let's hope he's having a drink."

"I can't see very well," said Jenny. " It's getting small. I don't think the man's come back."

There was another silence.

Then Jenny put up the glasses and said she could see no more.

"I have a feeling," said Mansel, "that there won't be much more to see. Anything else that happens will happen offstage. My God, is that the wireless?"

Above our heads there was a crackling noise.

"I think it's us," said I. "I may be wrong."

"Excuse me, gentlemen."

We turned, to face the officer with whom I had spoken for a moment the day before.

"The Captain's compliments, sir, and we are upon the high seas."

9

We Consider a Dimple

We had bathed and changed and had eaten an excellent dinner, squired by champagne. And now we were sitting, smoking, on Jenny's private deck.

"Looking back," said Mansel, "some bad mistakes were made. The worst was made by John Ferrers, who failed to let Palin know that Punter had been seen in the district, not far from Hohenems. Then I made a very bad one, by asking Olivia Ferrers to receive Diana Revoke. I've no excuse to offer. It was an error of judgment – which cost us extremely dear. Then we both made one, by going to Wagensburg. That was excusable, for we didn't know where to turn, and 'out of sight, out of mind'. We had forgotten Punter, because he had never shown up: but of course we should have remembered that he was advising Friar. And, but for Orris' lapse, that mistake would have been the end of us. I daresay we made some others – in fact, I know we did. When I deported Friar, I should have taken his life. When you deported Orris, you should have taken his. But that is the fault of the upbringing we have had.

"To be frank, I've not much to be proud of. You have, William, for pulling the whole thing round. Your retrieval of those gems was an epic. You'll never do anything greater, however long you live. But the fact remains that, though we

260

have brought it off, it has been an untidy business from first to last. I mean, not one to be proud of. Nothing clean-cut about it. Up to the last, it was on the knees of the gods."

"Be fair," I said. "We got off to a rotten start. We were in it up to the neck the very night we arrived."

"I'm going to be fair," said Mansel. "You're perfectly right – we got off to a rotten start. But that is not the reason why we only got home by a very short head. The reason is clear as paint. From first to last in this business, we have suffered from a complaint from which, thank God, we have never suffered before. And that complaint was *fear*. Not fear of losing our freedom or even our lives: but fear of betraying our charge. There lies the explanation. If the gems had been ordinary treasure, we'd have had them out of the country within three days. But because they were what they are – ten times as precious a thing as the world has ever seen, risks that were hardly risks seemed to be very grave dangers...we dared not do this or that...we were obsessed by precaution...we went all lengths to mislead the unfriendly eye...thus causing ourselves incredible inconvenience and generally failing to see the wood for the trees.

"Now, to be perfectly honest, I don't think we can be blamed. The burden we had to carry was very sore: the responsibility, greater than any two men should take. And that, I think, is the answer and the excuse for the haphazard way in which we have done the job."

"Of course, you're right," I said. "Their value has been a nightmare from first to last. So far as I can remember, we've never worried before; but this time, as you say, we've never done anything else."

"I think that's true," said Jenny. "You both look quite different already. And when William first came aboard, I saw the strain in his eyes."

"I'm not surprised," said Mansel. "It has been a very great strain. Day and night, from the moment we left the castle twenty-nine days ago. The strain was eased a bit, when William got back to Jade and I got his wire. But it was always there, and it began to get tighter the moment we reached Trieste. Germany missed a chance there. Greed, of course. She told Italy something, but not enough. If she had told her the truth, they'd have pulled down The Heart of Gold, to find those gems."

"She couldn't," said I. "It was an Italian collection, transferred to Austria."

"So it was," said Mansel, laughing. "Talk about being hoist with their own petard." He stretched luxuriously. "Ah, well… It's all over now."

"I'd like to say this," said Jenny. "I haven't heard every detail of all you did: but I know how you left the castle, stayed at St. Martin and went to Wagensburg: I know William joined the troupe and how the gems were transferred from the car to the weights: and when you run down what you've done and talk about its being haphazard, I don't think you're being fair. When people are being hunted, they have to – to – What's the word I want, William?"

" 'Improvise'?"

"That's right. They have to improvise. You never expected to leave the castle so soon: you never expected to have to leave Wagensburg. You were carrying weight enough, without being hunted like that. It mayn't be as clean a job as you usually do, but I don't believe anyone else would have ever got home."

Mansel picked up her hand and kissed it.

"You're very faithful," he said.

"Tell me one thing," I said. "Friar was out of his depth in the countryside. But what was the matter with the police?"

"The Boche was the matter," said Mansel. "No doubt about that. You know as well as I that they hated his guts. With what result? That the moment his back was turned, they put up their feet. They never even trailed Friar. Had they taken that trifling precaution, they would have had the gems. When you were in that barn, you were at their mercy for more than an hour: and you were never touched. And two days before, when you were waiting for Bell, Kerrelin knew very well that you were somewhere about. He knew very well who'd made a mess of the Boche, for only a giant could have poked his face like that – I mean, I've had Bell's report... But because he liked you and because he hated the Boche, he took no cognizance of it. And there's the Boche for you. His spawn will work for him, but nobody else. Born to serve, he is the beggar on horseback, 'playing such tricks before heaven as make the angels weep'. Except by brute force, the Boche will never rule. No decent man will work for a beggar on horseback, a gimcrack laird. Look at the Kaiser – a shirt that was stuffed with sawdust, a parody of a man. And he is typical. Austria is a gentleman: Germany is a cad. But the cad has acquired the power: and very soon the gentleman will go down. I very much doubt if the Ferrers will get their furniture out."

"Jonathan's right," said Jenny. "Germany is a cad. She is the cad of Europe, as England is the peer. Where are the gems, William? You haven't told me yet."

I turned to look over my shoulder. The coast was clear.

"In the parrot's cage," I whispered. "That's why we let you suffer his evil tongue."

Jenny closed her eyes.

"And I never guessed. But how did you do it, William? I mean, there's nothing to show. And we bought the cage together..."

I told her the truth.

"That was terribly clever," said Jenny. "I could not think why you brought me so rude a bird. But now I see. The Customs fell for him, because of his wicked tongue. So they never thought of his cage."

"To Jonathan, all the glory. Such a ruse would never have entered my head."

"No glory," said Mansel. "I'm rather ashamed of myself. But we had to be careful, Jenny, and that seemed the surest way."

"Fear," said I.

Mansel threw back his head and laughed.

"I won't say you're wrong," he said. "The great thing is – it came off."

Our voyage to Fowey was an idyll, the remembrance of which is joyous and always will be so. We 'fleeted the time carelessly, as they did in the golden world'. The weather was always fair, and we had to ourselves the finest yacht on the seas. And the gems were under our hand, in the parrot's cage.

On our last night but one on board, when we had just turned in, Jenny went down on her knees and took my face in her hands.

"My blessed darling," she said, "it is the world to me to see you yourself again. When you came aboard, I was shaken, because of the look in your eyes. Before, when you have come back from one of these shows, for weeks you have talked in your sleep. This time you have not talked; but when, in the night, I have leaned over your bed, your eyes have been open, William, although you were fast asleep. And that I have never seen... But, for the last two nights, your eyes have been shut. Promise me, my darling, that never again will you undertake such a charge. If you must strain your body, that I can bear; for you can endure as can no man – not even Jonathan. But I cannot bear it – that you should strain your soul. Both of these things are mine – you gave them to me: but, while I will lend your body, I will not lend your soul."

"I promise you, Jenny," I said. I put an arm round her neck. "To tell you the truth, it was the shock that did it – the shock of learning that the weights had been left behind. That was the most dreadful moment that I have ever known. It 'murdered sleep', my darling. When I got back to Jade, I fell into a stupor, for many hours. Call it sleep, if you will; but it was not natural. For night after night after that, I rested and sometimes dozed:

264

but until your arms were about me, I never slept. And now you have made me well."

My wife was counting – upon the loveliest fingers I ever saw.

"Tonight at sea: tomorrow at Fowey, but we shall sleep aboard: and the day after that, at home." She sat back on her heels. "I've simply loved this, William. The voyage out was very quiet, but I was never dull. The Captain was very polite; and I used to go up on the bridge, and sometimes he would allow me to take a turn at the wheel. But all the time I knew I was coming to you. And then we got to Trieste – and then...you came...Then I got to know Colette – she is the sweetest thing, William: if I had to choose her a surname, I'd call her 'Loyal'. And now we've come back together, you and Jonathan and I. It's been as perfect as any dream could be. It's been like the old days, my darling, when I was a little girl. But Maintenance is our home. With Bell and Sarah and all the others about us...the meadows below the terrace and the rookery in the elms...the fire in the library and the scent of pot-pourri on the stairs...the precious smell of the stables, and Romford and Ringlet, lying down in their boxes – and not getting up when they see that it's you and me..."

I lifted her off the floor and into my arms.

"There's no one like you, Jenny – I've told you that before. There never was anyone like you. You'd charm a – I really believe you could turn that swine of a parrot into an honest bird."

Jenny kissed me.

Then she laid her cheek against mine.

"He's very much better," she said. "You see, I've been teaching him English: that's the way to make him forget his French. And he's getting on. This morning, all on his own, he said 'I love Colette'."

"You wicked girl," I said.

Jenny gurgled with laughter and brushed my cheek with her lips.

The next morning, while she was bathing, I visited the bird. (He dwelt, under constant supervision, in a stateroom two doors from ours. By day the door was locked: by night, either Bell or Carson slept by his side.)

"Well," I said, "you viper, and what do you know?"

The parrot looked at me.

Then –

"Adam and Eve," he said. And then, "We both like lions."

It was about three weeks later that Mansel showed me a letter which must be set out.

SECRET

My dear Mr Ferrers,

The Trustees feel – and they hope very much that you will agree with them – that the acquisition by the Museum of this incomparable collection should not be announced, nor should the gems be displayed for two or three years.

When once it is made, such an announcement will cause a worldwide sensation, and, though the Trustees may refuse to disclose your name, the Press of more than one nation will be sure to use every endeavour to come by the truth. This, just now, would not be so hard to pick up: and if it were published, apart from anything else, Austria, would, under pressure, request the return of the gems. But after two or three years, the scent should be cold.

I feel that I must repeat that the Trustees hope very much that you will understand and agree with their point of view.

Until they are to be displayed, the gems will lie in a strong-room which is being specially built. They will, of course, be open to your inspection at any time.

Believe me,

Yours most truly,

—

The wisdom of this proposal, nobody could have denied: and I think we were all relieved that our, something pregnant, secret was to be still preserved. But in his reply, Ferrers made it quite clear that Mansel and I must be admitted, too, to visit and examine the treasure whenever we pleased: 'for,' he said, 'but for the courage, endurance and resource of these two gentlemen, the gems would not be lying in your Museum today.'

Which was uncommonly handsome, as Mansel and I agreed.

Colette married Palin before September was out, and in November he brought his bride to Wiltshire, as Jenny had begged he would do. That was a great reunion, and Mansel came down from London, to make it greater still.

Colette being gone, Jasper disbanded the troupe and became the host of an inn in the South of France. And a splendid host he made, as I can testify.

The reformation of Custom – for so we named the parrot – was soon complete: I never saw a parrot so quick to learn: but I think this was due to Jenny who talked to him as to an equal, a privilege which the bird most plainly prized.

John Ferrers declined the peerage he might have had; "for, for one thing," he said, "others deserve that honour far more than I; and, for another, if I am to be a lord, then my cousin must be one, too, for the gems belonged to us jointly, and what I have done, I have done in both our names."

After much tribulation, Olivia and he and Palin contrived to bring to England rather more than half of the contents of Hohenems, including, to our surprise, most of the beautiful silver which Palin had shown to Friar. (By Mansel's advice, the hallmarks were filled with wax and the silver was suffered to tarnish, till all its beauty was gone: then it was packed with a number of kitchen vessels and battered electroplate: so nearly all escaped. But some very fine candelabra, which could not be so disguised, were stopped by the Customs and sent to a Salzburg Bank.) Two of the rarest pieces, the Ferrers insisted on giving to Mansel and me. We were very loth to accept them, because we felt they had given enough away: but they declared that, if we would not have them, then they should follow the gems; so an exquisite salver by Lamerie lies in our hall. And, to my great content, they sent Colette a pearl necklace to wear on her wedding day.

Now safes are not built in a day – or even a month, and Christmas was drawing near when I had a note from John Ferrers, to say that the gems were in place. So it came about that, one brave December morning, almost six months to a day since Mansel and I had left for Austria, Jenny and I were taken down to the vaults. And there, in a brand new strongroom, all to themselves, cleverly lighted by hidden electric lamps, the gems which had cost us so dear were lying on fawn coloured velvet, beneath a sheet of plate glass.

Though we knew little of gems, we, both of us, gasped. To say that they filled the eye conveys nothing at all. The brain itself was staggered by such a majestic sight. Had there been half a dozen, we must have been deeply impressed, for no one, however benighted, could ever have failed to remark the size and splendour of the stones and the almost incredible cunning with which they had been carved. And here were not six, but one hundred and twenty-seven flawless stones…the vast majority bigger than any that I had seen…and every one carved by a master, a sculptor in miniature… And when I say 'master', I mean it. The men that carved those jewels knew more than their mystery. Humanity herself looked out of those precious stones. Humanity grave and learned, Humanity wanton and gross, Humanity bold and brutal, Humanity gentle and sweet. Laughter and tears and horror, pride and wisdom and hate, courage and love and remorse – half the emotions we know were there portrayed. I beg that you will not ask me how it was done, for no man, I think, could answer a question like that. How did the men of the East produce their ivory balls 'laborious orient ivory, sphere in sphere'? But there the wonder was lying, before our eyes.

The deputy curator was speaking.

"I have, I may say, a lifelong acquaintance with gems, but never had I imagined such glorious workmanship. The carving of precious stones is extremely rare. In all my life I have only seen four examples. And they in no way compared with the least of these. My theory is that Pope Alexander the Sixth just swept the board. By hook or by crook he garnered what sculptured gems there were. And here is his collection, as gorgeous today as it was when he amassed it." He shook his head. "I am glad I have lived to see it, and that's the truth.

"It was in a bad way when it came. The gems had been drenched with water, the cotton wool about them was full of sand. Whoever handled them can have had no idea of what they were worth."

"They – they weren't damaged?" said Jenny.

"Mercifully, no. The elements cannot damage such things as these. Violence alone can do that. Cleaned and polished, they might have come straight from the bench."

"Did you do that?" said Jenny.

Our friend inclined his head.

"I shared the honour, madam."

"They do you the greatest credit. May we look round?"

"Of course. Mr Chandos is one of the three who have that privilege."

Side by side, very slowly, we passed about the case, feasting our eyes upon perfection – upon stones of incredible splendour, wrought by the kiss of the chisel into yet more incredible works of art.

Beneath each gem was a label...

Medusa, looking out of a ruby – and out of an emerald, too: Cupid and Psyche, smiling upon each other – from two enormous sapphires, set side by side: Hera and Dionysus – the latter's eyebrows were raised and he looked excessively bored:

pious Aeneas and Ovid, with a wicked look on his face: Ariadne and gross Silenus, a little more than 'just nicely' – the work of some superman: Nero in emerald, cheek by jowl with a ruby from which Euripides was lifting a plaintive face: Paris and Menelaus, with, peering between them 'the face that launched a thousand ships': Pallas Athene, disdainful, and Aphrodite, demure – this was especially lovely, and I can see it now: Alexander the Great and Aristophanes: Cleopatra and Horace – the latter smiling upon some reminiscence: Hephaestus, his eyes looking sideways, and Homer, blind: Odysseus, with drooping eyelids: Andromache, in sapphire, stony with grief: a Yawning Boy and Cicero, very precise: the Minotaur and Vespasian: Pontius Pilate and Sappho and Numa Pompilius: Pan, consumed with laughter, in emerald green, and Proserpine in sapphire, wearing a listless air: Jeremiah and Circe, her pupils up to her eyelids – a brilliant interpretation of Homer's sorceress: Cyclops, in ruby, staring, and Cyclops in sapphire, blind: Juvenal – and Judas, in ruby, the picture of haggard guilt: and, greatest wonder of all, a most magnificent diamond, cut into the head of Hermes, wearing his winged hat.

I whispered in Jenny's ear.

"You see that one called *Bacchante*, third row and two from the left?"

"Yes, I've got it, William."

"That's the only one that I've ever seen before. We were packing them into the Rolls, and Jonathan unwrapped it and put it into my hand."

The curator was watching us closely.

"One of these interests you?"

"All of them interest me. I was drawing my wife's attention to the *Bacchante*. The one cut out of a ruby. I – think it's wonderful."

"Forgive me if I'm mistaken. I thought I heard you say that you'd seen it before."

"As a matter of fact, I have."

The curator stared.

"Where did you see it, Mr Chandos?"

"In the greenwood," I said. "A man put it into my hand."

The curator smiled.

"A vision, perhaps."

"Let's say – an incarnation."

The curator raised his eyebrows.

"You may be right, Mr Chandos. If you are, it was some time ago. These gems have been off the map for over four hundred years."

"Then I must be mistaken," I said. I peered very close. "The lighting is very good, but daylight would be better still, Of course, I saw mine in the daylight. My *Bacchante* had a dimple, the most bewitching feature you ever saw."

The curator stared at me, and the colour drained out of his face.

"How – how did you know?" he breathed. "I've tried for hours to place it so that the dimple showed."

"What a shame," said Jenny. "Mr Curator, my husband is pulling your leg. As you said just now, the gems were off the map. But he is one of the men who put them on it again."

We became *personae gratae*. The curator asked no questions and so was told no lies. But for more than an hour he made us free of the lore which he had mastered, and magnified for us both the lovely miracle.

"No expert on earth," he said, "could ever appraise this collection: as well appraise Westminster Abbey…'Rockbottom', 'sale room', 'cost price' – such expressions lose their meaning within these walls. Who can appraise virtue? And virtue went out of their authors into these documents. Who can appraise history? And history, tradition, romance are shown forth by these matchless gems. That emerald Medusa belonged to Beatrice d'Este: those heads of Helen and Hector, to Lorenzo the Magnificent: that glorious diamond Hermes, to a Doge of Venice: that head of Pliny to one of the Dukes of Milan:

Odysseus was brought to Michelangelo, who took it straight to the Pope: Caesare Borgia gave that Fawn to his father in 1501: and so on… In my time I have seen many treasures – of jewels, of painting, of sculpture, of silver and gold: but never in all my dreams have I imagined a splendour such as this case presents."

(He was right, of course. But for me the expression 'cost price' will never lose its meaning, so far as those gems are concerned: for the cost price of their removal – and nothing else – was four men's lives, and, very nearly, five.)

At the last, he opened the case, took out the glowing *Bacchante* and laid it in Jenny's palm.

"Now you can see the dimple your husband saw. Think of the fearless hand that held the chisel that dug it; think of the eye that saw it before it was dug; and think of the heart behind them. Hand and eye and heart have been dust for centuries; but the dimple will always remember that brilliant partnership. Myself, I cannot conceive a fairer monument."

With that most moving tribute, I think I may fairly close this true account. Could they but speak, those fabulous gems could tell a thousand tales, and every one more signal than that I have just set down; but for me they will always remember a wisp of a path in the mountains towards the break of day, and a man and a maid, heavy laden, the one, herself near spent, supporting the other's efforts and guiding his failing steps.

DORNFORD YATES

AS BERRY AND I WERE SAYING

Reprinted four times in three months, this semi-autobiographical novel takes the form of a conversation between members of the Pleydell family; in particular Berry, recalling his childhood and Oxford days, and Boy, who describes his time at the Bar. Darker and less frivolous than some of Yates' earlier books, he described it as 'my own memoir put into the mouths of Berry and Boy', and at the time of publication it already had a nostalgic feel. A hit with the public and a 'scrapbook of the Edwardian age as it was seen by the upper-middle classes'.

BERRY AND CO.

This collection of short stories featuring 'Berry' Pleydell and his chaotic entourage established Dornford Yates' reputation as one of the best comic writers of his generation and made him hugely popular. The German caricatures in the book carried such a sting that when France was invaded in 1939 Yates, who was living near the Pyrenees, was put on the wanted list and had to flee.

DORNFORD YATES

BLIND CORNER

This is Yates' first thriller: a tautly plotted page-turner featuring the crime-busting adventures of suave Richard Chandos. Chandos is thrown out of Oxford for 'beating up some Communists', and on return from vacation in Biarritz he witnesses a murder. Teaming up at his London club with friend Jonathan Mansel, a stratagem is devised to catch the killer.

The novel has equally compelling sequels: *Blood Royal, An Eye For a Tooth, Fire Below* and *Perishable Goods*.

BLOOD ROYAL

At his chivalrous, rakish best in a story of mistaken identity, kidnapping and old-world romance, Richard Chandos takes us on a romp through Europe in the company of a host of unforgettable characters.

This fine thriller can be read alone or as part of a series with *Blind Corner, An Eye For a Tooth, Fire Below* and *Perishable Goods*.

DORNFORD YATES

AN EYE FOR A TOOTH

On the way home from Germany after having captured Axel the Red's treasure, dapper Jonathan Mansel happens upon a corpse in the road, that of an Englishman. There ensues a gripping tale of adventure and vengeance of a rather gentlemanly kind. On publication this novel was such a hit that it was reprinted six times in its first year, and assured Yates' huge popularity. A classic Richard Chandos thriller, which can be read alone or as part of a series including *Blind Corner, Blood Royal, Fire Below* and *Perishable Goods*.

FIRE BELOW

Richard Chandos makes a welcome return in this classic adventure story. Suave and decadent, he leads his friends into forbidden territory to rescue a kidnapped (and very attractive) young widow. Yates gives us a highly dramatic, almost operatic, plot and unforgettably vivid characters.

A tale in the traditional mould, and a companion novel to *Blind Corner, Blood Royal, Perishable Goods* and *An Eye For a Tooth*.